W9-BWC-299

"IT'S NOT MY FAULT!
I DIDN'T DO IT!"
QUARK SHOUTED.

Security Chief Odo stared at the carnage that used to be the main floor of the Promenade. Shopwindows had been shattered, a section of the bulkhead had blown inward and another peeled back, as if someone had been looking for something but wasn't too particular about cleaning up afterward. The lighting flickered and sputtered, and some places were not lit at all.

Around him were the bodies of those who had been shopkeepers or Starfleet officers or Bajoran tourists visiting the station.

"Why hasn't Security done something about the bodies?" Odo said aloud. "Isn't there anybody left alive on this station?"

He stood quietly, shushing the gibbering Ferengi. Aside from themselves, there was no noise that he could hear . . . not even the air recirculators.

Deep Space Nine was absolutely silent.

Look for STAR TREK Fiction from Pocket Books

Star Trek: The Original Series

Star Trek: The Next Generation

Star Trek: Deep Space Nine

About the Author

DAFYDD (pronounced DAH-veth) AB HUGH seemed perfectly normal until one day in 1987 when, on his way to meet DA Jim Garrison with vital evidence on the Kennedy assassination, he was abducted by a "long, cigar-shaped" craft piloted by Men In Black (MIBs).

Since then, Mr. ab Hugh and his puppet friends have written both science fiction and fantasy, including the Arthur Warlord saga, about a British SAS agent pursuing an IRA operative back in time to the days of King Arthur (*Time's Fell Hand* and *Far Beyond the Wave*), and the Jiana series (*Heroing* and *Warriorwards*). His novelette "The Coon Rolled Down and Ruptured His Larinks, A Squeezed Novel by Mr. Skunk" (*Azimov's,* August 1990) was nominated for both the Hugo and Nebula awards.

Mr. ab Hugh privately insists he is really Volteron from the planet Volteria.

Most Pocket Books are available at special quantity discounts for bulk purchases for sales promotions, premiums or fund raising. Special books or book excerpts can also be created to fit specific needs.

For details write the office of the Vice President of Special Markets, Pocket Books, 1230 Avenue of the Americas, New York, New York 10020.

FALLEN HEROES

Dafydd ab Hugh

POCKET BOOKS

New York   London   Toronto   Sydney   Tokyo   Singapore

The sale of this book without its cover is unauthorized. If you purchased this book without a cover, you should be aware that it was reported to the publisher as "unsold and destroyed." Neither the author nor the publisher has received payment for the sale of this "stripped book."

This book is a work of fiction. Names, characters, places and incidents are either products of the author's imagination or are used fictitiously. Any resemblance to actual events or locales or persons, living or dead, is entirely coincidental.

POCKET BOOKS, a division of Simon & Schuster Inc.
1230 Avenue of the Americas, New York, NY 10020

Copyright © 1994 by Paramount Pictures. All Rights Reserved.

STAR TREK is a Registered Trademark of Paramount Pictures.

This book is published by Pocket Books, a division of Simon & Schuster Inc., under exclusive license from Paramount Pictures.

All rights reserved, including the right to reproduce this book or portions thereof in any form whatsoever. For information address Pocket Books, 1230 Avenue of the Americas, New York, NY 10020

ISBN: 0-671-88459-X

First Pocket Books printing February 1994

10 9 8 7 6 5 4 3 2 1

POCKET and colophon are registered trademarks of Simon & Schuster Inc.

Printed in the U.S.A.

CHAPTER
1

MAJOR KIRA NERYS WAS AMAZED that the unknown ship had made it through the wormhole at all.

Every instrument display in Ops maxed out, Kira felt a tingle creep along her flesh, and Lieutenant Jadzia Dax announced "Ship coming through," all simultaneously.

Kira stared at the main viewscreen through bloodshot eyes. Ordinarily, she enjoyed watching the wormhole flower into existence, disgorge a ship, then disappear as if swallowing itself. At the moment, she cared only that whatever chose to happen did so *quietly* and did not increase the pounding in her head.

The day in Operations was slow, fitting Kira's mood. Dax sat at her science console, looking impeccable as usual. Every strand of hair pulled back into the omnipresent ponytail, face freshly scrubbed, uniform glittering, neck spots sharply defined.

In contrast, Kira's hair clung to her scalp oddly, despite her shower, and her reflection in the morning mirror had looked more glowering than usual, matching her morning-after mood. At her insistence, the lights were dimmer than usual.

Commander Benjamin Sisko had been in his office since Kira came on duty, and she had not seen him through the entire watch. From her vantage point, all she could see of Chief Miles O'Brien was the top of his head as he rummaged in the systems core beneath the main viewer.

The peculiar ship that had just come through caught Kira's attention even through her haze as it limped out of the wormhole. Dax gracefully tapped at her console, increased the magnification before Kira even asked.

The ship's hull was breached at a dozen points. One bubble-shaped warp pod was damaged, leaking a thin stream of coolant behind the ship; the other was sheared off entirely. In places, the metal hull was peeled away from the ship like the dangling skin of an accident victim.

Chief O'Brien looked up from repairing the Ops air-recycling duct long enough to say "Jesus"; then he lost interest and returned his attention to the circuitry. His hair was more scruffy than usual, and sweat beaded his forehead: the interior of the duct was hot and humid.

"Is anybody even alive on that—thing?" asked Kira, standing behind the lieutenant. Quiet as she tried to make her voice, her head still pounded so hard she winced.

The major raged silently to herself. *Damn that saucer-eared Quark and his Ferengi wine!* She had gone into Quark's Place the night before for a few innocent drinks of synthehol; but the Ferengi, in a typically disgusting attempt to get her drunk enough to say yes, slipped some vile, Ferengi wine into her glass instead of synth.

Real wine . . . with *real* alcohol. Fortunately, Odo had noticed that Kira was sloshed and hauled her back to her quarters before she began dancing on tables or offering to fight any man in the joint.

The downside was that Odo (and apparently everybody else) refused to believe it was *Quark's* idea, not Kira's, for her to swill Ferengi wine all night . . . or at least, they all pretended not to believe her protests; she could not be sure.

"You wouldn't think so, would you?" Dax replied brightly. She seemed to Kira to take special delight in being even more cheery than usual, as if somehow sensing that Kira was hungover. "But the pilot seems alive and unhurt. And no dead bodies aboard. Either he was alone or he threw them all out the airlock before passing through the wormhole. He's hailing us."

Dax precisely stabbed the comm-link button with her fingernail. Kira jumped at the noise.

"Lonatian freighter *Square Deal*," croaked the voice; "come to dicker, eat a meal. Captain Square-Deal Djonreel; for docking rights I do appeal." Audio only; Dax was still trying to resolve the video.

The major stared at Dax, who could barely contain her smile. Kira turned back to the screen. "Major Kira. Deep Space Nine." Her throat was raw, and her voice croaked almost as badly as the captain's.

"Docking here with us is fine," added Dax unnecessarily.

O'Brien jumped into the act, not even looking up from the transporter circuitry. "Long as you don't moan and whine."

Kira glared first at one, then the other. "Would you two stay off this official line?" Then she winced, silently swore a Bajoran blasphemy. She had *meant* to say "official communication."

"Doesn't scan," said Dax.

The voice replied, surprised. "Such wit, such grace, from all of you. I just came through. What do I do?"

Finally, Dax synched in the visual display. Square-Deal Djonreel, if that was in fact his name, looked like a Bajoran festival lamp with eyes: onion-shaped head so brightly lit by his interior lights that it hurt Kira to look at it; big, round hole at the top, probably his nose; mouth obscured by two flaps of "onionskin" flesh dangling from just below two bright pink target circles, which might have been eyes. Kira had never seen his race before.

Another damned Federation weirdo. Why can't everyone just look normal, like a Bajoran?

Kira spoke carefully, making sure none of her words rhymed. "Take docking pylon five, Captain Sq—Captain Djonreel. Just take your—your manipulating digits off the controls; Lieutenant Dax will tractor you to the pylon." It was the safest course of action; from the look of Square-Deal Djonreel's ship, it could lurch out of control at any moment.

Should I disturb Sisko? Kira debated. *Should I swallow my pride and ask Bashir to fix up my hangover? Should I run gleefully down the Promenade with a carving knife, killing every Ferengi I see?* At last, she said "Dax, keep an eye on the wormhole. Whoever shot him up might come after him."

Major Kira finished her stroll around the operations table, glancing at each station. Everything was working, amazingly enough. Then she returned her console, closed her eyes, and rubbed her temples, dreaming up ingenious punishments for Quark and whoever invented doggerel.

The object of Kira's fury sat blissfully unaware that his life hung by the thread of Kira's civility. Quark, the Ferengi owner of the social "hot spot" on DS9, Quark's Place, stared into the ornate, antique Ferengi treasure chest that contained his hoard of gold-pressed latinum, carefully gathered over many years selling drinks and—other things.

Since it was a slow business day, Quark had decided to take an uncharacteristic but much-needed three-hour holiday away from business. He initiated a very special program in one of the holosuites, a program to which only he knew the code key, and sat now in a dank, moldy dungeon that smelled of centuries, gloating over his latinum.

Quark felt safer opening his treasure chest in such an environment.

Unexpectedly, a crack of light appeared in the midst of

the ancient, stone wall. Quark stared. The crack widened, opening into some sort of secret door.

"That's not in the program," Quark puzzled, then realized to his horror that someone was *opening the holosuite door,* ignoring the OCCUPIED sign, and in a moment would actually see Quark's treasure!

The Ferengi frantically scooped the bars of gold-pressed latinum into the chest, carelessly dropping one on the ground. Before he could pick it up, Quark's timid older brother Rom poked his impossibly ugly face through the unexpected door, leering at Quark and his latinum. Quark slammed the lid on the chest, then hopped up on the wooden plank table, sitting to block Rom's view of the Ferengi artifact.

"Ah. Quark. I thought I might find you here."

"What an amazing deduction, Rom. And the only clue you had was that I *told you* I'd be in holosuite two. I also told you not to disturb me."

"Oh. Am I disturbing you?"

Quark rolled his eyes. Thank cash that Rom's son Nog showed rather more intelligence and promise than his father. "What is it, you irritating, earless little *philanthropist?*"

Rom gasped at the obscenity; flustered, he reached behind him and dragged yet another person into Quark's private fantasy: a strange, brightly lit onion with legs. "Th-th-this is Captain Square-Deal Djonreel. Says he must speak to you. Urgent. I-I-I . . ."

"Should get back to the bar," finished Quark, barely containing his rage at the interruption of his holiday.

"I should get back to the bar," suggested Rom, skulking back out of view with an obsequious Ferengi cringe (number four—the "relative's cringe").

"What do you want?" demanded Quark, then realized it could be an important client. "Sir." He made a halfhearted cringe (number one—*I cringe on general principles; now what do you want?*), still irritated by Rom.

"Box," said Captain Square-Deal Djonreel. "Locks. Offer deal—a real steal."

His chest burst open and a limb stretched forth, holding a large box marked with the seal of the Cardassian empire. Despite long years serving all the disgusting races that frequented Quark's Place, particularly the Cardassians, Quark's stomach churned as the captain's other limbs twitched and writhed in bright, orange goo. Square-Deal Djonreel was only the second Lonat that Quark had ever seen; the first time, he actually fainted, ruining one of his father's perfectly devious business deals. Quark unconsciously rubbed his bottom, remembering his father's subsequent "discussion."

Why can't everybody just look normal, like Ferengi? he thought.

Quark reached out, not leaving his perch, and took the box. It was definitely Cardassian, even older than his Ferengi treasure chest. The seal was from the Uta Dul dynasty, more than a century old, and *unbroken*.

The Ferengi stared greedily at the box, itself worth more than Quark's entire personal fortune, and tried to bore his vision straight through the Kuluk-metal sides to peer at the mysterious, enticing contents.

Unfortunately, a Cardassian seal was not something one could hammer open or pick with a swizzle stick. The Cardassians used "force shield" seals for their most important possessions; the seals required a precise sequence of radio-wave frequencies broadcast into them. A wrong frequency would cause the seal to detonate, destroying the box contents and possibly the face and hands of the unskilled locksmith.

Few Ferengi knew how to pick a Cardassian seal; Quark was one of those few. At least, it had seemed straightforward enough the last time he had done it.

The box was heavy. Quark gingerly shook it, hearing a satisfactory rattle of stuff. "What's in the box?" he asked, trying (without success) to sound bored and uninterested. "Um . . . um . . . I hope not rocks," added Quark belatedly, realizing the rhyme was forced (and lame).

Lonats always spoke in rhyme for some insane reason. They claimed that their poetry was subtle, supple, and graceful in their native language; but the Universal Translator turned it all into nursery verse. If you rhymed back at them, you often got better deals.

"Don't know. Didn't show. Sold it to me sight unseen; must be something pretty keen."

Quark looked up from the Cardassian box and noticed that the captain was staring down at the bar of gold-pressed latinum that fell when Quark scooped up the rest. "Ah . . . ah, Square-Deal Djonreel," said the Ferengi, trying to distract the captain from the shiny bar. "I really can't be—philanthropic. Don't you even know the topic?"

The Lonat glowed, finally figured out what Quark meant. "Ancient alien artifact. Probing more would lack in tact."

"I haven't much, and that's a fact. But I can offer, ah, the princely sum of two bright bars of latinum."

"*Two?* You villain! What a laugh. Fifty wouldn't equal half!"

"Fifty! I mean, you can't believe I'd offer fifty; you know Ferengi must be thrifty." Quark reached up, rubbed his ears while thinking. "I'll give this deal my best refinement. I'll try to sell it on consignment."

Square-Deal Djonreel pondered, alternately glowing and dimming, flapping his onionskin mouth. "Despite the pain it is to sever, I cannot dicker here forever. Consignment you shall have consent . . . *if* we settle on percent."

Quark licked his lips, beginning to enjoy the game. "I run the risks in such a sortie. I say we split it sixty-forty."

"Forty percent? That's my cut? You take me for some kind of nut?" The captain moved closer, menacingly.

Not good, thought Quark. Djonreel would insist upon at least fifty percent.

The saving grace was that Lonats were not very good at

lightning calculations . . . a fact that any good Ferengi considered a perfectly acceptable bargaining tool. "All right!" said Quark. "All right! Don't start to pound. How does sixty-fifty sound?"

Square-Deal Djonreel dimmed to merely bright. Something seemed fishy, but he could not quite tell what. But even more than humans, Lonats hated more than anything to seem hesitant or uncertain in a deal.

He did the best he could. "More Ferengi bunko tricks, the . . . bottom price is sixty-sixty."

Quark grinned crookedly, feeling his pointed teeth with his tongue. *Tricks-the with sixty?* When a Lonat resorted to such a feeble rhyme, he was severely rattled. Bracing himself, he stuck out his hand, took the captain's appendage. "Your cut of the sale will be recorded. Till you return it will be hoarded." Quark intended to take sixty percent of any sale, then give the rest to Djonreel; as the agreed split—sixty percent to each partner—was clearly impossible, any Ferengi court in the sector would consider Quark's interpretation close enough to pass muster.

Square-Deal Djonreel dimmed almost to the luminescence of a normal being. He was not happy with his own performance in the complicated dance of the deal. *Probably expected at least some up-front latinum,* thought Quark.

"And now I must depart this place," said the captain, "and head out into deepest space." He took a last, longing look at the bar of latinum beneath Quark's dangling feet, sighed a deep amber, and turned around. He stared in confusion at the dungeon wall where a door had been when he came in.

"End program," gloated Quark. No sooner had the words escaped than he found himself sitting on air instead of a fine, Ferengi jailwood table. He flailed his arms and fell heavily to the deck.

As Square-Deal Djonreel squelched through the door, Quark again rubbed his aching bottom, wondering what

the mystical connection was between Lonats and that
portion of his anatomy.

Constable Odo stared in utter amazement at the wall
display. *The wretched little Ferengi has finally done it,* he
thought; *he's driven himself mad with his debaucheries.*

Odo sat in his security office, behind the heavy but
utilitarian desk, watching one of several wall displays
that continuously showed parts of Deep Space 9. Odo
had a standing rule: no matter who or what else was
displayed, at least *one* screen must always be following
the station's public enemy number one—Quark.

At this moment, Quark was huddled in one of his own
holosex suites, running some ghastly prison program and
talking with the pumpkin-headed Lonat in the most
bizarre fashion.

As the conversation proceeded, Odo briefly wondered
whether he could use the weird, nursery rhyme negotia-
tion to persuade Dr. Julian Bashir to transport Quark to
a psychiatric facility on Bajor for his own protection.

Odo had just awakened from his bucket, and his brain
was still a bit fuzzy as the pieces fell slowly into place.

Still, the event was weird enough, even for the disgusting Quark, that it warranted investigation. Odo stood,
made sure none of his features or clothing had run, and
boiled out the glass door of his office toward Quark's
Place.

Unless the little hood is having me on. Was it possible
the Ferengi had discovered Odo's hidden "spy-eye" in
the holosuite and was trying to trick Odo into making a
fool of himself?

The constable had installed the bugs when Dr. Bashir,
who would not tell him why, asked him to. Before the
doctor's request, Odo was so repulsed by the thought of
what went on in the suites that it never occurred to him
to watch.

But Bashir insisted that they be installed, muttering
something paradoxical about Lieutenant Dax and Major
Kira being eternally grateful, even if they never found

out about it. That way, Odo could "keep an eye on things" even when not physically present, disguised as an article of furniture, a rug, or a bottle of Quark's vile spirits.

No, thought the constable; *Quark may be clever, but even he wouldn't routinely sweep private holosuites for hidden bugs*. After all, he was not a Cardassian.

Odo pushed into the Promenade, then turned sideways to swim through a mob lined up to play The Gokto Lottery. The constable scowled: he could not remember seeing an application from the Bajorans to run a game of chance. *Have to talk to the commander about it. Or better yet, Kira.*

The station was full to overflowing from the latest wave of tourist ships to the wormhole. With the tourists had come a yammer of merchants, a mummer of missionaries (all faiths), a fraud of mountebanks—and of course a lift of pickpockets, a shiv of muggers, and a deviant of flashers, Ferengi, and other perverts.

The political turmoils sweeping Bajor had crash-landed on DS9. Every other step, Odo had to duck under a banner or dodge a sign-waving, chanting crowd of Bajoran fundamentalist or antifundamentalist (tolerationist?) protesters. The current fashion for the orthodox "Bajor for Bajorans" was dark blue, gray, and black, while the progressive faction preferred light and sky blue.

For some reason, none of the Bajorans these days liked red, but it was still a popular color among the hordes of tourists, come to gawk at both the wormhole and the riots.

The sea of sentiency made Odo squirm, longing even for the days of Cardassian rule: at least then, there was a sense of decorum, decency, and above all occasional *silence*.

The holding cells were jammed so full of "detainees" awaiting either trial or a one-way ticket off Deep Space 9 that three of Odo's men had a full-time job just keeping them from killing each other. The constable had already converted a cargo bay to an emergency jail, getting Chief O'Brien to divide it up with portable force shields.

Growing annoyed at the sea of intelligent and nearly intelligent beings that washed against him, Odo put his arms together and shifted them into a wedge like a "cowcatcher" on an old-fashioned Earth *loco-motive,* a wheeled engine that pulled cargo along a railed track. He ploughed toward Quark's, brushing the people aside.

When Odo reached the den of iniquity, he was amused to discover that Quark was not benefiting from the mobs. There were now so many merchants selling out of inexpensive pushcarts on the Promenade, with virtually no overhead, that they easily undercut Quark's prices for everything from synthehol to legal gambling. In fact, the Ferengi had recently become quite the moralist, demanding that Odo, Kira, or Sisko himself "do something" about such disgusting, wide-open marketeering on the Promenade.

Even Quark's notorious holosex suites ran mostly empty, since most of the worlds represented on DS9 these days had sexual needs so pedestrian and boring that they would never dream of paying for an elaborate, sexual holodeck program.

Quark's Place was a huge, three-story facility, the largest private operation on DS9. Where the "exterior" of the Promenade was banners and bunting, the constant rumble of the rabble, beggars, miners, and assorted nuts inside Quark's was a completely different universe: the casino had fewer of the dregs of the sector but was, if anything, *more* sleazy, dangerous, and illicit than the Promenade itself.

The bar was stuffed floor to ceiling with glitzy, flashing lights, the well-dressed, and thousands of kilos of ersatz jewels—though Quark would have hotly disputed the adjective.

Any of the hoi polloi who wandered in were subtly steered toward a Dabo table in the corner, away from the "pressed and groomed" crowd in the rest of the club.

There were so many colors visible at any one time, it often hurt Odo's eyes, used as he was to more spartan ways. The most exotic colors, of course, were the syntheholic (and supposedly alcoholic, though Odo had never caught the Ferengi) drinks mixed by Quark himself, with occasional help from Rom.

Quark bragged that anybody could get *anything* in Quark's Place; the gnomelike Ferengi was not amused when Odo agreed, naming a number of exotic, sexually transmitted diseases. "My holosex suites are the cleanest in this sector!" raged Quark, growing redder by the second.

Odo entered Quark's place just in time to see the Ferengi scuttle from the holosuite, down the stairs, toward his safe, the Cardassian box tucked securely under one arm.

"Good evening, Quark," said Odo, making himself curl his mouth up in what he hoped was a menacing smile. "What have you got there? More bars of latinum? Brekkian narcotics? *Stolen cultural artifacts?*"

Quark started and glared suspiciously at Odo. "Never mind what I have here. My business is my own. Something I can do for you, Odo? Would you like a nice holosex session with a Ferengi harem?" His own grin was more of a leer.

Odo straightened, then increased the effect by making himself several centimeters taller. "I've no interest in your disgusting perversions, Quark. But I do have a legitimate interest in sealed, Cardassian boxes that might contain anything—such as a new plague virus or explosive device."

Quark twisted his body around to conceal the box. "What makes you think it's a sealed, Cardassian box?" he demanded, suspicious.

"The Cardassian seal around it."

Quark peeked down at it. "Oh. So I see. Well, I'll be sure to tell you what was in it. Now goodbye."

"Quark, I understand you caring nothing for your own continued existence, since nobody else does. But we do care about the safety of this station . . . and you are *not* going to open that box without complete scans first. Conducted by Chief O'Brien and Dr. Bashir."

"But—but then everybody will know what's in it!"

"Oh dear, you mean you might have to actually sell it honestly, with full disclosure? Yes, I do see where that would be a problem."

"Odo, thank goodness. Don't scare me like that! For a moment, I thought—"

Quicker than even the greedy Ferengi could move, Odo stretched his arms out like grappling hooks, seized the box, and wrenched it from Quark's hands.

"*Thief!* I'll have you arrested and locked in your own cells, Odo!"

"Stop whining, Quark. You'll get your precious box back, just as soon as O'Brien and Bashir assure me it poses no danger to the station." He turned toward the door, took three steps, and felt the Ferengi breathing on his back.

Odo stopped suddenly, and Quark ran into him. "And where are you going?"

"If you think I'm going to allow a shapeshifter to handle my property without watching him every step of the way, then you must think I'm a credulous cretin." Odo opened his mouth, but before he could speak, Quark interrupted. "Don't even think it! You're in enough trouble, lifting other people's perfectly legitimate property, without adding slander to your crimes."

Rolling his eyes, Odo strode off toward the infirmary. Try as he might, he could not shake the stubborn Ferengi, who stuck closer to him than his own shadow.

CHAPTER
2

ODO STOOD IN the Ops system core, hands clasped behind his back, scowling down at Chief of Operations Miles O'Brien.

The constable was in a bad mood. First, Dr. Bashir had scanned the Cardassian box, declaring it free of any known dangerous contaminants. Now O'Brien insisted that it appeared to be nothing more menacing than a box of old junk.

There were a couple of potentially dangerous (because unknown) devices, but nothing was set to explode or do anything significant when the box was opened.

"Are you certain, Chief?" Without some plausible reason, Odo would have to simply hand the box back to Quark to open at his leisure.

O'Brien bristled, but hid his offense behind an Irish smile. "Oh, I think I've been around a tricorder or two in my time," he said. "Nothing dangerous about the box, though I can't say much about the contents until I can examine them independently."

"Can't you tell what they are?"

"There are a couple of unknown items. I think one is an ancient Cardassian directed-energy weapon—"

"A weapon!"

"—completely drained of power. It's been sitting in there for over a hundred years. The other is from a culture I've never seen before. But I don't think it's dangerous; it has hardly any power reading at all."

"An unknown artifact?" Odo's eyes gleamed. This might be sufficient to pique Commander Sisko's interest.

"You heard the chief," grumbled Quark; "it's not dangerous. Thank you very much for your opinion, Chief O'Brien. Now, if you don't mind . . ."

This time, Quark was the faster. Odo reached for the box, but a reddish pink blur licked out, seized it, and left Odo to grab a handful of air.

Quark charged up to Ops proper and took three steps toward the turbolift before he felt the constable practically stepping in his footsteps. "Where do you think you're going?" demanded Quark.

"I should take you into custody for illegal receipt of alien cultural artifacts."

"There's no crime in a simple, honest business deal."

"Honest? With a Ferengi involved?"

"I'll let that pass this time, shapeshifter. Now you let *me* pass, and—"

Odo padded after Quark. "Alas, you are right. I don't have enough evidence to take the box from you. But I *will* be present when you open it, if you can defeat the Cardassian seal. And if anything even looks iffy, I'm bringing it right back here and bother Chief O'Brien again."

Without glancing up from his diagnostic display, O'Brien said, "Oh, no bother. No bother at all. That's what I'm here for, day and night. And while I'm at it, I can dust your furniture, clean your windows, and mop your lobby."

"Dust? Mop? Chief, what *are* you talking about? Surely you're not telling me the cleaning servos are down again?"

O'Brien sighed deeply. "No, Odo. Never mind. Go away." He made a dismissive gesture with his hand, and Quark stepped into the turbolift, followed by his shadow.

Quark and Odo argued for fifteen minutes about whether Quark could open his box in private. They stood in Quark's office, small but comfortable by Ferengi standards, though Odo seemed to find the gilt-and-bejeweled columns garish.

Finally, Quark decided it was hopeless. Actually, he found the situation neither so incomprehensible nor outrageous as he pretended; even the Ferengi was a little nervous about an artifact from the Gamma quadrant so alien that Chief O'Brien did not have a clue as to what it did.

But of course, Quark still defended his unabridged right to absolute privacy with the ringing tones of moral dudgeon worthy of a Ferengi Supreme Contract Arbitration barrister.

At last he subsided, panting in exhaustion. He opened a drawer in his ornate, white-and-silver Louis XIV desk from Earth (replicated, of course), and extracted an "ear-pricker," a miniature, tricorder-like Ferengi device for springing locks—used only for perfectly legitimate locksmithing purposes, naturally. He inspected the Cardassian seal.

The seal wrapped entirely around the box, exerting a force shield designed to interact unpredictably with force manipulators, energy beams, or brute, physical tools. Theoretically, only the matching Cardassian key ring could open it; but since Garak, the only Cardassian left on DS9, was not extraordinarily likely to help a Ferengi open a Cardassian strongbox, Quark had to rely on his own initiative.

"Give it up, Quark," said Odo. "You can't break a Cardassian seal without destroying the box, and you know it."

"Nonsense, Odo. Where's your spirit of adventure?"

"Adventure is for children and those with undeveloped minds." I accept the world as it is."

The Ferengi tool glowed satisfactorily blue in the room dimly lit by ersatz candlelight as Quark traced the complex geometry of the field. He did not trust the readings, however, since the seal was specifically engineered to thwart lock picking. Quark preferred to depend upon his own experience and native Ferengi cleverness.

He adjusted the frequency of the ear-pricker to half a phase *ahead* of the frequency cycle it read and gently probed the force vortex that corresponded to the "keyhole." Even before the ear-pricker beeped a warning, Quark felt that something was wrong and let go of the contact button. He stepped quickly back, but his probe had been deft and fast enough that the seal did not react.

Quark rolled the phase shift back a quarter cycle to plus-ninety degrees and tried again. This time, he felt the ear-pricker catch hold of the field the way it should. He gently rotated the vortex until the ear-pricker flashed amber, warning of imminent field breakdown, then stopped.

"First tumbler," announced Quark. Odo stared, his mouth slightly open.

Suddenly, Quark felt, rather than heard, a stealthy presence at his office door. He had left strict instructions that no one was to disturb him for any reason.

Without moving from his position, he called out "Rom—unless DS-Nine is falling into the wormhole, you had better vanish before I count to one. One . . ." Footsteps rapidly pounded up the hall and down the stairs.

Quark picked up his tensor and activated it to match the ear-pricker's beam, holding the first tumbler in place. "Must work quickly now," he said, half to himself and half to Odo, "only have a few moments before the field realizes it's being picked."

He thought back to his early years, working for his

father, gathering vital information about the content of locked boxes before an auction. How else was an honest Ferengi to know what to bid on? He had once before worked on a Cardassian seal.

In that case, the second through fifth tumblers all corresponded to the notes of an obscure Cardassian musical chord . . . probably the mnemonic used by the owner to remember the combination.

Quickly but carefully, Quark spoke into his desk console: "Computer, display most popular Cardassian chords containing the frequency"—he looked at the ear-pricker readout—"four-forty-eight cycles per second in increasing order of popularity." Quark's throat clenched; he risked his beautiful Ferengi face on the unknown contents of a Cardassian strongbox. But it was simply the merchant-prince's burden.

Instantly, six chords appeared on the display.

The six most popular chords containing the Cardassian musical note Divak, 448 cycles per second. Only one was named after Divak itself: Divak eight and two.

I get one shot at this, he thought, wiping sweat from his ears. "Here goes nothing, I hope," said Quark.

He set the ear-pricker to 672 cycles, the next dominant note in Divak eight and two (Daka-nan, the eighth note of the nine-tone Cardassian scale, as Divak was the fourth). Quark grimaced, averted his eyes, and pressed the contact button. He felt the field flicker, and his heart almost stopped. Then the beam caught, allowing the Ferengi to twist the second layer of the field negatively.

The next note, Daka-tul high, was 576 cycles "sharped" up to 588. This was the critical test, because Divak eight and two was the only chord that contained Daka-tul high. If the field held, then Quark had picked the seal, unless it was based on a chord so obscure the computer could not find it.

He set the second tensor tone to hold layer two in position, and was just about to probe with the ear-pricker at 588 cycles when he suddenly remembered that a century ago the Cardassian scale was based on a larger spread than the current scale. The Emperor Somebody-or-other had shortened it to force his own barbaric musical tastes on everybody else.

As a result, chords had changed slightly.

Sweat dripping onto his shoulders, a dry-mouthed Quark gasped a second query. "Computer—what Cardassian musical chords a hundred years ago contained the two frequencies four-forty-eight and six-seventy-two cycles per second?"

This time, only one chord displayed, an obsolete chord called Divak four and five high. The note at 588 cycles did not appear; had Quark continued, the seal would have realized it was being picked and self-destructed.

It was only the sheerest luck that Quark's second frequency, 672 cycles, did not cause the same result.

Swallowing hard, the Ferengi reset his ear-pricker to the next frequency in the century-old chord; the third force-shield layer slid forward smoothly.

The last two frequencies were easy, and the seal retracted into itself, sliding off the box onto Quark's desk.

"I don't believe it," snapped Odo, clearly annoyed that the Ferengi had succeeded. Quark opened the box.

"Here, now," said Odo, finding a new objection. "Is that box your property?"

Quark gazed speculatively at Odo, trying to figure out whether the constable actually had inside information, or had just taken a lucky guess. "No, but it's in my care. I'm selling it on consignment. I have to know about what it should bring . . . it's only fair to my client."

Odo grunted, but could not press the question further without revealing his knowledge, thus revealing his spy-eye.

He discarded the outdated Cardassian disruptor immediately. Its only value was as scrap material to be shoved into a replicator for "mass credit."

There were three squatty statues, each more grotesque than the last: two were Cardassian religious icons, the third of unknown origin but having some similarities. "Might get some Cardassian anthropologist interested," mumbled Quark unhappily. Together, he could not imagine them fetching even 400 grams GPL after splitting with Square-Deal Djonreel.

The box and its seal were valuable in themselves, of course; but Quark preferred to buy them himself, setting a fair price (then paying the Lonat captain his forty-percent share, as agreed).

Only the final item showed real promise, more in its mystery than any intrinsic value.

The unknown, alien device was larger than a phaser, smaller than a tricorder. It was roughly shaped like a hand-sized belt buckle, sharply, almost brutally angled, more like Cardassian than Federation design. But it had none of the studied crudity that had been the style in the Cardassian empire for two hundred years.

Instead, the device was intricate and subtle. Tiny sucker-pads made it stick to the box, to Quark's hand, to the table when he yanked his paw away. It was made out of a dark gray material, an alchemical marriage between metal and plastic, light and strong, but malleable.

But it had a memory: Quark pressed hard on one surface, indented it. After a few moments, it slowly undented itself, returning to its original shape.

There were no obvious physical buttons, but Quark's ear hair stood up straight in the force aura surrounding the device.

"Well, Odo, what do you think it could be?"

"I don't have the slightest idea, and I have no more time to waste on you. I have a station full of less successful criminals than you to jail. Hand it over."

"It's mine!"

"For *testing*," explained the constable, wearily.

"But what if that oaf O'Brien accidentally destroys it while testing it?"

"Then you can pay that pirate captain half of the nothing you'll get for it."

"You *were* listening!" Quark leaped up, the device in hand, glaring about his office. "What were you disguised as this time? Where were you, you shifty—wait! We didn't do the deal here . . . we did the deal *in the holosuite.*"

Quark turned incredulously toward Odo. "Why, Constable," he purred, "you dirty old shapeshifter!"

"I was not spying on your holodeck sexcapades!" Odo shouted.

Quark whirled around, back to Odo. When he turned back, he held the alien device in one hand, the ear-pricker poised dramatically over it in the other.

"Stand by to be dazzled," he whined in the typical Ferengi mix of pomposity and terror of the unknown.

"No!" commanded Odo. "Put it down! I will *not* allow you to jeopardize this station just to make a few measly bars of—"

Quark pressed the contact button, probed the force vortex. The ear-pricker matched frequencies immediately at 914 cycles per second; there were no locking mechanisms at all. The vortex was a switch, not a keyhole.

Deep Space 9 lurched beneath the Ferengi's feet until he thought he must be standing sideways on a vertical bulkhead, rather than the deck. The lights flickered twice, then vanished into a soupy blackness surrounding a rippling bubble of relative normality.

Quark stood at the center of the bubble, but it extended barely far enough to include Constable Odo.

The Ferengi went west, but his stomach lurched south. Squealing like a stuck Greeka pup, he dropped both ear-pricker and alien device, and felt his body rolled flat like cookie dough. He blinked his eyes, found himself lying on the deck in eerie silence. A dim, blue glow lit the office: it was the emergency lighting he had installed in Quark's Place after the big poker-game fiasco.

The emergency lighting was dim, as if it had been on for days. It should have been as bright as normal.

He climbed shakily to his knees, rubbing his aching ears. A puddle quivered on the floor, filling the Ferengi with a nameless dread, to which he instantly attached a name: Odo. The puddle drew into itself, foamed up into a column of constable, solidifying into the familiar, featureless face of the shapeshifter.

Odo glowered, as if to say *I meant to do that.*

Something was terribly wrong, but for a moment, Quark could not identify the problem. Then he noticed his sensitive ears were sending an urgent message: silence, silence, silence.

The normal noises of the station had vanished. The confused babble of clients shouting, laughing, bellowing, and singing drunken space chanties had shut off like a light switch. Even the normal, low grumble of Deep Space 9's fusion reactors was missing.

He stared at the constable, a horrific thought growing in his head. "Odo!" he gasped. "I've gone deaf! Call Dr. Bashir, hurry!"

Odo sighed in relief and slumped against the desk. "Thank goodness," he said. "For a moment, I thought I'd forgotten how to form ears."

Quark edged toward the office door, listened to the noiselessness. "Um . . . if we're not deaf, Odo, then— what happened to everyone else? What happened to the whole rest of the station?"

He turned back. Odo stared at him with his unblinking, remorseless eyes. "Maybe you made them all *go away,*" he said, so softly the Ferengi almost did not hear him . . . and wished he had not.

Quark stooped and picked up the alien device instead of his beloved ear-pricker. He could not have said why. As he stood, he felt a metal band clamp around his bicep; it was Odo's hand, which he had shifted into a manacle.

The constable touched his communicator. "Odo to Ops." Silence. "Odo to Ops. Major Kira, are you available?" More silence. "Anybody? Ops, Engineering, Security? Chief O'Brien, can you get the lights on in Quark's Place?"

He looked down at the communicator, frowned. "Blast. Yet another equipment failure. At least the Cardassians kept this place in fine fettle. All right, let's take a little stroll," said the constable, voice tight.

"Do we have to?"

Odo propelled Quark out the office door and down the stairs. The brilliantly colored lights of Quark's Place were dim and flickering; even the rotating lasergraphic dome that the Ferengi was convinced made patrons gamble harder was still, its hypnotizing beams of laser light unseen.

Something was on the floor, a bundle. A blanket. Irrationally fearful, Quark averted his eyes; but Odo dragged him toward it, stopped and stared.

"I think you'd better look at this," said Odo.

Compelled now by morbid curiosity, yet still as reluctant as before, Quark slowly bent his neck to bring the bundle into view. It was a man. A Ferengi. It was Rom.

Rom was dead, covered with dried blood from a dozen wounds. Quark felt clammy sweat on his ears, blood rush to his face. Guilt percolated through him as if he had actually killed Rom himself.

Maybe I did . . .

No! I am a Ferengi, he thought, *not a human. We don't panic. We only cringe as rational beings. Get ahold of the deal, Quark, you miserable mark!*

He bent slowly, faced Odo across his brother's body. "This isn't my fault, you know. I had nothing to do with this. You're my witness!"

"I didn't see a thing, Quark. Don't count on me for your alibi; I was a puddle of liquid, remember?"

There were fourteen circular puncture-holes in Rom's back, two of which had been fatal.

"These were made with considerable force," said Odo. He made a pair of long fingers and gently probed one of the holes.

Quark pressed his lips together, fought down a rising gorge, and felt faint.

"Here we are," said the constable, his voice professionally neutral. He pulled his fingers out, shrank them to normal. They gripped a flattened cylinder of soft metal, approximately ten millimeters in diameter. Odo stared in amazement. "Do you recognize this, Quark?"

"It's not mine!" whined the Ferengi, cringing back in the approved fashion, hands over face (number eight: *You caught me with my fingers in the biscuit tin, but society's to blame*).

"That's not what I meant. I mean, do you recognize what kind of weapon this is?"

Quark peeked between his fingers. "Chemically propelled rifle bullet," he squeaked. "Probably a fullautomatic, considering the number of bullet wounds."

"That's what I thought. Now, Quark, how did you happen to become an expert on historical weaponry?"

The Ferengi stopped cringing. In a huffy voice, he said, "People pay good money for ancient guns. If I can't price a Klingon Chordat-77 or an Earth 30–06, how can I fix a profit margin?"

Odo dropped the bullet at Quark's feet. "All right. Price that."

His terror and anguish dispelled for the moment by the magic words, Quark gingerly picked up the deformed bullet, plucked a jeweler's eye from his pocket, and examined the evidence. After a moment, he shook his head. "It's an odd caliber. Never seen it before. Four point eleven millimeters, expanding to about nine and a half on impact. Nose is hard, remains intact; this thing is supposed to penetrate armor, Odo."

"Now, why would someone use it on a shopkeeper?"

Reminded of where the bullet had been taken from, Quark instantly dropped it as if it were a live, poisonous insect. "Rom," he whispered, stroking his brother's cheek. "What did you do? I told you there was no percentage in resisting a robbery."

He looked up at Odo to ask whether Rom had had a phaser, but the constable was staring across the room. "There are more bodies over there," he said in a quiet voice.

They found four other bodies, all shot by the same sort of chemically propelled bullets. Quark recognized three of them as customers, and the fourth he thought he had seen at the Dabo table, but could not be certain.

"Is there anything missing, Quark?" Odo asked.

"Missing?"

"Taken. Was anything taken by the killers?"

"Taken?" Quark still stared across the room at his brother, not understanding the question. "Taken? Oh, you mean stolen?" Suddenly reminded of Ferengi priorities, he ran to the safe, punched the combination. Inside, and untouched, were the six bars of gold-pressed latinum and thousands of chips he kept as the house "bank." He checked the shelf behind the bar; his expert eye told him that not a single bottle of expensive, imported synthehol and quasilegal alcohol was missing. The automatic transaction machine had not been tampered with.

Even the kylarghian fire gems on the Dabo table were untouched. Not a single item of value was taken.

"How peculiar," announced Odo in typical understatement.

Quark was aghast. "You mean—they did all this for some reason other than *loot?*" His scandalized tone indicated that he might have forgiven them otherwise.

Odo tried his communicator again, to no effect. "I don't like this," he said; "somebody should surely have heard the weapons discharge. Where is everybody?" Once again, he changed his hand into a flat band, wrapped it all the way around Quark's arm, and melded the fingers, making a closed manacle. "Come on, let's put you in custody and figure out what happened here."

"Custody!" Quark was too shocked to protest further as Odo dragged him out the door onto the Promenade.

Both cop and Ferengi stopped in confusion: the Promenade was as devoid of life as Quark's Place had been. Dozens of dead bodies were piled in heaps along the bulkheads.

Even with his arm held in Odo's rigid grasp, Quark managed to cringe—a remarkable display of contortionism. "It's not my fault! I didn't do it! It's you—*you* did it!"

Odo stared at the carnage that used to be the main floor of the Promenade. Shopwindows were shattered, a section of the bulkhead blown inward and another peeled back, as if someone were looking for something and not too particular about cleaning up afterward. The lighting flickered and sputtered, and some places were not lit at all.

Why hasn't Security done something about these bodies? Who would simply stack them like cargo? Isn't anybody left alive on this station?

He stood quietly, shushing the gibbering Ferengi. Aside from what they made themselves, there was no noise that he could hear . . . not even the air recirculators.

If they're out, we have only five days before the oxygen content falls below human and Bajoran tolerances. If the heat doesn't fry them first.

As a matter of fact, it did feel hotter than normal. Since temperature variation made little difference to Odo until it got extraordinarily high or low, he had not noticed.

Odo's pocket security pack was still functional. It informed him that the air temperature was 50 degrees Celsius, 122 degrees Fahrenheit.

They walked slowly across a cracked and buckled floor, wary of tripping. He checked his chronometer; the time seemed correct, about one hour since he had left Chief O'Brien.

The constable shook his head. "Something's—stop whining, Quark—something's not right about the time."

He dragged the Ferengi over to a pile of ten or twelve bodies, stooped, and examined them.

He pulled a corpse back, laid it on the broken deck. It was hard to see in the dim, flickering light. Little as Odo knew about human biochemistry, bodies should not putrefy that quickly, even at the current temperature. If he had to guess, he would estimate the bodies to be at least two or three days dead.

"Oh no," he said, quiet tones cutting through Quark's guilt with a stronger emotion: fear.

"Oh no? Oh no *what,* Odo?"

"Quark, do you have a chronometer that isn't tied in to the station computer?" The Ferengi began feeling in his pockets. "No, no," amended Odo, "I mean somewhere in your tavern. Not in your pocket."

"Uk. Well, yes. I have an antique Klingon clock in my office. Battery-powered."

"Let's go." As soon as they reentered Quark's Place, Odo stopped the Ferengi. "And a torch."

"Torch? Why not a flashlight?"

"That's what I said," said Odo, "an electric torch. A flash. Do you have one?"

"Are you kidding? After the lighting went out when I was trying to hold the big game, I—"

"Yes or no?"

Quark glared. "Behind the bar."

Odo walked him over, and the Ferengi retrieved his beautiful, expensive new hand torch. The constable immediately confiscated it.

"Hey! That's my property!"

"I may need it for the investigation."

"What investigation?"

Odo looked down at Quark from a height; the constable's lips were pressed together tightly. "Whether I can raise anybody or not, even if we're the only people left alive on this station, *I am still the constable.* And I *will* conduct an investigation. Any questions?"

Quark shrank back, blinking. "No. No questions."

"Klingon clock. I have a terrible feeling I know what's happened."

Quark pointed up, back toward his office. Odo took the stairs four at a time, Quark stumbling behind, hand still in Odo's handcuff-grip. In the Ferengi's office, Odo found the clock and studied it, trying to remember the native Klingon time and date system.

"Quark . . . will you please confirm what this piece of machinery displays?"

"Can't you even read a clock? It says—no, that's wrong. The batteries must be low."

"What does it show?"

"It says it's, um, ten thirty-five, stardate 47237.8. But that's wrong . . . that's three days from now."

It all fit: the temperature, the decomposition of the bodies, the lack of response to the communicator signal, the Klingon chronometer.

"No, Quark," said Odo; if the shapeshifter had had a stomach, it would have turned. "It's *not* wrong. Your blasted device locked us into a static-time bubble for three days! And somehow, during that time, something or someone attacked and destroyed Deep Space Nine."

He shoved his face close to the Ferengi, beyond fury. "We're it, Quark! We are all that survives! And if no one has come to help by now, I suspect they aren't coming at all."

Kira sat at her console in Ops, humming softly to herself. She felt so much better than she had yesterday that she almost forgot herself entirely and sang a verse of "The Dear, Green Place." Sisko was in his office, and all was right with the station.

Quark had done such an effective job at hiding out that no one had even seen him for more than a day. Oddly enough, Kira had not been able to find Constable Odo, either.

"Wormhole," said Dax for the sixth time in as many hours. The wormhole was much busier these days than when Bajor had first taken over the Cardassian station.

"Cardassian?" guessed Kira.

"Nope."

"Borg?"

"Not this time."

"The prophets have come out of their holy realm to guide us in our endeavors?"

"No such luck." The Trill poked at her control pad causing the ship to materialize on-screen.

It was truly an interstellar ship, completely unstable anywhere but the zero-g of space. Eight small, black, rectangular solids, each no bigger than a runabout, were connected by spaghetti-like strands of tubing that looped among them in a complicated dance. Some swirls were large enough for a humanoid; others were undoubtedly power conduits.

Several of the tubes poked out into space and ended with wide-open mouths or muzzles. Kira felt a premonition of danger; her combat experience told her those were weapons—of a sort she had never seen before. They were not the round, solid-state contacts she saw on the business ends of phasers or disruptors.

"Don't recognize them," Dax said. "Major, they might be visitors *from* the Gamma quadrant, rather than returnees from here."

"Really?" Major Kira thumbed her communicator. "Commander."

Sisko's voice responded immediately. "Yes, Major?"

"Monitor three. Check it out."

A slight pause. "Who are they, Major?"

"Dax thinks they're from the Gamma quadrant."

"I'll be right down."

High above them, Sisko's office door dilated and disgorged the commander of Deep Space 9. Kira wondered, not for the first time, how he always managed to have a uniform so crisp you could cut bread with the creases and boots so shiny you could bounce a laser off them.

She tried not to watch him too obviously as he elegantly descended the stairs, lithe as a festival dancer.

Good thing his nose is so disgustingly smooth, she thought; *otherwise there might be a certain temptation.* . . .

"What makes you think it's a Gamma ship, old man?" Sisko asked Dax upon reaching the operations table.

"First," she answered, ticking points off on her fingers, "it doesn't match any Federation, Cardassian, Romulan, Borg, or Bajoran ship designs. Second, it's using a refined particle-accelerator drive, rather than impulse or fusion. And third," she concluded, "it reached the wormhole, so it must have warp-speed capability; but there is no antimatter on that ship. So they must use something we've never developed ourselves."

"No antimatter?" repeated Chief O'Brien, popping up from behind his engineering console.

"Hail them," ordered Sisko.

Dax did so, then stared at her display. "I think they're running through every possible radio and subspace frequency, trying to contact us. Ah, they found our communications bandwidth. Audio only, there's no visual."

"Put it on—" Before Sisko could say "screen," Dax piped the audio signal through the Ops intercom.

"You will surrender your prisoner or be destroyed," said a flat, emotionless voice.

"Shields up!" commanded Kira. O'Brien did it himself from engineering.

"They're speaking Cardassian," said Dax, "but they're not Cardassians."

"Open a channel, Lieutenant. This is Commander Sisko of the Bajoran and Federation station Deep Space Nine. We are holding no prisoners from the Gamma quadrant."

The aliens' response was quick and to the point. "Prepare to be boarded," they announced.

CHAPTER
3

FOR AN INSTANT everybody in Ops paused, holding his breath. Then they all began talking at once.

"Dax—get us some help," ordered Sisko. At the same moment, Kira tapped her communicator: "Odo! Odo, answer me!"

Nobody responded to either Dax's subspace message or Kira's emergency call.

"They've put a shield around the station," exclaimed O'Brien; "it's stopping subspace communications."

"Can you break through it, Chief?" asked Dax.

"Security! Kira here, priority one!"

"Chief," asked Sisko, "are our own shields holding?"

"No, sir; yes, sir," said the chief, responding first to Dax, then Sisko. "We can't break out, but they can't break in, so far."

"Kira," said the commander, "this constitutes an attack. Fire phasers. Burn their noses a bit."

Kira's fingers ripped across her console almost too fast to see. She was unable to lock the phasers on, so she directed the fire visually, using the computer to triangulate on the alien ship from several views.

She fired two short phaser bursts, one at each propulsion pod of the alien ship. The ship apparently had no shields, and the blue phaser streams struck their targets.

Incredibly, the phaser blasts reflected like lasers off a mirror.

"Commander," said Kira, barely controlling her amazement, "did you see—?"

"I saw," said Sisko. His calm voice cut through her tension, relaxed her just enough to fire an immediate barrage along the entire length of the alien hull, again sighting visually, since the phasers refused to lock on target.

Wherever the phasers struck, they reflected; one shot actually returned directly at DS9.

Kira ducked involuntarily, but the reflected shot missed Ops by a hair. "O'Brien!" she shouted.

"Incoming!" announced Dax. "Large, metallic—Kira, it's a torpedo of some sort."

Kira tried to lock on to the torpedo but was as unsuccessful as before. She took a few potshots at the torpedo, but it was too small to hit. "Sisko!" she exclaimed. "I can't hit the damned thing!"

O'Brien shouted from his own station. "Don't worry, it'll just hit the shields and . . ."

They all stared; the torpedo flared blue-green for a moment, as if passing through a pane of colored glass. Then it continued, as if it did not even notice the station shields.

Sisko leaned over his console. "Batter up," he said, smiling grimly.

"What are you—" Kira started to ask, then saw on her own instruments that the commander had activated the tractor beam. Instead of trying to lock on to the missile, he simply swept the tractor beam through a plane that intersected with the torpedo.

The device rebounded from the tractor-bat, spun off above the station. "Damn," said Sisko, "foul ball!"

"What in blue hell is that thing?" demanded Chief

O'Brien, staring at his sensor array. "A chemical explosive . . . and it went right through our shields like they weren't there. Thank God the commander knocked it aw—"

A white light flared on the screen, brightening until the automatic filters blocked it out. At the same time, every electronic display in Ops blinked off, then flickered back on again.

"Security here—Major Kira, *are you all right?*"

"Hunh? Oh, sorry." Kira realized that security had responded several times to her call, but she was so occupied by the battle she had not heard. "Find Odo immediately. Urgent."

"Aye, sir."

Sisko frowned, still apparently the calmest one in Ops. "How could a torpedo slide right through our shields?"

He looked to O'Brien, Dax, and Kira, but each stared blankly.

"Sir," said the chief, "I think we may have a worse problem than that."

"Incoming, number two!" shouted Kira. This time, she did not wait for the commander; she used the tractor herself. She did not have Sisko's years of practice with a baseball bat, but she had sufficient time to use the computer to help her aim. She struck the next torpedo cleanly, and knocked it far away before it exploded.

"What do you mean, Chief?" asked Sisko.

"Sir, when that thing exploded, it knocked our shields down for a half second. During that moment, I picked up an energy transfer."

"What happened?"

"Sir—I think they beamed some people aboard."

"Where?"

"Promenade."

"Incoming three!" Kira was kept busy for several minutes as the alien ship fired missile after missile. Each cut through the shields as if they did not exist, but Kira batted each missile away.

"Somebody's got to go hunt them down," said the commander, "round them up and hold them until we can figure out what they want. Where's Odo?"

"Gone," said Kira, unable to take her eyes off her console. She barely nicked one missile, and it exploded close enough to actually rock the station. "He doesn't answer his call. I've got security out looking—"

"I need somebody experienced with in-station disturbances . . . either you or O'Brien."

Sisko looked from one to the other, debating which he could least spare from Ops. Kira, however, knew that if she so much as stepped away from her console, she might miss the next "station buster" bomb the invaders fired.

On the other hand, Dax could temporarily take over engineering, if necessary. Thus, O'Brien was the most expendable at that moment.

Kira looked at Sisko, shook her head.

"O'Brien," snapped the commander, "beam directly to the Security office and find those invaders." Sisko tapped his communicator. "Security! The station has been invaded by hostile forces; Chief O'Brien is beaming over to you . . . he'll locate the invaders, and you take them out. And find Odo! Out.

"Sisko to Bashir."

"Bashir here, sir," said the doctor's eager-to-please voice.

"We're under attack."

"Attack? Is that what that was?"

"Casualties might be coming your way. It could get heavy, Doctor—we've been boarded by what might be a strike team. They're on the Promenade."

A pause. "I understand, sir. I'll prepare."

"If you want to relocate to a safer location, I'll understand."

This time there was no hesitation. "No, sir. Everything is here, and I really can't move it. I'll be all right."

"It's your decision. Sisko out."

While the commander spoke, Dax transferred all the engineering functions to her own console. O'Brien ran to the transporter pad, veering past his console long enough to activate the energizing touchpad. He vanished in a swirl of transporter sparkles.

Sisko's voice cut above the tumult. "Dax, try the photon torpedoes. Kira, see if you can knock one of their own bombs at them—then Dax will hit them with a photon torpedo right after their own explosion. Two can play this game."

Sweat dripped down Kira's face, but she could not remove her hands from the tractor trackball even long enough to wipe her sleeve across her forehead. She blinked stinging sweat from her eyes. "Three, two, one, shoot 'em, Dax."

Kira knocked the bomb back toward the alien ship just as Dax fired a full spread. A strange tube projected out from the alien ship and fired a steady stream of tiny pellets at the bomb, spraying them so quickly it looked like a fire hose.

The stream missed, but was quickly swerved to intersect the bomb's new trajectory. The missile vanished in a hail of pellets.

But in the confusion, Dax's photon torpedoes slipped right past. They exploded, yawing the ship.

"Got 'em!" shouted Dax. "Did some damage, too. Incoming, Kira."

The new missile was not well aimed, probably thrown off course when the ship changed position while still controlling it. Kira did not catch a big enough piece of it to knock it completely away. It exploded, much too close, and again DS9 shuddered under the impact. The shields fluttered, failed again momentarily.

"Second failure," said Dax; she looked up, unhappy. "Another team beamed aboard."

Sisko tapped his communicator, informed O'Brien and Security of the new invasion. "Dax," he added, "have you found a way to break through the communications shield?"

"Sorry," she said; "I tried every channel of subspace and even regular radio and microwave. Nothing."

The commander turned to Kira. "Major, program a probe to eject from the station and contact Bajor as soon as it clears the shield."

She raised her brows, annoyed that she had not thought of it herself. It took her thirty seconds to program the probe with the unusual instructions; she nervously watched her instruments, dreading another bomb attack while she was occupied. But the alien ship was quiet, possibly as a result of their last attack.

"Ready," she announced.

"Launch."

Kira launched the probe. It streaked directly away from the alien ship, on the other side of DS9. She hoped the station itself would shield the probe from the ship.

The invaders were merely playing dead. They fired a barrage of six bombs at the station. Frantically, Kira swung the tractor beam wildly, knocking back the four most direct shots. Two looked wild, and she was forced to ignore them.

They were not wild. The other two shots exploded on two sides of the probe, crushing it between them like a hammer striking an anvil. The probe was obliterated long before it breached the communications shield.

Dax fired another photon-torpedo spread, two of which struck the ship, battering it.

For a long moment, nothing happened; both DS9 and the alien ship paused, took stock of the situation. Then the ship began to back slowly away from the station.

"Hold your fire," ordered Sisko, "they're withdrawing."

Kira finally wiped her dripping brow. "What about the strike team inside the station?"

"You stay here," he answered. "Let's see what O'Brien and Security can do. And find that blasted constable!" Sisko looked at her and grinned. "I can't spare you from the batter's box, Major."

"What?"

"Never mind. Just stay where you are. Dax, get damage reports and send maintenance crews. Kira, patch me stationwide."

"Aye, sir." She opened the stationwide channel, then nodded at the commander.

"This is Commander Sisko," he said, voice still professionally calm. "I regret to inform you that Deep Space Nine has been attacked by an unidentified hostile force. For the moment, the battle has broken off. But there are invaders inside the station. Everybody must evacuate the Promenade *immediately*. Return to the habitat ring. Above all else, *do not hamper Security*. Return to the habitat ring—that is a direct order. Sisko out." He turned to Kira. "Major, get me a continuous feed from O'Brien; I want to know everything that happens *before* it *happens*."

Chief Miles O'Brien's heart pounded like a fusion pulse-wave; he wondered if it meant he was about to explode, as it would in a fusion reactor.

O'Brien had become an engineer because after his experiences in the Cardassian war, he could not bear the thought of killing another living being . . . even a Cardassian.

He was a friendly man, a family man; he wanted nothing more than a wife to love, a child to take care of, and a steady job working with his hands—*well, perhaps a wee, tiny bit of adventure,* he admitted. But not this; not something that endangered Keiko and Molly.

He walked as quickly as he could past the operations table to the transporter pad, resisting the temptation to run. As he passed his engineering console, he typed the coordinates of the security office and flicked the switch to Energize.

He stepped aboard the pad and felt the familiar, comforting vibration as his body was torn apart, molecule by molecule, stored, broadcast, and reassembled in the middle of a large room.

The Spartan room that adjoined Odo's office was

packed with grim, determined security forces. Desks were shoved to the side to make room on the floor for a weapons inventory. A Bajoran rushed past with an armful of phaser rifles, another with a box of hand phasers.

God help me, thought O'Brien. *I'm a lover, not a fighter!* Husband, father, engineer, amateur magician, raconteur, and three-fisted drinker . . . never a warrior!

Lieutenant Moru, number two officer in Security after Odo, covered the vulnerable glass doors by lowering the interior blast shields, heavy plates of metal that would theoretically protect the security office from attack.

"O'Brien?" she asked. He nodded. "Here." Moru tossed him a tricorder. "Find the raping bastards."

"Yes, sir."

Just then, Commander Sisko spoke to the station, told everyone to evacuate the Promenade toward the habitat ring. O'Brien laid the tricorder on a desk and took a moment to program it to search for anomalous alien genetic patterns.

He slowly rotated through 360 degrees, sneaking a glance at the Bajoran lieutenant. She looked harder than Kira, even tougher than the old security officer on the *Enterprise,* Tasha Yar. She could probably have given Lursa and Bator, the sisters of the Klingon Duras, a run for their money.

"There's twelve of 'em, sir," he said, pointing toward the side bulkhead. "I think they're near Quark's Place."

The school! For a moment, he looked in the other direction, toward Keiko's schoolroom. Then he decided that the best way to protect his wife and daughter would be to confront the aliens where they were now, before they had a chance to wander around to the other side of the Promenade.

"Move out," commanded Moru, cradling a huge phaser rifle in her bare arms.

They dashed out the security office door, leaving half the garrison behind to defend it, if necessary, and double-timed toward Quark's.

The Promenade was in an uproar. Civilians walked or ran toward the connecting tunnels to the habitat ring. Banners were trampled underfoot, but some of the Bajoran religious protesters could not even let off their verbal sniping long enough to cooperate in the evacuation.

Shopkeepers were shooing tardy customers out and locking their doors; some carried irreplaceable "treasures" in their arms or on floating pads.

Moru took point, O'Brien right behind her, followed by the other twenty members of the security platoon. "Wait—wait," said the chief. Moru held up her hand, halting the column.

"Just around the curve," O'Brien whispered. "Now there's fifteen of them bunched up in the middle of the deck, twenty meters ahead."

Moru nodded, put her finger to her lips. She made a complicated set of hand gestures, and the platoon fanned out into half a chevron, swept forward slowly.

There was no mistaking the invaders. They looked as if they had stepped out of a holoplay about extragalactic storm troopers.

They wore gray-and-black armored suits with shiny black "bubble" helmets and carried a strange-looking weapon that O'Brien had never seen before. Moru reached back, pushed O'Brien behind the line; he was only too happy to comply.

Lieutenant Moru spoke through a Universal Translator PA system in her own helmet: "Don't you move! Anybody who hears this voice, *don't move* or you will be shot." Half the civilians froze; the rest either dropped to the ground, hands over heads, or fled screaming.

The platoon strode forward in step, phaser rifles leveled at the invaders.

The aliens did not bother responding verbally; they leveled their own guns.

Moru's security platoon fired first. Phaser beams lanced out, and every shot hit its target.

The bright red phaser light cut the air and struck the

invaders' armor. The beams reflected off in a kaleido-
scopic swirl of high-intensity energy bursts.

The reflected phaser blasts fired in every direction,
depending on the angle of the piece of armor they struck.
Holes burst through bulkheads; store windows disinte-
grated in a shower of glass. One of the security women
was caught in her midsection by a blast on the highest
setting; she collapsed, dead instantly.

The invaders were not even affected.

They returned fire, and Miles O'Brien thought the
gates of hell had opened wide. Their guns used some sort
of chemical explosive to propel projectiles, like the
gunpowder firearms that humans had used centuries ago
on earth, and they were *loud*. He covered his ears and
crouched down behind the security team for cover.

The invaders' firearms kept shooting, and shooting,
and shooting, firing rounds so quickly that they func-
tioned almost like directed-energy weapons.

"Computer!" shouted Moru. "Force shield nine-one
up!"

Between the security force and the invaders, a shield
popped up, shimmered protectively.

"Retreat, regroup," ordered Moru. O'Brien stayed
behind the lieutenant, watching the invaders intently to
see how they would react. "Force shield nine-three up,"
added Moru; another shield popped up behind the
invaders, trapping them.

The invaders calmly walked toward the security platoon. Their leader carried only a small, hand-sized
firearm, rather than one of the big rifles carried by the
others.

They reached the force shield, stood immobile for a
moment. "Inspecting it," said Moru; "next they'll try it,
then try to shoot through it." She turned back to
O'Brien, grinned. "Then, all of a sudden, they'll become
great believers in diplomacy."

"I hope you're right, sir," said the chief; privately, he
had a very bad feeling about the attack.

As Moru predicted, the invader leader strode forward,

directly into the force shield. The shield crackled, and electricity discharged all around the invader's armor, outlining it. The invader continued walking, unimpeded by the shield; its comrades followed, jogging toward the platoon.

Moru stared, astonished. "Fire!" he shouted. "Hit 'em with everything!"

The platoon fired phaser shot after shot, but they reflected from the invaders' armor. The invaders shouldered their rifles as they advanced, raked the security team with automatic fire. Security personnel dropped to O'Brien's left, ripped open by the high-velocity projectiles.

One of the invaders at the center of the group, using its companions as concealment, raised a different weapon over their heads, and fired a large projectile into the platoon.

In sudden epiphany, Miles O'Brien, a former soldier in the Cardassian war, understood it was explosive. He rolled to his knees, then feet, and just before the invader fired, he pelted back around the curve of the Promenade bulkhead.

The concussion knocked him off his feet from ten meters away, sent him sliding along the deck, stunned but uninjured.

The security platoon fared less gloriously. O'Brien snuck a quick peek back, saw three of them in full flight, badly injured and shooting wildly.

Then he turned and ran back toward the security office—hearing another explosive concussion behind him as he ran. He felt like a coward for not staying and getting killed, even though he knew it was much more important that someone survive and warn the commander.

He burst through the security office door, was caught by two burly security men. "Gone," he gasped; "killed them—all of them!"

"Who killed whom?" demanded a security chief.

O'Brien sucked air into his burning lungs, wincing as

his bruised ribs complained bitterly. "They—they got us. All of us. No survivors except me." He looked the security chief in the eye. His nametag read C EWIN. "We're in big trouble, Ewin. They've got some kind of armor . . . phasers don't affect them."

"Not at all?" asked Ewin, having trouble with the concept.

"It doesn't *shield* from a phaser blast . . . it *reflects* it perfectly. Phasers, phaser rifles, probably not even the station's entire phaser array would affect a single one of them. We need something more powerful, something with a brute-force kick like Irish whisky."

"Christ on a crutch," snarled Chief Ewin. "Toborhan! Find us a big hammer in the weapons lockup—we've got to hold them here on the Promenade . . . if they get into Ops or the habitat ring, we may as well abandon the whole station!"

O'Brien tapped his communicator. "Sisko."

"Sisko here," said the voice.

"They've got—"

"I heard," said the commander; "I've been listening. Chief, can you make a phaser overload on cue?"

"I . . . a phaser grenade?" He thought for a moment, phaser schematics flashing like holovision in his head. "Sure, I guess."

"Get up here and make us some phaser grenades. Security . . . who's in command down there, now?"

"Cory Ewin, sir," said the burly, black-haired Welshman.

"Find something harder to hit them with and *hold them on the Promenade*, Ewin. O'Brien will be back as soon as possible with that phaser-grenade hammer you're looking for."

"Aye, sir," said Ewin, staring dubiously at a hand phaser. "O'Brien," he asked quietly, "can you really make these things explode?"

"Sure, and it's easy," said Miles O'Brien; "you readjust the—"

"Don't tell me," said Ewin, holding up his hand; "I *don't* want to know." Shuddering, he put the phaser back on the table.

The dead station was utterly silent. The complete absence of the normal tumult still shocked Odo. The constable would never have believed he could actually *miss* the hurly-burly of miners, tourists, religious fanatics, and boisterous Federation crew members that normally inhabited Deep Space 9.

Three days later. How could three days have suddenly "gone missing"? And what could have happened to DS9 during that time to kill so many?

And where was Security? Where were the command crew?

Odo had almost gotten used to the blue-white, flickering lights on the Promenade. At least, it was sufficient to let him avoid the worst of the glass and metal shards on the floor.

He squatted near a body that was stiff from rigor mortis. He stared at what used to be his second-in-command. She, too, had been killed approximately two days ago, when Quark and Odo had been in the "time bubble" for about a day, with two to go before they woke up.

It's maddening, thought Odo; *worse than being in jail. At least in jail you have some idea of the passage of time.*

"Your wounds are all in the front, Lieutenant Moru," he said; "I just wanted you to know I noticed that." He reached down, tried to shut her eyelids; but they were dried open and would not move. She had been dead for two days, and in that time, no one had closed her eyes.

The disrespect bothered Odo nearly as much as Moru's death itself.

She had left her right arm and a lot of blood back up the lightning-lit corridor, just outside Quark's Place. But she had still managed to scramble backward, firing all the way. Her phaser rifle was drained of power, whether by repeated firing or by her assailants, the constable could not tell. She died a hero, defending DS9 against . . . against what? Who had attacked, and why?

The attack made no sense, the sort of exuberant injustice that literally made Odo's flesh creep, for he grew so agitated that he almost lost control of his shape.

Nothing of value appeared to be missing; no invaders seemed to remain aboard; and after three days (if the Klingon clock could be believed), no one had come in response to a distress call that would have sounded *automatically*, even if everyone in Ops had died.

Odo slowly walked back to where he had left the Ferengi. The curve of the Promenade was invisible in the flickering gloom, giving the illusion of infinite distance.

Quark had been busy; all the bodies were arranged neatly with sheets drawn over them. The little pink bartender and petty villain sat on his haunches, staring up the corridor toward what was once Quark's Place, the finest gambling and holosex hall in the sector.

"I did it," he whispered, "didn't I?"

"I'm sorry? What did you say?" Odo bent close.

Quark stared at the deck. "That's what you want, right? A confession? Well, surprise, Odo; you heard right . . . I confess."

The constable was so amazed he could find no words. Quark continued. "It—it *had* to be the device. What else could . . . oh, gods of commerce, Odo, I must have killed them all!"

The Ferengi wrapped his arms around his ears. It was not a standard Ferengi cringe; Odo realized to his shock that it was good, old-fashioned, honest guilt. A real emotion. "If you had told me yesterday," he began, "that I would ever hear a Ferengi—"

"Is there anybody left alive? Sisko, Kira . . . Dax? Is Jadzia Dax left alive, or has that loveliness been ripped apart by high-velocity projectiles?"

"I don't know, Quark."

"Bashir? Rom? Garak? N-Nog?"

"I don't know." Strangely, the taste of triumph at

obtaining Quark's confession turned to ashes on Odo's lips. It was no longer of any importance that the Ferengi admit his guilt. "Rom is dead, Quark."

"I forgot."

The constable watched the Ferengi, felt a very unaccustomed emotion: pity. In all his days since waking up in the med lab, Odo could not remember feeling sorry for a criminal, until today. And for Quark, possibly a mass murderer, yet!

"I must be losing my mind," he marveled. "Or my nerve."

"I—I . . ." Quark stared furiously, helplessly at the deck. "I—I take—full responsibility for my actions, Odo."

Odo stared in amazement. Hesitantly, he touched Quark on the shoulder, tried clumsily to pat it.

"Odo, I demand that you arrest me for—for murder." The Ferengi looked straight at Odo, eyes sunken, ears flushed and pulled back until they were nearly parallel to his head.

"At most, negligent homicide, Quark. Perhaps not even that."

"You saw what happened. I switched the field, then suddenly all this!" The Ferengi looked pointedly at the pile of shrouded bodies, the ruined stores, the collapsed overheads.

Odo found himself in the odd position of defending Quark's innocence to Quark himself. "But how could you know what was going to happen? Quark, I work for justice, not the law of an eye for an eye! Besides, if I put you in storage, who's going to help me explore what's left of this station, figure out what happened and what to do next?"

"Odo, if it's really been three days, why hasn't a ship come? How long does it take to respond to a distress call?"

"See?" said Odo. "There are too many unanswered questions to pick a suspect just yet. Make you a deal, Quark; a plea bargain. You plead no contest for the moment, and I'll release you on—um—one bar of gold-pressed latinum bail. All right? A deal?" Odo extended his hand.

Quark stared at it as if he had never seen one before. "Bail?"

"Yes, it means you're free to move about the station."

"I know what bail is, you shifty Cardassian relic! How much did you say, one bar?"

"One bar."

"That's—that's wildly excessive! Bail is supposed to keep criminals from running away; where would I *go?* No, Odo . . . oh no, I should be released on my own recognizance!" Quark pounded the deck as he made his application. He yelped, subsided into silence, rubbing his wrist.

"Well, it looks like the old, familiar Quark has decided to rejoin us," said Odo.

"Yes, well . . ." The Ferengi glanced at the stacked bodies, then quickly away. "Let's get moving, see what we can find. Maybe some of this ruined junk will be salable, at least."

They rose and started their first exploratory trip around the Promenade.

"You know," said Quark, speaking pro forma, without any real conviction, "if we're really the only two left on DS-Nine, we could claim salvage rights. All we need is a Ferengi barrister who can convince the judge. . . ."

CHAPTER
4

O'BRIEN STAGGERED as the station rolled again. After a long slumber, the invading ship had apparently awakened. Nearly thirty minutes had passed since the invaders attacked DS9 without provocation.

He looked at his tricorder, saw the angle that indicated invader-direction begin to bend.

"They're moving again!" announced Chief O'Brien. He watched the readout, mentally tracking the invaders' progress around the Promenade. "Jesus and Mary," he breathed, "they're heading away from us—toward the school." He looked up at Ewin. "Keiko!" he explained, face drained of blood.

The chief heard distant thunder, the force of an explosion striking some faraway part of the station.

"Keiko? The schoolmarm? What about—"

"She's my wife."

Ewin stared for a moment, puzzled. Then the words sank in. "You're *that* O'Brien?" he exclaimed. "All right, steady on. She's probably already evacuated. Which way should we go, left or right?"

For a terrible instant, O'Brien could not even call to

mind the station diagram. Then he shook his head, dispelling the cobwebs of fear. "Neither," he said. "They've sent scouts out in both directions around the main Promenade level. But if we go up to level nine, we can cut directly across through the emergency power conduit. Ah, if it's not in use."

"Lead on, Macduff," said Chief Ewin.

O'Brien jogged across the corridor to the access ladder; the turbolifts were too close to the alien advance line in either direction. *It's LAY on, Macduff, you illiterate Welshman,* he thought; *and Macduff was Scottish, not Irish.* In fact, Miles O'Brien had made the same mistake only a week before, and Keiko had corrected him, more or less hilariously. She took great amusement from the discovery that she knew Shakespeare better than her Irish husband did.

That was one of the times he gritted his teeth and loved her.

The station rocked and rolled under another impact. "Commander," asked O'Brien, "what's going on up there?"

Kira answered instead. "We're busy," she said tersely; "carry on, I'm monitoring you as best I can—"

A *boom* sounded over the communicator, so loud that the chief jumped. The explosions from their own photon torpedoes sent an earsplitting crack of white noise through the communicator channel.

Despite his chubby frame, O'Brien shimmied up the ladder so fast he outdistanced the more physically fit but less agile security platoon. He opened an access panel, then waited long enough that Ewin could watch as he crawled through the opening.

Inside was a narrow, white tunnel. Running down the middle was a roughly cylindrical lattice of ferrotite bars, the magnetic containment grid that channeled and directed the flow of microwaves that powered the station.

Even outside the grid, in the narrow space between bulkhead and the conduit itself, he could feel the surge of the microwaves (which Starfleet engineering regulations insisted could not be felt by humans). They caused the hair on his hands and neck to flutter. He pulled a spanner from his belt, hesitated for a moment in front of the circuit pad. The security platoon squeezed through the access hole after him.

"They're using the emergency conduit," he explained to Ewin. "Must be running shields, phasers, and something else big, like tractors, all at the same time."

"Would it fry us if we stepped inside?"

"Probably. And don't touch the grid, either."

He took a deep breath, continued. "I can reroute the power flow, but . . ." He thought of the station suddenly losing power for a few moments, while the power couplings realigned. He thought of Keiko, Molly, the school.

"Commander?" he said.

"I've been following off and on," said Sisko's voice out of the air, crackling with static from proximity to megajoules of broadcast power.

"If I transfer power, you're going to lose it for a couple of seconds while the couplings retune and align to the new flow."

"Negative," said Major Kira's voice, fainter; she was shouting across Ops, not having hands free to slap her own comm badge. "The invader ship has fired fifteen torpedoes at us so far; we need shields, phasers, and tractor beams *continuously.*"

"Dax," said Sisko's disembodied voice, "is the schoolroom evacuated?"

During the slight pause, not a single security officer breathed.

"No, sir," said the lieutenant. "Mrs. O'Brien informs me she has not been able to get out yet, and several of the children are with her. Including Jake."

"And Molly?" asked O'Brien.

"Proceed with the power shift in twenty seconds," ordered Sisko. "Lieutenant, fire a full battery of photon torpedoes, set to detonate in eighteen seconds directly in the line of sight between the invader's sensor array and the station. Maybe we can make them blink."

Behind him, Chief O'Brien heard Ewin softly counting: "One hippopotamus, two hippopotamus, three hippopotamus . . ." O'Brien looked at his wrist chronometer; the security chief was as accurate as a metronome.

At ten hippopotami, O'Brien cracked the panel cover and removed it, careful not to touch the "hot" grid.

At fifteen hippopotami, he inserted the spanner into the upper isolinear deck, snagged the routing packet junction node.

At sixteen hippos, Dax's voice announced "torpedoes away."

Two seconds later, multiple peals of thunder echoed through the comm link, forcing everyone to clap hands over ears. Ewin continued his count, unperturbed.

The instant that Ewin ate his twentieth hippopotamus, O'Brien thumbed the contact on his spanner, reversing the node. Almost immediately, he felt the power slack, die.

"Down," he advised. The security platoon began to stir, but O'Brien held his hand up for them to wait.

"Up!" shouted Kira. O'Brien let his breath out; if the power had not come back on-line, he would have had to re-reroute it back through the emergency conduit again.

He slipped very carefully between the ferrotite bars of the containment grid into the conduit itself, being very careful not to so much as brush against them. Even with the flow shut down, the grid still maintained a static electrical charge "hot" enough to kill a man instantly if he was not wearing the proper protective clothing—which none of them were.

When the platoon saw that he did not appear to fry, they quickly followed, being equally careful around the grid. The luck gods were smiling, and nobody stumbled.

"Come on," said O'Brien, sprinting along the catwalk with new urgency, now that he knew Keiko was definitely in the war zone.

They had to crouch as they ran to avoid brushing the

ferrotite, which slowed them considerably. Even so, they reached the opposite side of the Promenade much more quickly than they would have circumnavigating the perimeter.

Just as they reached the other side, another near miss caused the entire station to swerve violently to their left. O'Brien staggered, fell to the deck. He clutched at the catwalk, teetered precariously for a moment, then recovered facedown on the walkway.

Petty Officer Dahnu slipped, fell against the side of the conduit. The explosion of electrical discharge nearly deafened the chief. He stared in horror at the dead Bajoran man he had never met. Dahnu's face was contorted in a silent scream of agony.

Ewin pushed insistently at O'Brien's shoulder blade. "Come on, man. Move it, move it! Time enough later, right?"

Shaking, the chief slipped out between the ferrotite bars of the grid, careful to the point of paranoia not to touch the metal. As the other men and women exited, O'Brien padded softly to the corresponding access panel, and peered through the grille without removing it.

His stomach contracted; below them, a knot of ten invaders milled arrogantly in the promenade, guns in hand, while two pairs of their comrades dragged shopkeepers who had been slow to evacuate out of their stores to the habitat ring.

The Promenade was eerily deserted except for the tableau below them. The invaders used an odd sort of Universal Translator; it translated the words well enough, but the tone came across as harsh and mechanical—not like the Borg, but like an executioner's song.

Of each Promenade merchant, they asked the same question, which sounded like a declarative statement through their translator: "Where is the other one like us."

As O'Brien watched, frozen in horror, the interrogator

casually executed each merchant who had no answer to the question, which meant all of them, since nobody even knew what the inquisitor was talking about.

O'Brien watched three executions: the first was a Ferengi spice trader, who cringed, bowed, and scraped before being murdered.

The second was a Bajoran woman who looked like a somewhat older and fatter version of Kira. *A relation?* he wondered. She was defiant, refusing to give in to the fear she must have felt. A brave woman. The grand inquisitor put a bullet in her head without a second thought.

The shot echoed around O'Brien's skull as a third person was hauled to the question. "Where is the other one like us," asked the inquisitor, voice as harsh and discordant as the previous two times.

Suddenly, Miles O'Brien recognized the man, another Bajoran: he was the gruff matie who sold the ever-popular "glop on a stick," a Bajoran favorite that O'Brien had learned to like. What was his name? Doran. Loran, something like that.

"You're looking for the other one, the one that looks like you, right?" The inquisitor said nothing, waited for Doran to continue. "I saw him . . . they've—he's hidden. They took him off the station." Doran looked from rifle to armor to shiny, black helmet.

O'Brien could tell from Doran's face that he was lying through his teeth.

"He's not here," continued the Bajoran, licking his lips nervously; "and if you don't immediately stop killing us, you'll *never* find out where he is."

Still the inquisitor stood silent; but he also had not shot the man yet. He waited, patiently.

"Odo took him," said Doran. "Took him off the station."

Come to think of it, where is Odo? O'Brien wondered whether the Bajoran glop-merchant might be telling the truth. Maybe Odo *did* take the "other one" away.

In any case, the story was good enough that the rest of

the invaders had also stopped interrogating and executing the mall merchants.

Slowly, the inquisitor raised his hand-held firearm, pressed it against Doran's throat, pointed upward toward his brain.

Doran licked his lips. His voice sounded dry, scratchy. "O—Odo, the c-constable. He's got your friend. Got him—took him off the station. Not to Bajor! No, the . . . the other way." Doran's face suddenly brightened. "Through the wormhole. Yes, took him through the wormhole to the Gamma quadrant. *That's* where he is."

No! O'Brien pressed his lips together hard to stop himself from shouting *No, you idiot, don't tell them that! That's where* they *come from!*

Doran continued, oblivious of his miscalculation. "A couple of days ago, two days ago, Odo took your friend through the wormhole to—"

The explosion from the inquisitor's gun sounded louder than all the rest, probably because it was both unanticipated and thoroughly expected. Miles O'Brien jumped, slumped back away from the panel.

"It's hopeless," he said. "They don't care. They don't feel. We're flies to them." He nodded to Chief Ewin, handed him three "phaser grenades" he had assembled, keeping the last two for himself. "Lay on, Macduff," whispered O'Brien, "and damn'd be him that first cries, 'Hold, enough.'"

But in fact, a different quotation ran through his brain, from *King Lear*, the one Keiko disliked the most. It stuck in O'Brien's memory for days:

> As flies to wanton boys, are we to the gods;
> They kill us for their sport.

"Odo!" cried Quark. "Here, look at this."

The constable straightened, quickly strode to where the Ferengi peered around the Promenade bend. There was clearly no danger; the self-protective Quark would not have been idiot enough to shout at Odo after finding a living enemy.

Whatever happened, it had begun two days ago and was all over a day before Quark and Odo came out of time-freeze.

The shapeshifter walked past Quark and around the curve of the inner bulkhead. Then he stopped short, speechless. Even in the darkest days of the Cardassian occupation of Bajor, he had never seen such casual carnage.

At least thirty bodies of Promenade merchants lay where they had fallen or been thoughtlessly tossed aside. Each had a single bullet wound in the head, causing instant death.

The stores themselves were ripped apart, much worse than Quark's Place had been, as if a lunatic with an asteroid-mining phaser had carved bizarre, geometric patterns in the walls, floors, even ceilings of DS9's Promenade. Somebody was looking for something . . . or *someone*.

In the midst of the floor were the remains of yet another security platoon.

Odo lost his shape for a moment, so stunned at the sight. He started to shrink into himself before realizing, concentrated on restoring the "Odo" shape. Quark, unable to tear his gaze from the morbid fascination of annihilation, did not even notice.

Odo dropped to hands and knees and examined the battle scene from line-of-fire level.

Casualties were one hundred percent; but there were a lot more missed bullets around the men and women, indicating they had taken the enemy by some surprise, perhaps wounded some. Looking back in the apparent direction of the platoon's fire, Odo saw deep phaser burns in every surface, but fewer in direct line of fire.

"Quark, use your analytical skills. What does this suggest to you?"

The Ferengi, looking distinctly bluish white, stared from the butchered security platoon to the other side of the battle, his brows lowered in confusion. Suddenly he gasped. "There are almost no phaser burns behind where the bad guys were standing."

"Which suggests?" Odo knew very well what it meant, but he wanted to hear another person express the same viewpoint; Quark, apparently being the only other living entity on DS9, was elected.

Quark looked back at the constable. "That—they were wearing some sort of personal shields that deflected phaser blasts?"

Odo nodded; it was the same conclusion he had drawn. "Even the station shields *absorb* and reemit phaser energy as microwaves. They don't perfectly reflect it."

"What's the difference?"

Odo answered impatiently. "Absorbing such energy *uses* energy; every blast weakens our shields, and eventually they fail, letting a shot through.

"But if these—assassins—can reflect phaser fire without having to absorb it, they're . . ."

"Invulnerable?"

Odo stood, shaking his head. "I don't believe in invulnerability. But there are stories."

"Stories? Of invulnerable assassins?"

"The Cardassians tell stories, tall tales about . . . no, forget it. They're just a myth. Bogeymen to frighten Cardassian children into obedience."

"Who are?"

Odo turned the bodies over. The highest-ranking petty officer present was Chief Ewin, along with the only senior chief left after two had died in the first engagement. With Ewin and Moru both dead, that left Lieutenant (j.g.) Turnan in command, Ensign Turnan-Dai as XO, and no enlisted personnel above the rank of CPO.

In two short battles, probably fought within a few minutes of each other, judging by their proximity, Odo's security squadron had lost its executive officer, all but one department head, and the four senior noncoms. They had been devastated.

Quark wandered slowly among the bodies of the

merchants. "I know these people," he said, voice shaky. "I didn't like them; they were always complaining about the casino—said it brought a bad element to DS-Nine. But I—I told them that it just sucked up the bad element that would be here anyway, kept it from polluting their dainty emporiums.

"I didn't like them, but . . . but I *knew* them all. Do you understand what I mean?"

"I understand. You must know, Quark, that there were not many people on this station that I would call friend either, or who would call *me* friend. I haven't found their bodies yet, except Lieutenant Moru; she and I understood each other very well. But I must assume that the rest are dead as well, or they would have cleaned this place up, gotten it back in working order."

"Even if you didn't like them, you knew them," said Quark, not sure if he were talking to Odo as much as to himself. "You wouldn't want to see *this* happen to them."

"To anyone. But I understand what you mean. I've never seen anything like this before. Despite what Major Kira may tell you, the Cardassians did not generally mow down their Bajoran prisoners like they were so much wheat."

Constable Odo pressed his lips together grimly, continued examining the crime scene—*battle* scene.

"Concussion marks," he said, running his fingers over the deep indentations in the outer bulkhead. "I was not aware we had any explosive devices on this station; but these were obviously projected at the enemy from our security team."

"Didn't work," Quark pointed out unnecessarily.

"Maybe they did. It might have killed an enemy, and the rest of them might have taken the body along or transported it off the station."

Odo crouched, crawled along the ground near the impact crater. Finally, he found what he sought: tiny fragments, presumably from the bomb. When he had collected a dozen or more, he sifted them in his hand, mentally trying to piece them together.

At once it clicked. "Clever human," he breathed, impressed. "Quark, do you know what this was?" The Ferengi shook his head, and Odo answered his own question. "This used to be a hand phaser. Somebody hot-wired it into a bomb, a grenade."

"One of the security officers?"

Odo shook his head this time. "The only person who could do it is Chief O'Brien. Well, perhaps Lieutenant Dax as well. They must have realized the invaders or mutineers had reflecting armor, decided to try a brute-force explosion."

Silence; Odo looked up. Quark was not listening, staring down the corridor instead. The constable followed his gaze, saw what had caught his eye.

The schoolroom set up by Chief O'Brien's wife, Keiko, had been attacked. It was torn apart worse than it had been when Vedek Winn's terrorist faction had bombed it.

"Nog!" cried Quark. He sprinted down the corridor toward the ruined schoolroom, and Odo pelted after him.

A dangling beam blocked the upper part of the doorway, delaying Odo. The shorter Ferengi was not impeded. Odo ducked underneath, shrinking himself by thirty centimeters. Searching through the rubble, they found the bodies of two Bajoran children, but no Nog or Jake Sisko.

The schoolroom resembled the toybox of a very destructive child: it was a perfect square filled with rubble that surrounded a blast site where something had exploded very powerfully. But among the broken bulkheads and shattered desks, there were odd discrepancies of chance . . . such as the three computer terminals against the back bulkhead, which were completely unscathed.

"Maybe he wasn't here," suggested Odo. "You know he often plays hooky."

Quark looked back at Odo; they both knew that Keiko had recently given Rom a stern lecture about the commercial advantages of school, and Quark's older, more gullible brother had practically kicked the boy's behind all the way to the schoolroom.

Jake, of course, rarely skipped school.

Quark found a debris tunnel, squirmed along it to investigate the rear of the classroom. Odo found a clear spot and grew until his head brushed the ceiling, looking down from above.

The expensive Federation computers that the children used were untouched and untaken, another clue that piracy had not motivated the attack. One display was still on, but it was almost too dim to see.

That's odd, thought Odo; he looked back at the Promenade itself, realized the exterior lights were dimmer than they should be, as well.

If the fusion plants were operating normally, everything should be as bright as normal. *They must be off-line, somehow,* he deduced. But even on battery power, normal station operations would not drain the power for years.

Something must be pulling a *lot* of juice, enough to burn out the batteries after only three days. Offhand, the only system Odo could think of that drew that much power was the station shield. But if the shield was on, how did the invaders get aboard? Were they *already* aboard, an in-house mutiny?

He turned his head, looked down, and saw *her.*

At first, all Odo could see was a pair of feet, too small for a man, too large for a child. He stepped over a fallen support beam with his still-giant legs, then shrank to normal size.

A woman was definitely pinned beneath a collapsed bulkhead. She was not moving or making noise.

"Quark," Odo shouted, "give me a hand."

The two of them managed to struggle the bulkhead off of her body. Tossing it aside, Odo knelt to examine her.

It was definitely Keiko O'Brien, recognizable by her raven black hair and Japanese features despite the gaping bullet wound in her forehead. One glassy eye stared at them, an accusing glare: *Where were you? Why didn't you protect me and the children?* The other eye was swollen shut.

"I'm sorry," said Odo. Quark looked away. "I'm sorry, Mrs. O'Brien. I failed. I wasn't here." He pulled her out of the rubble, causing a mini-cave-in. He laid her body flat.

Wordlessly, Quark handed him a cloth wall-hanging, a painting of both the inside and outside of DS9, created by the younger children; Odo spread it over Keiko's body. It was too short to cover her completely, so he left her legs exposed.

"Failed?" asked the Ferengi. "And what would you have done if you'd been here, Odo? Died with the rest of them?"

"If necessary. If that were all I could do."

"Then who would be left to warn the Bajorans and the Federation about the attack?"

Odo snorted. Typical Ferengi reasoning, justifying failure. "I wasn't here, where I should have been, to defend the station." He glared a long time at the Ferengi, as if daring him to contradict.

"Keiko was killed by a bullet," continued the constable; "other than her swollen left eye, she has no other injuries. The bullet was fired from a short distance away, I would guess, since the wound is surrounded by embedded grains of powder, which are probably the remnants of the propellant.

"This raises an interesting question: Why is the schoolroom torn apart by multiple bomb blasts?"

Quark shrugged. "Somebody trying to fight back?"

"It would have to be after she died," Odo pointed at a gaping wound in Keiko's thigh. "She took bad shrapnel here, but there's no evidence of scabbing, or even leg convulsions."

"Revenge, then," suggested Quark.

"Of course. But who? Security is decimated; if the

civilians had any sense, they'd withdraw down the connecting tunnels to defend the habitat ring."

The constable frowned. "Quark, this was no ordinary attack or terrorist rampage. These invaders destroyed practically the entire security force. Without them, Deep Space Nine itself would be in imminent danger of being lost."

"Destroyed? Or taken over?"

"Somebody jumped them, jumped them hard. It wasn't the Cardassians, the Romulans, or the Borg. Quark, somebody came through the wormhole from the Gamma quadrant and destroyed this station."

Despite his fear, Chief O'Brien was about to follow the security platoon as they boiled out of the emergency-power conduit, but Ewin stopped him. "You ain't a soldier anymore; you don't even have a rifle," he pointed out. "Besides, we need you to make more of these phaser grenades." He pushed O'Brien firmly back toward the grid.

Cory Ewin's action saved O'Brien's life.

The plan worked; the security platoon caught the invaders by surprise, fired into their ranks at will.

Dozens of blasts erupted from the security team's phaser rifles, striking the invaders unimpeded at the highest setting; but every shot reflected off the invader armor, whirling and splitting into multiple beams of intense red light, deadly to everyone except their intended targets.

O'Brien ducked his head, the acrid smell of ozone burning his sensitive nostrils. Aghast, he saw the invading aliens turn casually into the full brunt of phaser fire and raise their chemically propelled projectile rifles.

He fell to his stomach as they opened fire. Thunder reverberated in the corridor, drowning out the screams of agony as security men and women were torn apart by the bullets.

Blood sprayed as O'Brien had never seen before, covering everything and everybody. He gasped as a stream of fluid struck him in the face. Nothing even in the terrible Cardassian war had prepared Miles O'Brien for such raw carnage.

In addition to people, the invaders' guns shredded bulkheads, control pads, and anything else in the line of fire. The soft, indirect lighting of the Promenade, designed to maximize civilian comfort, turned into the harsh glare of exposed filaments and yellow-sparking electrical discharges. O'Brien's ears rang so he could barely hear the cries of the dying; a blessing, he decided.

Ewin survived the first assault, lobbed an "O'Brien surprise" into the middle of the invaders. It exploded with a roar that hurt even O'Brien's bruised eardrums and a flash that would have blinded any unshielded eyes that saw it. The chief covered his eyes, and the platoon wore flash-suppressors.

Three of the invaders were knocked down, one apparently dead or severely wounded, the other two shaken but still functional. Miles O'Brien silently cheered from his vantage point; it was the first casualty inflicted on the enemy by station personnel.

Then he watched, sickened but fascinated, unable to turn away, as the remaining invaders loosed volley after volley until the entire platoon was dead. Not a man or woman escaped, and Ewin was not able to throw any more grenades.

As far as O'Brien knew, the entire Promenade security force had been killed. "Commander Sisko," he whispered.

After a moment, Sisko's voice responded, the gain turned so low O'Brien could barely hear the commander.

"They got us," said O'Brien. "There's nobody left. There's no security! The core section is now completely undefended."

The invaders conferred, too far away for the chief

engineer to overhear them. Then they split up, half heading upsection, the rest downsection.

Suddenly struck by a thought, O'Brien whispered, "Sir? Commander?"

"Sisko," said the voice.

"Can't you lock on, transport them into the brig?"

"Sorry, Chief. Kira tried. We can't get a lock on them—they're jamming us."

"Keiko! Get a lock on Keiko and the kids, beam them to Ops!"

"Some sort of electromagnetic disruption field," said the commander; "we can't lock on anything."

"For God's sake, Commander, do something—*they're headed toward the school!*"

Suddenly Kira's voice cut through the conversation. "O'Brien, I've almost got a lock on *you*. Is there anything around you that could be blocking their ECM?"

He looked around, suddenly realized what it was. "The magnetic containment grid! The static charge must block out their electronic countermeasures."

"Get in the grid," ordered Kira. O'Brien barely slipped through before she continued. "Locked— beaming you to the schoolroom—energizing."

His gut wrenched as he materialized in a corner of the room, holding the last two phaser grenades, one in each hand.

The worst problem with combat use of transporter technology is that dematerialization and materialization both take *time*. While they continue, you exist in a state halfway between dream and daylight, more myth than reality.

As the world of Keiko's schoolroom slowly phased into existence around him, Chief Miles O'Brien could only watch, impotent, as the inquisitor slowly raised his gun. Time seemed to slow; O'Brien's brain could not propel his sluggish body to coalesce any faster.

The inquisitor's finger tightened on the trigger. Nearly solid, O'Brien tensed the muscles he would need to charge across the room and catch the invader in a flying tackle, simultaneously shoving Keiko toward a small, open access hatch he noticed at the back of the room.

She could fit; the invaders in their bulky, armored suits could not.

Almost . . . almost solid . . .

CHAPTER
5

KEIKO O'BRIEN heard the evacuation order in the middle of a lesson on the Federation Prime Directive. Unsure what was going on, she began hustling the children out the door, making them leave all their personal effects behind—computers, book data clips, antiques for show-and-tell.

The older children left immediately except for Jake Sisko, son of the commander, and Nog, Rom's son and Quark's nephew; the former stayed because his father would have, the latter because Jake stayed.

Molly O'Brien was also still present; at three years old, the daughter of Keiko and Miles O'Brien was too young to find her way back to the habitat ring by herself. She was being a very brave girl, not crying at all.

Jake paced nervously, running his hand over his very short, black hair. Unlike his Ferengi friend Nog, Jake had actually lived through a brutal attack by the Borg . . . the attack that had killed his mother, Jennifer, Commander Sisko's wife.

Keiko felt a flash of guilt as she remembered; Captain

Jean-Luc Picard of the *Enterprise* had led that attack as "Locutus," while controlled by the Borg.

The younger children became frightened, and Keiko had to hug them, calm them down. She had managed to get all but two little Bajoran girls out the door when two soldiers in some sort of black and gray armor walked into the classroom.

One stepped to the side, covered the room with his weapon. The other walked up to Keiko. "Where is the other one like us," it asked in a voice so neutral that Keiko could not even tell whether it was male or female.

Holding Molly behind her, Keiko stared in astonishment at the inquisitor. "I . . . I don't understand the question," she said.

"Where is the other one like us," it repeated.

Keiko thought she caught a movement in the corner of her vision. She resisted the impulse to look in that direction, which would have drawn the inquisitor's attention.

"Is there another one like you on board?" she asked.

The soldier paused a long moment. Letting her eyes roam, Keiko suddenly realized she could see a reflection in one of the display terminals. Jake Sisko had crawled across the floor on his belly, shielded from the inquisitor's view by a line of desks. Somehow, he had silently worked free an access hatch where the floor met a bulkhead.

It was small—too small for the armored figure before her; but big enough for the children and possibly herself.

"There is another on this facility who looks like us," stated the inquisitor in its flat tone. "The other signaled twenty-eight hours ago. Where is the other being held."

Keiko felt rather than saw Molly crouch down. She could not see Jake either, but she presumed—she prayed —that he was urging Molly to crawl under the desk with him.

Keiko hoped the Bajoran girls found the escape route; she could not see them, or Nog, for that matter. But at that moment, only one person mattered to her: Molly O'Brien.

"If the other is being held prisoner, it—I mean he will be held in a Security holding cell."

The inquisitor raised its hand weapon, pointed it at Keiko's head. "You will take me to the Security holding cell," it said. It moved forward, grabbed hold of her shirt.

Keiko realized an instant too late that she should have walked forward herself; from its new position, the inquisitor could now see the access hatch.

It looked over her shoulder, saw the escape in progress. The inquisitor chittered a word that was not translated by its Universal Translator, followed by "small animals escaping—kill them."

This time she did not hesitate. Keiko launched herself at the inquisitor with such unexpected force that she bore it to the deck with her.

Oh God, I never thought it would end like this! She surged forward, covering the inquisitor's helmet with her body as it tried to wrench her free.

Keiko looked up, screamed. Her beloved Miles was just materializing in the schoolroom. *"Run!"* she screamed. *"Run, run, run!"*

The inquisitor managed to grab her hair, yank her head back. She saw the enormous barrel of his gun point directly at her face.

Thunder reverberated in her head, echoing round and round before finally dying out.

Keiko O'Brien had a few, confusing glimpses of light, vision, pieces broken apart, the shattered remains of her brain unable to mentally process the stimulus sent by her visual cortex, still intact in her occipital lobe.

Oh God . . .

The light slowly faded, died completely. A voice spoke, possibly her own.

"Miles—"

* * *

Miles O'Brien saw his wife's head jerked forward into the invader's gunshot. She fell backward across the desk behind her—*her* desk.

As if in a horrible nightmare, he was paralyzed, unable to move, unable even to scream.

Keiko was unambiguously dead. No human being could survive a wound like that. Keiko, his only beloved, his fair colleen, the one who made life alive, would never again smile, laugh, love, or even spat with him.

O'Brien stared dully, entire body numb. His brain was already exploding when he thumbed both contacts on his phaser grenades simultaneously, threw one at the feet of each invader. He made no effort to get out of the way of the blast.

Keiko called to him. *I'm coming,* he told his wife. She was always calling him; she loved him.

The inquisitor rose, turned toward O'Brien. At that moment, the grenades detonated.

The invader's armored body slammed into the chief, driving him back into a bulkhead and blackness.

Blackness.

Gray twilight. Dawn—

O'Brien blinked, came to consciousness. The schoolroom was wrecked, worse than it had been after the terrorist bombing a while back. One of the invaders was helping the other limp out the door.

O'Brien tried to rise. He would have jumped them from behind, tried to break a neck, if they even had necks. But his body would not respond.

How funny, he thought; *the bastard saved my life by walking between me and the grenade.*

Then he remembered Keiko. For many minutes, he could only listen to distant shots and explosions, screams of the dying, while tears ran down his face. He could not move to wipe them away.

At last, O'Brien managed to get some feeling back into his limbs, get them to respond feebly. He wriggled on his belly toward the open access hatch.

Now's not the time to die, he thought. *Now's the time to live, to pay the buggers back for me own, fair, sweet colleen.*

Quark caught Odo's arm. He silently pointed at an open access hatch behind Keiko's body. In the explosion's dust and rubble, they both saw the clear track of something heavy being dragged or dragging itself through the hatch, the trail still clearly visible even after two days in grisly company.

"Maybe we should . . . follow it," said Quark, swallowing.

Odo nodded. "Stay behind me," he counseled.

"I thought you'd never ask."

Odo stepped over the remains of a school desk, dropped to all fours in front of the hatch. He wriggled into it, followed closely by Quark. As soon as the constable saw that the hatch led to a tunnel that went on for some distance, he shrank his limbs into lizard legs for easier travel.

Quark let out a short scream, instantly stifled. "Damn it, Odo—you could at least warn a person before you turn yourself into a monster!"

Enjoying the jest, Odo let his head flow into his neck, caused it to bulge out again where his rear end had been, stretching the new neck behind him until his face practically touched the Ferengi's. "Perhaps your own monstrous soul would be more comfortable in a body like this," he suggested.

Quark recoiled so panic-stricken that he banged his huge head on the tunnel ceiling. He stared, eyes as big as saucers, revulsion written so plainly on his face that Odo almost felt sorry for an instant.

He reversed the metamorphosis, continued down the tunnel with his head facing forward.

They crawled for what seemed like hours through the black tunnel, guided only by their two hand torches, before finally stopping.

Quark gasped for breath. "I'm a businessman, not a miner!" he declared angrily.

"I thought all gnomes liked caves," said Odo.

The tunnel terminated at a junction: corridors branched left and right, while a ladder led up. The ladder was blocked by an emergency hatch.

"Unless we're completely turned around," continued the constable, "that ladder leads up to the upper core and Ops." He restored his normal shape, stood and mounted the ladder.

When he reached the hatch, he said, "Security override, Constable Odo. Verify." There was no response. "Blast, I forgot the computer's down."

Odo reached up to the control pad, which glowed a dim green. He looked back down at Quark. "Avert your eyes," he ordered.

"Why?"

"Because I'm about to type my private access code, and I don't want you to see it."

"What possible difference could it make *now?*" demanded Quark, peevishly.

Odo scowled down at him; with a Ferengi curse, Quark turned his head and stared at the opposite wall. The constable quickly typed the code, then pressed the emergency open relay. As the hatch slowly rolled back, he watched a message flash on the display.

"That's odd," he said; "there was an attempted illegal access two days ago."

"Who?"

"Jake Sisko. He was denied entry by the computer."

Quark bolted up the ladder so fast he almost dislodged Odo. "Nog? Jake and Nog were here? Then he must have gotten out of the schoolroom!"

"We don't know about Nog. Evidently Jake tried to access Ops, presumably to join Commander Sisko, but the computer turned him away."

"Where did they go after that?"

"Left or right, I suppose. I would have to use a tricorder to follow the DNA spoor. But we're going up now."

Quark gazed down the ladder at the junction below. "Maybe you should go up to Ops, and I'll—"

"Don't even think it," said Odo. "There are a hundred twists and turns in these conduits and access tubes. It would be like trying to follow a rabbit down a rabbit hole." The hatch finished opening. "Besides," added Odo, "we have a better chance of finding them both using the station sensors . . . if we can get the computer back on line, that is."

Quark sighed. "I guess you're right, much as it pains me to admit it. Lead on, Macduff."

Mk'doff? Some obscure Ferengi reference? Odo continued up the ladder, mildly perplexed.

Ops was nowhere near as badly torn up as Quark had expected. It was riddled with bullets in places, almost at random; but there was no machinery smashed, there were no displays burst open, and Commander Sisko's office was not bombed.

Odo walked around the operations table, staring curiously at the controls and instruments and trying to assess damage. As many times as he had been there, the constable seemed to know virtually nothing about how it all worked . . . but of course, that was Odo all over, totally unconcerned about anything except station security and harassing Quark.

Quark walked to the main-sensor-array display at Lieutenant Dax's science console. Dax! Was the belle of DS9 still alive? He shook his head; evidence indicated that nobody had survived.

Not even Nog, else he would eventually have returned to Quark's Place, the most familiar spot on the station.

Quark blinked rapidly, shoved the thought far back in his hindbrain, where the higher cortical centers of profit and loss could not access it. Time for a full accounting later.

Ops was three stories high, as tall as Quark's Place, from the systems core well, where O'Brien spent much of his time, up to Commander Sisko's office high above the main floor. In between heaven and hell sat the huge operations table, around which Dax, Kira, another engineering officer, and even Sisko himself would sometimes sit, fooling around with their consoles.

Several of the consoles had bullet damage, including Dax's science console, where the main sensor controls were located.

First, are there any bad guys still out there? He slid his finger back and forth on the touchscreen, sweeping the sensors around the complete globe surrounding the station. They were alone, unless somebody had a cloaking device of some sort.

"Hey, don't touch that," snarled Odo. "This equipment belongs to the Federation and Bajor. Don't monkey with anything, you might break it."

"I'm not going to *break* it, you officious little policeman."

"Well, just leave it alone."

"Oh? And who's going to locate the boys? You?"

Odo looked worried somehow, even though his sculpted face did not reflect any more emotion than usual. "I'm sure I can learn enough about the instruments to—"

Quark ignored the rest of Odo's remarks, quickly performed a level one diagnostic check. "Shields are still up, but the sensors indicate there's nothing out there. So I'm shutting them off. That'll stop the battery drain.

"There's damage to most of the secondary systems, including sensors; I can't say exactly what or how much, though.

"Logs indicate that twenty-three million messages were sent to Starfleet, obviously on automatic, but no response was ever received. I think there's some sort of force shield around the station that blocks all communications."

Odo stared in openmouthed astonishment. "How do *you* know how to work this equipment?" His tone of voice implied that he would be less amazed if Molly O'Brien, Keiko's toddler, had done it.

Quark smiled nastily. "Why Odo, surely you remember I once commanded DS-Nine."

"Oh. That."

"In any case, I had a life before I opened Quark's Place, you know. I shipped with my uncle Rank—"

"How appropriate."

"I shipped with my uncle Rank," he continued, "on a Ferengi Nondisclosure-class merchant ship called the *Margin.* Where do you think I got the money to buy the place in the first place?"

"Burglary and extortion?"

Quark continued quickly, ears flushing. "Ferengi instrumentation, while superior, is basically the same as Federation, Cardassian, and Romulan, since the same laws of physics apply."

"Hm." Odo crossed his arms, watched the Ferengi narrowly as he fooled around on each console. Quark frantically tried to remember anything beyond the first-year apprentice basics of Instrument Class.

Despite his brave talk, he knew he did not know enough to get them off the station or even refine the sensors enough to locate a particular person on DS9 . . . particularly with the main computer off-line.

Quark discovered with delight that Dax had set up a number of macros to automatically perform the routine tasks, one of which was to open channels with Bajor, the Federation, or the nearest starship. After some fumbling, he activated the macro, stood back, and watched the subspace call.

```
tx 28827.33.4123.A bajor HiCoun → open
wait handshake............................................
```

The dots slowly crawled across the screen. At last, when they reached the right side, the display changed.

```
tx 28827.33.4123.A bajor HiCoun → terminate
NOR
contact not established → diagnose? :Y
```

Quark touched the Accept touchpad; after an instant, the words "unable to diagnose problem" appeared below the display. *Of course. The computer is down, you fool.*

If there had been a mechanical problem with communications, Quark realized, the level-one diagnostic, which used hardwired circuits rather than the computer, would have detected it. Thus, either there was a logic fault in the communications system, or more likely, the force shield set up by whoever destroyed the station was still up. If he knew more about the sensors, he could probably detect it; but it was not worth the time it would take to learn.

He had a more important task.

Just for thoroughness, while he was trying to remember everything he knew about sensor tuning, he activated Dax's communications macro two more times.

```
tx 28827.33.4123.A bajor HiCoun → terminate
NOR
contact not established → diagnose? :N

tx 28911.05.1001.A FedStarSixCom → terminate
NOR
contact not established → diagnose? :N

tx 99401.99.7***.* StarFleet anyship → terminate
NOR
contact not established → diagnose? :N
```

The sensors, as with all Federation equipment, were designed to be easy to operate. But "easy" was a relative term. The Cardassians undoubtedly thought their computer was easy to operate; but Quark had listened to at least a thousand complaints by Chief O'Brien over glasses of synth that it was rigid, recalcitrant, and reluctant . . . and O'Brien was a trained engineer.

At least the Federation believes in "help" screens, thought the Ferengi. *Thank Tariff for small favors.*

Most of the allegedly helpful explanations of sensor

functions were so much gibberish to Quark, who had never attended Starfleet Academy. The laws of physics might be the same for Ferengi and Federation, he thought, but the laws of product design were radically different.

Quark's Ferengi heritage ultimately served him well: by persistent, relentless poking into areas he was not supposed to go into, he finally managed to shift the sensors from mass-detection to biological systems.

He initiated a shipwide scan—a necessity, since he still had no idea how to narrow the scope.

Quark stared at the display, at first not comprehending what he saw. Then he shouted as if he had just spun a Cluster on a doubled and redoubled Dabo wheel.

"What? What is it?" demanded Odo.

Quark jumped, whirled around. For a few peaceful moments, lost in the intricacies of instrumentation, he had actually forgotten that the annoying constable was still with him.

"The display!" he croaked, jabbed a finger at the screen.

Odo stared. "Oh, ah," he said, obviously in a total fog.

Quark explained. "Biological—I set the sensors to biological scan and scanned the station. Look." He pointed at hundreds of crisp, sharp spikes. "There are people still alive here! Dozens of them!"

Then the screen flickered, and the spikes disappeared. "Uh-oh," said the Ferengi; now the screen clearly showed there was *no one* alive on DS9 . . . not even themselves.

Then the spikes reappeared, but they were inverted, indicating some kind of weird "anti-life." They began to march across the screen from right to left.

"What does *that* indicate?" asked Odo.

"That the sensors don't work," squeaked Quark. He felt his face flush bright pink with embarrassment, remembering the diagnostic check that warned of sensor problems and seeing the bullet holes.

A terrible thought occurred to him: Suppose the

mass-detection sensors were also malfunctioning, and there was an invader ship out there?

Quark had just dropped the shields!

He decided that in this case, silence was certainly the better part of disclosure. What Odo did not know might still kill them both; but if Odo did find out the danger Quark had put them in, the Ferengi might be the only one to die.

"So," said Odo, with his customary and uncanny knack for knowing precisely the most embarrassing questions to ask, "all you can say for sure is that the invaders' ship has left the vicinity, right?"

"Ah—ah—n-no, I can't say anything else for certain. For sure. I mean, absolutely."

"Hm, probably returned to report victory and bring reinforcements for a general invasion. How lovely . . . and all because your loathsome device kept me from being here to . . ."

"To what? What incredible feat could you have pulled off if you'd been here?"

"To arrest them," he finished lamely.

Quark leaned forward eagerly. "Look—we know Nog and Jake escaped the schoolroom—"

"No, we know *Jake* escaped."

"Yes, yes, but isn't Nog always with him, much as I used to chide the child for hanging around a human? So surely we can conclude that they, at least, found a hole to survive attack, right?"

"Quark, that was two days ago. A lot can happen in two days." He looked around the empty Operations Center.

A world can crumble in two days, he thought.

"Well," said Quark, "I guess there's not much else we can do here. Wait, did you check the ship's chronometer?"

Odo nodded. "It basically matches your Klingon clock, though your clock is eleven minutes fast."

"Yes. I've apparently neglected to reset it for the past three days."

"Let's go."

"Where?"

"Back to the junction where Jake couldn't get into Ops."

"I thought you said it was useless, like following a rabbit down a rabbit hole!"

The constable shrugged. "Fortunately, I happen to *have* a tricorder to follow the DNA spoor."

The Ferengi stared in amazement. "You lied!"

Odo regarded Quark with a reptilian calmness. "I said I would *need* a tricorder to follow Jake's trail; I never said I didn't *have* one."

"You—!" Quark bit off the rest of the sentence; in his present predicament, it would be contraeconomic to finish.

Chief O'Brien stared at his chronometer, incredulous. It read 1607. *Four hours?* How could only four hours have passed since the invaders attacked?

Subjectively, it was less than one; he had been out for some time.

Emotionally, it felt more like forty.

He scuttled brokenly along the conduit crawlway, climbed the cold and sticky emergency-access ladder, and identified himself to the computer for the Ops access hatch.

He scaled ten more levels of DS9, grateful for the first time that the ladder on each level was staggered from those above and below—otherwise, the temptation to simply let himself fall all the way back and join Keiko might have been irresistible.

The lights flickered. *Must have shot up some junction nodes,* he thought. Ordinarily, this would have infuriated the chief; today, it did not matter. Nothing mattered anymore except killing the invaders.

As O'Brien poked his head up into Ops, Kira was speaking. She sounded hesitant, as if broaching a subject so strange she was afraid it might anger Commander Sisko. "Sir?"

"Yes, Major?"

"Do you know what a militia is?"

The commander rubbed his chin. "Of course; classically, a paramilitary force of indigenous residents, banding together to repel invasion."

"Well, there are a lot of Bajorans on the station, sir."

"Yes?"

"And lots of us have experience fighting the Cardassians during the occupation."

"Yes?" Sisko was beginning to get annoyed. "Major, if you have a suggestion, just spit it out."

She chewed on a lip. "Experience fighting with impromptu weaponry and command structures or even as individuals."

"Major Kira, are you suggesting I order the civilians on this station to defend themselves because we can't protect them?"

"No, sir," she said; "just *some* of the civilians. You know that Colonel Bata Huri lives here now?"

Kira breathed the name with such reverence that O'Brien knew Bata must have been a great hero of the Bajoran underground.

Sisko nodded, apparently knowing about Colonel Bata. "How long would it take Colonel Huri to pull a militia together?"

Kira smiled. "I'll contact her; you can talk to her yourself."

"Major . . ." Sisko said. "This Colonel Bata; is she—good?"

Kira snapped back at him. "The Cardassians put a bounty on her, sir: ten million bars of gold-pressed latinum."

O'Brien leaned over, one foot on the ladder, and hopped onto the deck in Ops.

"Anyone ever try to collect?" Sisko asked.

"Sure," said Kira, curling her lip. "But only Cardassians."

Kira stopped in midsentence as she caught sight of the

chief, and stared as if he were a ghost. The rest followed her gaze, treating O'Brien to a moment of silence.

Then everyone shouted at once. An Ops tech ran over and helped the chief to his console chair while Dax, Kira, and Sisko crowded around.

"We thought you had left us, Chief," said the commander.

Kira explained, "When your signal feed just stopped after the explosion, we naturally assumed . . ."

O'Brien slapped his chest; all that remained of his communicator was half the mounting pin.

"Eh? Sorry, sir. I—I was shaken and—and didn't notice."

"Is . . . ?" Dax did not complete the question; she must have seen the look on O'Brien's face. "I'm sorry, Miles," she said softly.

He was thankful he did not have to spell it out; somehow, saying it aloud would make it more real.

"I can't stay here," he said.

"You'd better," argued Kira. "We need you to hold the place together while these bastards rip it apart."

O'Brien turned to her; she was the only officer on the station who had any experience with guerrilla warfare. "Sir, the phasers can't hurt them, but the phaser grenades *can*. At least they knock them down and stun them, and maybe we can do something to them while they're incapacitated. But that means I—"

"That means you have to make more and distribute them around the station," said Lieutenant Dax unexpectedly from behind them.

For a moment, O'Brien was startled that a young girl would understand before Kira and Sisko, who had both fought in combat. Then he remembered that she was not a young girl but an ancient, symbiotic entity: Jadzia Dax may not have fought in any wars, but it was a good bet that Curzon Dax or one of his predecessors had.

"Yes, sir," said the chief, blinking; his eyes were terribly dry. "It's the only thing we have that even fazes them."

Puzzled, Kira said, "I assumed we'd just slip it into the replicator and make thousands of them."

"Did you now?" asked O'Brien; he added a belated "sir" to soften the rebuke, since she was his superior. "Have you tried it, sir?"

"Well, not yet."

O'Brien smiled grimly. "Try it. You'll get a phaser grenade, all right: completely empty of power. Useless."

"Drained? Is it a safety mechanism? We can override—"

"The replicator can't create energy, Major. Trust me on this. I have to take phasers and make 'em by hand."

Major Kira gritted her teeth, turned away, smacking her thigh with her closed fist in frustration. Not for the first time, O'Brien thought she would look awfully pretty without the carefully layered horrors of a lifetime spent in the Shakaar.

Sisko put his hand gently on O'Brien's shoulder, respectfully but insistently propelling him away from the others. When they were alone, the commander spoke softly. "Chief, are you certain you're up to this? You can stay here or in Engineering and make grenades, and I'll have a security officer distribute them."

O'Brien looked through empty eyes at the older man, the only command officer on the station who truly understood what the chief felt at that moment. Sisko had been through it himself. "I can't hide, sir. I *want* to do it. For her."

"I understand."

"I know you do. Besides, I want to show some other techs how to make the grenades, just in case the invaders catch me, or . . ."

"You're not planning anything spectacular, are you?"

"Maybe," he admitted; "but not something useless and stupid. Where are they now?"

Sisko looked over at Kira. "Major? Are you scanning them?"

"I can't scan them directly," she said, "but all I have to do is see where the scanner blanks out, and that's where they must be. They're still working around the Promenade, room by room. I don't know why they haven't come up here, but let's not curse the rain that floods the border river.

"At least they've stopped shooting bombs at us."

"Maybe they ran out," suggested Dax.

Kira looked at O'Brien. "Chief? What does it mean, the other one like them? Who are they looking for?"

He shook his head. "Near as I can figure, sir, they think we're holding one of them captive somewhere. We're not, are we?"

Dax spoke up again. "I already checked that, Chief. All the people who Odo's arrested recently are Bajoran or some Federation race."

"And where the hell *is* Odo?" asked Kira, more to herself than anyone else.

Dax answered anyway. "Nobody has seen him for about a day. I queried the computer, and it says he's off the station—but there is no record of him leaving.

"For that matter," she mused, "Quark is gone, too. And nobody has seen him since he and Odo had a conference together in Quark's office."

"Quark," repeated the major; O'Brien shuddered to hear the tone of her voice. The bone-deep chill of death ran through Kira Nerys; she always frightened him a bit.

She lost her soul fighting the Cardassians, he thought, *and she's hungry enough to eat yours to replace it.*

"Give me all the phasers you've got," he said. "I'll make you a batch of grenades. Here, Lieutenant, let me show you how to do it."

"Let me know the moment they leave the Promenade," said the commander.

"Aye, sir," said Major Kira.

CHAPTER
6

MAJOR KIRA, still standing at her weapons console, turned to the commander. "Sir . . . I strongly advise we evacuate the civilians from the station."

Sisko pondered for a moment. "Agreed. We can bring them back later, if the situation warrants. Any thoughts on how you might do that, Major?"

"I assumed we'd drop the shields and beam—" She caught herself in midsentence. "Chief, would the transporter be able to lock on to its own pad?"

Without a word, he trotted over, stepped onto the transporter pad. Kira poked at her display again and again, swearing softly in Bajoran. Finally, she shook her head.

"Then it's going to have to be runabouts. That's better anyway; the civvies don't have to leave the habitat ring. O'Brien, you'll have to round up the civilians and stuff them aboard the runabouts."

"Sir," said the chief to Kira, his face grim, "let me show you how to make a phaser grenade." O'Brien started to open a phaser, but Kira stopped him with a withering glance.

"Are you joking? I can't recable a phaser! I can't even install a stereo data-clip reader. I kill people and break things. That's my job. *Your* job is to make phaser grenades."

"Yes, sir," said the chief. "But if I'm to go round up civilians, then I *can't* make phaser grenades. So I'll have to show you."

"Oh," she said, feeling dumb. She thought for a moment, tugging at her ear.

Sisko spoke quietly. "Major, you're going to have to go with Chief O'Brien and evacuate the civilians yourself."

"Me! But who's going to knock away the bombs?"

He looked askance at her. "Major, I was guarding home plate back in old Thomas Sowell Field before you were potty-trained."

"Really," she said, her tone rather stiff.

"Go away," said the commander; "that's an order. Round up as many as you can, children if you can find them; then march them to the nearest runabout and pack them off to Bajor."

"But sir," she protested, "when we launched the probe, they swatted it like a fly."

Sisko nodded. "All right, then *let me know* just before you launch. We'll fire a full spread at the invaders, blind them for a few moments . . . long enough to get the ship away.

"Look," he added, "they haven't lobbed a bomb at us in a couple of hours . . . I think we might have damaged something. Or maybe Dax is right. In any case, it's been a stalemate."

"Okay," said Kira, grudgingly turning over tractor-beam control to Commander Sisko. She turned to Dax. "Where are they now?"

The lieutenant checked. "Unfortunately, they've occupied the entire Promenade and blockaded the turbolift shafts. You'll have to break through to a crossover bridge."

"Never mind," said O'Brien; "we'll burrow beneath them."

They stepped into the cold, dark Cardassian turbolift. Just before entering, Kira asked, "Are you sure about this, Commander? Because I can handle both the photons and the tractors while Dax—"

"Out!" thundered Sisko, smiling faintly. He pointed at the turbolift.

"Are you ready, sir?" asked O'Brien. She nodded, and he said to the lift, "Level seven, maximum track." The doors slid closed; then the world dropped out from beneath Kira's feet.

She would have fallen, but the turbolift accelerated so quickly she was in zero-g for a few seconds. By the time she realized what was going on and braced herself, it was already coming to a crushing stop. She staggered out after O'Brien, dizzy from the trip. It was the fastest turbolift ride she had ever taken. *Maximum track; have to remember that.*

"Here's where it gets tricky," said the chief. "They've got decks nine through eleven, the Promenade, and the lieutenant said they blocked up the turbolift shafts. But we need to get down to the habitat-ring crossover bridges on level fifteen."

"So we use access ladders?" Kira asked.

"Are you kidding? That would drop us right in their laps. No, we're going to slip right by them like a snake under a garden."

Level 7 housed several large rooms that used to be the ammunition storage dumps back when the Cardassians ran DS9. Now the ammo dumps were used for auxiliary computer memory clips, attempting to bring the computing power up to Starfleet standards.

The turbolift opened into a six-corridor intersection between a permanent set of "temporary" bulkheads and room dividers.

O'Brien ran to a small door set a meter off the deck, placed his palm against a control pad. After a moment, the door slowly rolled open, revealing a downward-sloping tube.

Holding out one of his phaser grenades, O'Brien

cautiously poked his huge orange head into the tube. "Looks clear," he said. "After you, sir."

"Don't you want to go first?" she asked, feeling oddly reluctant to climb into the tube.

"I have to shut the door again," he explained.

"Hm. All right." Swallowing her unexplained fear, Kira Nerys hoisted herself into the tube, face first, and wriggled along it far enough that O'Brien could join her, but no farther. He did so, then palmed the door pad on the inside. As the thick hatch rolled shut again, Kira's ears popped in the suddenly lower air pressure.

"Where are we?" she whispered. Normal talking seemed a bit blasphemous in the slippery, sloping tube. The lights slickered off and on, randomly, frightening her further. *Probably just a combat-related power fluctuation,* she thought, unconvinced.

"Hub-shaft maintenance," answered the chief, as softly as she. "Sir, you may not enjoy this. It's . . . well, you'll see."

"What?" But O'Brien did not seem disposed to elaborate, so Kira crawled on.

"Is this shaft narrowing?" she asked suspiciously.

"Huh? No, not so far as I can tell," said O'Brien.

Kira stopped suddenly. O'Brien softly called out, "What's the matter, sir?"

"Nothing. I'm—just give me a moment." She breathed deeply for several seconds. *The walls are* not *closing in, the walls are* not *closing in,* she repeated to herself. For a moment, she had flashed back to the darkest days of the war, the occupation, the time she spent in . . .

Painfully, she resumed her crawl. The downward slope was only a few degrees, but she felt as though she were suspended by her feet over an abyss. "I never thought I'd have to do this again," she whispered.

Every so often, the station bucked and rocked from another explosion. Kira was frantic; the one time she contacted Ops, Sisko, now handling the tractor-bat by himself while Dax fired photon torpedoes, cut her off so quickly she was afraid to try again.

At last, Kira and O'Brien reached the end of the crawl. They faced an oily, geared metal hatch, like those leading to the docking ring. O'Brien pressed past the Bajoran major, trying not to think thoughts that would make Keiko angry, and typed his personal access code into the control pad.

The door clicked loudly, unlocking. Kira waited. "Well?" she said. "Now what?"

"Now we start cranking." The chief reached up to the manual-open crank, began rotating it briskly. The door slowly rolled back.

After several minutes of cranking, it was only half wide enough to admit them. "I'll take over for a while," Kira offered. O'Brien accepted gratefully.

"So why isn't the door working?"

"It is. It's a mechanical door. No servos."

Kira stopped and stared. "Why?"

O'Brien shrugged. "I guess the Cardassians didn't want anyone going through it."

"Well, you could have warned me. I have workout gloves."

"I didn't know."

She scowled. "Haven't you ever been through here, Chief?"

"Only in my diagrams."

At last the massive door had opened enough to let them pass. Inside was a huge, cylindrical shaft running up and down hundreds of meters. The only illumination came from the still-flickering lights in the tunnel through the door they had just opened. A thin filament, the size of a strand of hair, scintillated in the door light.

"What the hell is this?" asked Kira, staring in wonder. "I never knew this was here!"

"Has something to do with the Cardassian gravity generator . . . and it runs from level three all the way to the lower core. We'll take this to level fifteen, then cross back underneath the invaders to the habitat ring."

O'Brien smiled a bit grimly. "Look, there's something I should warn you about, Major: it's open at the bottom. You can literally fall out of the station here."

Kira stared incredulously at O'Brien. "Chief, I can't climb down eight levels on a piece of string—and you can't either!"

"Um, that's the other thing, sir. There's no gravity in there."

"Zero g?" she asked, confused. "But the gravity generators . . ."

"That *is* the gravity generator; part of it, anyhow. When we're in the shaft, we're inside the generator, which means *outside* the generator field."

She gingerly stuck her arm through the door; it did feel slightly lighter, as if floating in water.

"Now, be very careful," said O'Brien. "A little tug is all you need. Any more, and you'll break the filament, anyway. Let me go first, all right?"

"Be my guest."

Miles O'Brien squeezed his lithe bulk through the partially opened door, inverting himself in the process. He dangled effortlessly, upside down, waiting for Major Kira.

Nervously, she stepped through the door herself, a much easier fit. At once, she was falling. She clutched at the black filament as if it were the last tree branch before a cliff. Kira ended up rotating around and around the wire, her feet slightly scraping the heat-scored walls fore and aft, the narrow direction of the shaft.

"Stick your foot out, sir," said O'Brien; "you can stop your rotation."

She did so. Her stomach screamed, insisting it was about to lose what little it had eaten. Her inner ear informed her that she was plummeting to her death.

Slowly, she inverted to match O'Brien. It felt exactly the same, no matter how she oriented, just as the books said it felt. "Wha—why are the walls burned?" she asked, trying to quell the panic attack.

"I think the shaft sometimes recharges off the sun."

"You *think?*"

"I don't know much about Cardassian gravitational technology."

"What if it starts recharging while we're in here?"

"Um, I hope it doesn't," said O'Brien. "Starting travel," he said, tugging once, gently, on the line.

Kira began a hand-over-hand motion, suddenly found herself hurling at the chief. She crashed into him, caromed into the wall, losing her grip on the filament. She bounced past O'Brien, headed for the great outdoors—deep space. Just then, a hand latched on to her ankle, wrenched her to a stop.

O'Brien reeled her in like a fish. As soon as she could reach, she reanchored herself to the filament, gasping with retroactive terror. "Prophets! So the bloody Cardassians nearly killed me after all."

"Sir?" began O'Brien, diffidently. "If you keep tugging, you'll keep accelerating: there's no gravity to pull you to a stop. Just tug once; you'll keep going until you put the brakes on."

"Of course. I read about zero g in my crash course on orbital civil engineering . . . which consisted of an article in *Popular Starvoyaging.*"

"It's a boggle racket. You're always getting caught by something you didn't anticipate. I served a shore tour in the dry docks on Starbase Thirteen, putting the *Enterprise* together. That's why I requested to serve on her, five years later."

"Let's try it again." She smiled, a brief whimsy in the midst of tragedy. "You'd better keep an eye on me."

O'Brien tugged once, began to drift. "Keiko always loved zero-g biospheres," he said, as Kira followed.

Kira and O'Brien anchored themselves as well as they could in the zero-g shaft, turned the warped door crank handle. The level-seven door had been much easier to open than the gateway to level fifteen was. Of course, the gravity had helped.

At last, they opened it enough to squeeze through.

The crawlspace was identical to the one eight levels above; Kira would almost have believed it was the same tunnel.

When they reached the vent port leading out onto the outer core corridor, Kira listened for a long time, not allowing O'Brien to open the panel. This was as much to prove she was not really terrified out of her wits by the enclosed space as it was to ensure no invaders had gone this low yet.

At last she nodded. O'Brien cracked the panel, then opened it all the way. They clambered out, stretching the kinks out of their joints.

"Where's the nearest crossover? Can we take a turboshaft from here?"

O'Brien pointed to the right. They walked for two hundred meters through the silent, white corridor, found a connecting tunnel. A turboshaft ran along it, shuttling between the core section and the habitat ring. A turbolift waited patiently in the shaft.

"Let's do it," said Kira. "As soon as we get to the ring, we split up: you find the rest of security and the militia officers and give them your grenades. I'm going to evacuate everyone I can using a runabout."

"What is this militia you keep talking about?"

She squeezed his arm. "I don't know yet. We'll see what Colonel Bata's managed to do.

"In the meantime, in case we don't see each other again, thanks, um, Miles. And I hope you know Keiko is in a better place and still loves you." *And we're about to join her in that better place,* Kira silently added.

O'Brien frowned, nodded brusquely. They stepped aboard the turbolift, sent it careering toward the habitat ring—maximum track.

CHAPTER
7

CHIEF O'BRIEN could barely believe the change in the security team's demeanor. In little more than an hour, they had transformed from annoyed officiousness to righteous anger to haunted desperation as they heard first one, then another security platoon annihilated by the unknown invaders.

As O'Brien arrived at service bay four to distribute his phaser grenades, the team was deconstructing the repeated invader query—"Where is the other one like us?"—for some clue as to who they were, what they wanted, and what would make them go away. There was no longer talk of defeating them.

"'Where' could be an active question: Where is he now?" speculated PO2 Fleinn. "Or it could be more philosophical: Where will he come from, is he here yet?"

A nervous ensign, theoretically in charge, since he outranked the noncoms, but no more than twenty-one and without experience, tossed in his own speculation. "Maybe the key phrase here is 'other one.' They think we're harboring some dangerous fugitive, one who is like them, but 'other' than them."

The bay itself was huge, used for fixing gigantic asteroid-mining equipment. The ceiling was high, and the unpainted metal walls made it look like a prison.

"Sir," said O'Brien, "no disrespect, but does it really matter? Has anyone here seen any other person or life-form like them?" Some of the junior enlisted coughed and scuffed their feet, but no one spoke. "Then whatever they're looking for, it's not on Deep Space Nine," concluded O'Brien.

"But you canna tell them that," said PO1 Mari ni Connal, whose family came from the same Irish county that O'Brien's family came from a hundred years before. He thought of her as kin, nearly.

"I know. When you try, they just kill you."

"But I think it's oor only hope," she persisted. "If we can mak'em ken that we're speaking truth, that he's not here, what they seek, then they've nae reason to stay and keep killin'."

O'Brien shook his head. "If you can think of a way, let me know. In the meantime, the only thing that seems to faze them is a grenade in the face, and even that hasn't definitely killed one yet."

"Then I've got anayther thought," said Mari. "It occurs that a land-crawler has muckle-mare armor tae fore than aft. Perhaps a grenade in the *back* might be a wee, tiny more effective than the face?"

Chief O'Brien jabbed a finger at the woman. "Now *that* is the best suggestion I've heard." The other women and men on the security team mumbled agreement.

The ensign cleared his throat, and the considerably more senior noncommissioned officers all fell silent, respecting his rank. "Maybe what we need," he suggested tentatively, "is a two-pronged attack: first a diversion to turn them facing one way, then we hit them from the other side."

"Then what happens to the diversion team?" asked O'Brien.

Mari shrugged. "Belike they get blown apart like a ripe melon, lad."

"Just curious," said O'Brien. "All right, I'm off. Give me as many phasers as you've got; I've got to get grenades to this militia that Major Kira's on about, as soon as somebody tells me who and where they are."

"Oh," said the ensign—Jura? Dura?—his face brightening. "Here's a list, Chief." He pulled a data clip from a button-pocket, allowed O'Brien to plug it into his tricorder for a moment to copy the list, then retrieved it.

"Thank you, sir. Fare well, Mari; take care of the crew."

"Keep yourself, Miles. I'll recite a Hail Mary for Keiko . . . not that I expect she needs it."

"It's Molly I'm worried about," he whispered.

She clapped his shoulder, recited a verse from a very familiar song; fortunately, she spared them the pain of her "singing" voice:

> Ae fond kiss, and then we sever
> Ae farewell, alas forever
> Deep in heart-wrung tears I'll pledge thee
> Warring sighs and groans I'll wage thee.

"Bobby Burns was a Scotsman, not an Irishman. Everybody's confusing me with a Scot lately."

She shrugged. "At least he wasna *Sacsanach*, aye?"

A *Sacsanach* was a Saxon, an Englishman. Mari's family still maintained a lot of old, Irish traditions that everyone else had forgotten two hundred years back.

"Aye." O'Brien turned away, wishing he could smile to reassure Mari he would be all right. But she was one more reminder of his wife: strangely enough, considering their shared culture, Keiko had *introduced* them. Mari had been Keiko's aerobics instructor back on the *Enterprise.*

Fleinn handed him the bag of nearly thirty phasers. O'Brien slung it across his back, and was just about to proceed to the nearest name on his list when his communicator beeped.

"O'Brien," he said, tapping the insignia by habit, even though the line was probably already open.

"They found the crossover bridges," said Major Kira's tense voice from somewhere else on the habitat ring. "Bogeymen headed for the habitat ring along tunnels one and two, walking."

"No surprises," he muttered. "Understood, sir. Did you tell Ops?"

"Dax told *me.* They got a visual from a crewman who escaped. The invaders have done something, and now we can't even pick them up on our tricorders."

"What!" O'Brien immediately tried his own tricorder, confirmed that the scan now showed nothing but static.

"Christ, deaf *and* blind," he said.

Taking a deep breath, he slipped out into the corridor, slid down a ladder to level sixteen, and jogged toward the quarters of Bata Huri, a retired Bajoran colonel who now supposedly commanded a DS9 militia . . . if it was not just a figment of the Bajoran major's idealistic imagination.

Odo shook his head, staring at the tricorder reading. "No good. The spoor is two days old, and too many other people have crossed here before and after Jake passed by."

They were still in the crawlway, but it had widened enough that Quark could almost stand. The trail ended at a long, curved corridor stretching around the "vertical horizon" of the station's curve both left and right.

The constable looked left, saw an access ladder leading up and down levels. To the right lay tunnel two leading to the habitat ring. "Well, Quark, do we go up, down, or out?"

The Ferengi sat leaning against the bulkhead, contemplating. Jake's natural impulse would be to stay in the core, near his father, especially if he had Molly. But if Nog was with them, the boy would surely show enough Ferengi trade sense to get as far away from the combat as possible. Nog could be very persuasive, as Quark had had personal occasion to learn.

Out toward the habitat ring then, he decided.

Of course, one had to be clever in presenting one's input, particularly where police were concerned; they tended to hold a strangely low opinion of Ferengi in general.

"Up," said Quark; "he'll try to get to Ops again. Or else down, to the lower core. Anywhere but the habitat ring."

"Really," sniffed Odo. "Since I know from long, personal experience that you are invariably wrong when you try to be clever, I have decided we shall take the tunnel."

"Suit yourself," said Quark, as nastily as he could manage; "that's just the kind of rejection I'd expect from you."

They had followed the access crawlway as far as they could. It eventually led down to level fifteen and opened onto a corridor. Quark and Odo still saw the occasional body on this level, so it was safe to assume that the invaders had gotten to the habitat ring, as well.

The only question was whether Sisko had been able to evacuate the civilians beforehand.

The turbolift would not budge, so they trudged along the tunnel on foot.

The tunnel was long, straight, dark. It creaked loudly as the load of the entire habitat ring shifted. Window slits let in a view of the starfield, and when the station was oriented correctly, the wormhole. The stars crawled past the window as DS9 slowly rotated to share the magnificent view among all residents.

The station illumination ceased past a juncture box labeled JUNCTION NODE 97, which sported six bullet holes from an invader projectile weapon.

"They like the dark," Odo said, nodding at the junction node. They continued the trip in darkness, their footsteps echoing hollowly as if in an ancient tomb.

An emergency airlock door half blocked the tunnel mouth. The door was blown off its track by a powerful explosive . . . from the tunnel side.

"Somebody knew they were coming," said Odo, "and closed the airlock door. Probably wanted to trap them inside and evacuate the air from the tunnel. The invaders used a high-explosive shaped charge—almost no collateral damage—and knocked the door open."

"They came prepared," said Quark.

Odo nodded, barely visible in the slight starlight through a tunnel porthole. "This was not a diplomatic or trading team. This was a combat unit."

Odo squeezed past the door first, checking for telltale sounds that might indicate an ambush. The tunnel mouth was the perfect spot for one: anybody standing against the inner bulkhead of the habitat-ring corridor would be able to attack the invaders one at a time.

"If the civilians were going to make a stand, here's where they'd do it," he predicted.

Sure enough, the corridor looked like the aftermath of a monumental earthquake. The entire outer bulkhead was torn apart from a gigantic bomb blast, and every surface was covered with bullet holes and phaser scoring.

Even now, two days later, Quark could still smell a strong, metal-acid tang that he realized with a chill was probably the chemical propellant used by the invader firearms. Without air recirculators, the odor would probably linger for days to come, an olfactory tribute to the destruction of DS9.

They could not even walk normally, since the deck was torn apart, at times leaving gaping holes that could drop an unwary Ferengi two or three decks through twisted metal ribbons of deck material.

Quark leapt to a horizontal surface that resembled part of a wall, landing with an ominous echo. He stretched out his short legs in near darkness, his path lit only by the electric torch Odo carried, hoping the debris he stepped on was stable.

They found more bodies.

Odo was right; the defenders had chosen the airlock at the end of tunnel two to make a stand.

At least one hundred bodies lay where they had fallen defending their home against the invaders. The bodies were strewn randomly, as if flung by a massive explosion. The broken shards of a conference table, apparently a hasty barricade, stuck into bodies and in places, even into the bulkhead itself.

Quark saw holes in the overhead above piles of the resulting rubble, evidence of seemingly concentrated phaser fire into the roof for some reason.

The carnage lay unburied and visible all around; not the clear, bloodless death that a phaser dealt. Here was war in all its glory gore: severed limbs, splintered skulls, abdominal cavities opened for easy viewing.

"Rats," said Quark, seeing the vermin chitter and feed. "I didn't even know we had rats on board." They were the long, slinky Bajoran *krutus* rats that resembled furry snakes with eight legs.

Odo said nothing, not even to compare the *krutus* with Ferengi. He just shook his head sadly and pulled Quark along the pitch-black corridor, shining his confiscated torch directly before their feet so they would not fall into an abyss. They still saw only DS9 residents, permanent and temporary; there were no invader bodies.

Holding his breath against the smell, metal-acid mixed with the beginnings of rotting meat, Quark noticed a tool locker ripped open by ill-directed phaser fire.

He slid a drawer out, but it collapsed, spilling its contents to the deck, where some of the tools dropped into holes.

Fortunately, one of the items that remained was a powerful flash. Quark stooped and grabbed it, feeling justified, since Odo had taken his.

Quark and Odo climbed gingerly over deadfalls of metal debris, pathetic barricades against the invaders. Odo pointed at a dead Bajoran—rather, at her head and torso, since her legs were missing. "Colonel Bata Huri," he said; "undoubtedly the commander of this ragtag militia."

The "militia," presumably, comprised the dead Bajorans and humans surrounding Bata Huri. Most of the bodies showed evidence of a bomb blast.

"Fat lot of good they did," said Quark. Realizing his potential mistake, he cringed away from the constable; but Odo displayed no emotion. Perhaps he had shut it off to avoid confronting despair.

"At least they died like free men and women," said Odo.

Ahead was a collapse of ceiling that completely blocked the corridor, rising past where the ceiling should have been. It was at least two levels high.

Quark looked at it, looked back over his shoulder "Now what, O mighty leader? We can't go back; we'd just fall through a hole and be cut to ribbons. But we can't go *through* this, either . . . unless you thought to bring some mining tools?"

"We go forward."

"How?"

"We're going over the cave-in."

Quark stared incredulously. "You expect me to climb *that?*" he squeaked.

Odo looked at the Ferengi, raised his brows. "No, Quark. You can stay here, if you prefer. Maybe you can interest Bata in a game of Dabo to while away the days."

"Oh, you're a hoot. You're really a laugh riot, Odo. All right, who goes first?"

"I do," said Odo. "Try to keep up, won't you? I don't want to have to keep going back for you."

The constable crouched to hands and toes. His flesh began to ripple, flow. His legs shrank into his body, becoming thinner, strangely articulated.

Quark gasped, backpedaled so furiously he tripped over a militiaman's corpse. He jumped up, brushed himself off; no matter how many years he languished in the constable's presence, Quark could never get used to the sudden shapeshifting.

Odo continued to transform, sprouting several more pairs of legs. His arms turned into legs as well, and his head slid back along his body. At last, Odo had become a huge, grotesque, spiderlike creature with ten slender legs, each terminating in three-fingered hands.

"Betazed nectar-spider," he explained.

"Yes, I know," snapped Quark. "But aren't they usually about three centimeters long?"

Odo snorted, began to climb the deadfall. Quark followed cautiously, watching the constable: despite his graceful new appearance, Odo still massed the same as before, of course, much more than a Ferengi; Quark carefully observed which footholds were stable and which rocked or began to collapse.

Deadfalls were treacherous, as Quark was beginning to learn. By a quirk of the collapse, a thin, unstable layer of debris might cover a ten-foot-deep pit with sharp, twisted metal at the bottom. Breaking a leg would be easy with a moment's carelessness; death was not out of the question.

This particular deadfall was worse than a collapsed tree or rock cave-in. The ceiling above the corridor had collapsed, leaving a mountain of metal nearly two levels high blocking their path.

Quark balanced on a steel beam that teetered precariously. He reached up, trying to follow the multilegged Odo, and crawled across a cabinet door that buckled alarmingly beneath his weight. He kept his eye on the constable, choosing the best footholds from among the ten possible choices.

Odo was much heavier than a Ferengi; but by distributing his weight among ten rather than two legs, he lowered the kilograms per square centimeter below that of Quark's mass.

Odo stepped on a pipe that seemed stable. Quark followed exactly, but his own weight caused the pipe to roll, then twist.

The little Ferengi windmilled his arms as his stomach lurched sickeningly. Just before the pipe slid down the mountain, Quark leapt, landing gracelessly on a couch from the level above that had fallen through the hole. The pipe cascaded down the mountain, causing an avalanche in its wake.

At last, they crested the junk mountain, began picking their way gingerly down the other side. Strangely, Quark found going *down* harder than up: he dropped heavily onto a plastic box, and it collapsed beneath him. For a moment, he nearly leapt off the deadfall onto the deck that presumably waited below; finally, he caught his balance and shined his new, powerful flash down into the stygian darkness of the unlit habitat ring.

He could not make out the deck itself . . . either there was too much jetsam in the way, or perhaps the floor, too, had collapsed: in either case, Quark dared not leap blindly into the black.

He struggled to follow Odo, shining his torch back and forth to try to see what all ten leg-hands were grasping. When they finally reached the bottom of the deadfall, Quark's chest ached from his pounding heart.

As he caught his breath, he jabbed a finger at Odo. "Start talking! You said before you knew who these invaders were . . . if you don't tell me, you're—you're violating my civil rights as a resident here!" Quark panted; he was in reasonable shape for a Ferengi businessman, but the climb had been arduous, and more to the point, frightening. "Who the seven hells are they? Why did they attack the station?"

"You're not civil, and criminals have no rights," said Odo, distractedly. He stared down the corridor as if his eyes could pierce the blackness by willpower alone. *Yes,* he thought, *who the seven hells are they?* He had a suspicion, but he had no idea what sort of clue to look for to confirm or deny it.

"I don't know for sure, Quark. I've heard tales. . . ."

"Yes?" Quark was faintly annoyed. This was the second time that Odo had dropped a hint.

"They're not real, at least I've never seen documented evidence. Bogeymen that Cardassians use to frighten their children into obedience."

"You said that before. Almost the exact words," Quark pointed out. "Now why don't you try *explaining* them?"

"You're right; I should. There's no real name known for them; the Cardassians just call them—" Odo stopped, stared peculiarly down at a particular piece of wrecked metal. It looked like it was once a duct.

"Yes?" urged the Ferengi.

Odo knelt. There was a body in the duct. Irritated at the interruption by yet another corpse, Quark tugged at Odo's shoulder. "Come on, it's just another body. The corridor is full of them. What were you saying about the invaders, or assassins, or whatever they are? What do the Cardassians call them?"

Looking grim, the constable reached into the duct, grabbed hold of the corpse's belt. He could swear he recognized the lower half of that particular body. "Silence, Quark." Odo worked it out of its metal coffin, pulled it into the open.

Quark shined his flash onto the body, worked it up toward the face. Chubby but muscular, yellow shirt, curly, brown hair. Face frozen by death into the gritted teeth of anger and frustration.

The left part of his body, including arm and shoulder and the left side of his face, was blown clean off, and the remaining flesh on that side was severely burned. All of the skin was scraped off the fingers and knuckles of his right hand; apparently, he had not died instantly, had spent his last minutes of life madly clawing at the duct, trying to get out.

Chief Miles O'Brien stared up at them through his unblinking, dried and shrunken right eye.

The chronometer of Chief Miles O'Brien read 1854; *almost seven hours since the bastards hit us.*

He jabbed the touchplate outside Bata Huri's quarters.

After a moment, in which the colonel probably checked the outside-door display, the door slid open.

O'Brien blinked. At first, the girl who stood just inside the doorway looked like a Bajoran teenager, no more than fourteen or fifteen. "Is your mother home?" he asked.

"No."

"Oh. Is Bata Huri home?"

"Yes."

O'Brien waited. The girl did not move. "May I *speak* to Bata Huri?" he prodded.

"Certainly," said the girl, but still made no move to call Commander Bata to the door.

"Well, would you go *get* her? Please?"

"That would be counterproductive," said the Bajoran, gravely.

Chief O'Brien began to notice odd discrepancies. The girl's manner was dignified and mature; she had tiny wrinkles at the corners of her eyes. He mentally adjusted her age upward by a considerable margin, then made the conceptual leap. *"You're* Bata Huri."

"Yes, of course," said the commander with a slight twinkle. "Who else would I be?"

"How old are you?" blurted the chief. He winced; Keiko would have killed him for asking such a rude question of a woman he just met.

Bata Huri did not seem to mind, however. "I'm sixty-eight Bajoran years old," she proclaimed; "two years older than Master General Janri Kash himself."

"I'm sorry, sir. I was expecting—"

"Someone who looked like your Major Kira? That angry young gal looks like she just ate a squinchfruit! In any case, young man, or Chief, I should say, *my* commission isn't honorary. I really was a colonel before I retired here."

O'Brien stared in amazement. Now that he actually listened to her, he could hear the experience of decades in her voice, see her military bearing. She reminded him ineluctably of Captain Picard from the *Enterprise,* except that Bata Huri had hair.

How much did she know? "Are you aware of—"

"Commander Sisko contacted me a few minutes past. Nice young man; very unemotional. If we'd had a few like him on Bajor, we might not have needed the Federation to rescue us from the Cardassians. I called my team; we rendezvous at tunnel two in three minutes."

"Three minutes! We shouldn't be wasting—"

"We've plenty of time. Don't be impatient."

"Here," he said, handing her a bag with a dozen phaser grenades.

"Do they work?"

"Not entirely. But it's the closest thing we have aboard to a weapon that will actually hurt them."

Bata Huri glanced at the inside of her wrist. "Ready, dear? I mean, Chief? Let's go!" She grabbed a phaser rifle that was nearly bigger than she, bolted out the door so quickly she left O'Brien gawking at the hole in the air where she had been.

He tried to follow, was soon gasping for air. She moved like a monkey, skittering from one side of the corridor to the other so quickly he could barely keep up. Her rifle was always accessible, never quite pointed in any particular direction.

When they arrived at the barricades, meeting the rest of the DS9 militia ("This is only the first of them, dear," she told him; "more on the way, I hope"), he understood immediately why Bata Huri had been put in charge.

The men and women under arms for the station held Bata in awe; her slightest order was taken as a holy command.

There was no aura of superstition and religion surrounding her, as there was with the various Vedeks who had visited DS9. All that commanded obedience was Bata's own personality . . . *you could not say no to her.* It even affected O'Brien himself. *If my company commander had been like her,* he thought, *I might have stayed in combat line, instead of switching to engineering.* It was a sobering thought.

Under Bata Huri's direction, the militia closed the airlocks and set up barricades, stymieing the invaders. Their low-caliber bullets could not pierce the solid metal airlock doors.

Colonel Bata moved along the front line, whispering her new plan: "Fire into the ceiling above their heads."

"You want us to miss?" queried one Bajoran man, his face red with either fear or fury (or both).

"Phasers don't do a thing to 'em, Turiel—but they sure have an effect on the architecture."

O'Brien suddenly understood. "You want us to drop a ton of steel and chretite on their heads!" he guessed. Bata's smile was so motherly, it took away some of the pain from Keiko's death . . . for a moment.

"Shoot the floor out from underneath their feet, drop the ceiling on their heads—maybe that'll finally stop the bastards."

The Bajoran irregulars immediately began using the "Bata Tactic." O'Brien fired his personal hand phaser into the ceiling above the heads of the slowly approaching invaders, to no effect; then he was joined by four militia members firing the much more powerful phaser rifles.

Holes began appearing in the ceiling, but no rubble fell. "Don't use the highest setting," O'Brien shouted, "you'll just vaporize it! Use setting four—you want to heat it up so it collapses, not phase it out of existence!"

The bright red beams changed to a duller color. The invaders continued to advance, oblivious of the drama above their heads, their projectile rifles keeping the militia's heads down.

O'Brien heard a tremendous crack from the ceiling, so loud it reverberated even over the rifle fire.

So loud, the invaders finally heard it too. Their leader looked up, saw the red-glowing ceiling. He gesticulated calmly, waving his troops forward into a run.

They're going to clear the ceiling before it falls! O'Brien realized in sudden clarity.

Colonel Bata saw the same danger. Without hesitation, though her voice dripped agony, she shouted, "Hit them—hold them!" At her words, two huge Bajoran men leapt the barricade without a second thought, rushing into the certainty of bloody death. Startled by the unexpected charge, the invaders froze motionless; then they opened fire on the Bajorans.

The smaller man was struck twice, but he staggered on; the bigger man was a step behind, shielded from the bullets. Both crashed into the invader line at nearly top velocity.

The first four invaders went down in a tangle of limbs and armor. The rest had just begun to scale the scrumline when the ceiling exploded. Huge hunks of chretite and girders of press-steel tumbled like giant boulders, burying the invaders under what O'Brien estimated was at least six tons of garbage. A moment later, the "floor brigade" succeeded, collapsing the deck beneath the avalanche, causing it to collapse yet another level.

"Cease firing," said Bata quietly; her words cut through the hurly-burly of combat, and the irregular militia pulled back, assessing the damage.

For a moment, all was silent.

Then a great chunk of chretite shifted; a second rocked once, twice, finally fell over to slide down the rubble mountain. In the faint illumination from the core end of the tunnel, O'Brien saw an armored fist push up through the debris.

One invader struggled its way out of the impromptu tomb.

O'Brien lobbed a phaser grenade. It landed at the invader's feet, but the armored warrior kicked the bomb down the abyss before it exploded. O'Brien threw another, with a shorter fuse.

This one exploded directly in front of the invader; but when the smoke cleared, the invader picked itself up from its back, where it had been blown, and another crawled out of the pile of ceiling material . . . then a third.

The first invader opened up with its rifle, catching two militia defenders staring; they fell backward, gaping wounds in their chests.

Now the rubble almost exploded outward as the entire invader company dug their way out, apparently unharmed. They vaulted the pit, one by one, and continued to advance, laying down a murderous barrage of gunfire.

The report and explosive impact from the invaders' firearms reverberated in O'Brien's head like the hammer-beat of a hangover.

"Charge them!" screamed the enraged, panic-stricken man that Bata had called Turiel.

"Belay that," said Colonel Bata, her quiet voice somehow cutting through the explosive gas expansions that drove the bullets forward and the slap of the bullets themselves against the metal walls of tunnel two. Militia members who had begun to pick themselves and their weapons up for a charge sank back down to cover again.

"They're stunned—we can drive them back!" shouted the man who had called the charge.

"Maybe."

"Look! There's three invader bodies in the pit!"

From where O'Brien crouched, he clearly saw that the bodies were human or Bajoran. His stomach tightened sickeningly as he realized that they were probably hiding on level fourteen of the habitat ring, directly above the last section of the connecting tunnel . . . and that they were killed by O'Brien and the militia when they collapsed the upper deck upon the invaders.

I murdered them! he thought—then all at once realized something more urgent: Turiel's emotions were so out-of-control that he was hallucinating.

But Colonel Bata Huri could *not* see into the pit.

She raised herself up and tried to peer through the smoke; she tried to see if there really were invader bodies down there.

"No, get down!" shouted O'Brien, an instant too late.

A single slug caught Bata high in the shoulder. She made no sound, jerking convulsively as the high-velocity bullet punched a hole through her flesh and bone. Colonel Bata staggered back, fell on her back behind her troops, holding her shoulder and straining not to scream. Blood poured out of the wound like a squeezed sponge.

O'Brien shivered as he felt a wave of mingled terror and fury sweep the company. Within seconds, nearly three hundred men and women knew that Colonel Bata had been shot.

The chief looked from one grim face to another, saw only a burning need for revenge. It clouded their reason. They lacked the combat experience to counteract the rage they felt.

Bajorans were *very* emotional people. Raw emotion frightened O'Brien; it was uncontrolled, untidy . . . he saw too much of it in himself.

Turiel stood up. "Charge them!" he cried again, and this time there was no one to say no. Others took up the cry—"Charge! Charge!"

Bata's lieutenant, a retired policeman named Lakuta, frantically shouted for control, urging the troops to return to the Bata Tactic; but the instant-warriors took command of themselves, grabbed the airlock door, and rolled it back far enough to pour out into the corridor.

That was the cue for which the invaders waited. As soon as the airlock door was a third of the way open, the invaders halted, crouched, and fired a barrage of cover, while one at the back raised a larger gun over their heads.

The gun was a rocket-launcher; it flashed, then thundered with a force so great that O'Brien was blown backward by the air impact alone.

He rolled into a "duck and cover" stance on his knees, arms wrapped around his head.

The shell struck the airlock door and exploded, making O'Brien's phaser grenade seem like a small firecracker. The chief was thrown another two meters backward and struck by fragments of wood, chretite, and bone.

The few troops who survived the explosion staggered like blind zombies. They did not know where they were or what they were supposed to be doing.

Miles O'Brien turned his ringing head to the left, saw the remains of Colonel Bata: her legs had vanished, and she had taken shrapnel to the abdomen. O'Brien was amazed to discover that Bata Huri was not quite dead.

For a few seconds, her mouth opened and closed silently, eyes staring from the door to O'Brien and back to the door. He watched, mesmerized by her desperate attempts to give orders still, even in death. Then her head tilted, and she fell still.

O'Brien climbed to his feet, still shaky, and scrambled backward until he bumped into the outer bulkhead. His groping hand found an access vent, its protective grille torn off by the explosion.

He caught the lip, picked his feet up, and squeezed into the tiny opening just as the first invader loped through the flames and smoke. The airlock door was now permanently wedged open.

The invaders gathered calmly in the habitat ring corridor, assessing the damage. They shot the survivors, not even bothering to question them.

The undignified and useless death of Colonel Bata was the last straw for the chief. The emotional wave he had tried to keep numbed and dammed since the death of his beloved burst free. Red, bloody rage flooded his brain.

"You murdering bastards!" he bellowed, uncaring whether they heard him or not.

A pair of the closest invaders looked up, tried to find the source of the shout.

O'Brien reached into his satchel, extracted one of his remaining phaser grenades. He pressed the Arm button.

One hippopot—

The grenade, not having been reset from the default "0 seconds," exploded instantly.

CHAPTER
8

"THE TIME HAS COME," said Odo, brushing dust and dried blood from his hands, "to make a few preliminary deductions."

Quark stared at Chief O'Brien's body, pale in the torchlight. "I think we have more important matters to attend to," he said, stuffily.

"Burials? Quark, I'm aware of the elaborate rituals engaged in by Ferengi and humans and such, but—"

"*Please* don't use those two words as a compound noun, Odo. And a sheet over the chief's face would be fine. But I'm talking about Nog, and other survivors. We have to find them; it's the paramount concern."

"Our primary duty, Quark, is *justice.* In this case, since we know who, our paramount concern, as you put it, is to determine *what* they are and *why* they attacked the station personnel."

"Yes, you damned cop—justice *after* we find the survivors and care for them."

"What survivors? Quark, have you seen any?"

The Ferengi glared at Odo. "How can there *not* have been survivors? There are no invaders left, so it's fair to assume they were ultimately driven off. *Somebody* would have found a hole to hide in and escape death—and if anybody did, it would be Nog! And probably Jake," he appended.

Odo smiled. "The naive, first-cut deduction. It fails by inspection: *there are no survivors,* or we would have seen them by now. There are a lot of corpses with no obvious cause of death; the most logical deduction is that the invaders killed everyone, then left."

Odo waited for the Ferengi to object, but Quark remained silent; whether he was convinced or just biding his time, the constable could not say.

"First of all," continued Odo, "killing the station personnel was a secondary goal, not primary."

"It looks pretty primary to me!" Quark stared pointedly all around them, looking simultaneously outraged and nauseated at the haphazard bodies.

"Think, Quark: If the invaders meant to simply kill everyone and *not* take over the station, why bother transporting a strike team? Why not just blow it up with their ship, then escape back through the wormhole?"

"Maybe they did want the station."

"Then where are they? They obviously won; clearly there's no command personnel left, or they would have taken a runabout out past the subspace blanking field and sent a distress call. And there's no wrecked invader ship out there, so we didn't manage to kill them all.

"There is only one logical answer: They came here looking for something—information, some person or item, or treasure—and proceeded to conduct a very thorough, room-by-room search of Deep Space Nine."

"But did they find it?"

Odo shrugged. "We don't know yet. My guess is no, or they would have left before killing everyone."

"They *did* leave before killing everyone," Quark pointed out. "We're still alive."

"We were in a static-time field," Odo reminded him. "In any case, why kill"—he paused for a moment, recollecting the exact number of DS9 residents at the moment—"five hundred seventy-three out of five hundred seventy-five crew and civilians if you've already found what you so desperately want?" The constable shook his head, frowning. "No, Quark, the safest bet is that they killed everyone they found and did not find what they wanted, despite a thorough search, then decided it wasn't here, and left. So either it *wasn't* here, or it was very well hidden."

His eyes narrowed; at exactly the same time, Quark's widened. "No! You can't pin *this* on me too!"

"Really? It makes perfect sense, Quark. What better place to hide something than inside a static-time field? Let's see it, Quark."

After a long pause, during which Quark sulked like a child caught with Daddy's phaser, he reached into an inside pocket of his jacket and removed the Gamma quadrant device, tugging to pull the sucker pads loose.

"Yes, of course," said Odo; "your Lonat villain doubtless stole this from the Gamma quadrant, and its rightful owners followed him to DS-Nine to demand it back."

"No! That's ridic—that can't be right."

"Oh? And why not?"

Quark thought furiously, fluttering his hands in agitation. Odo waited patiently, realizing he had the little Ferengi dead to rights.

At once, Quark gasped, then relaxed. Smirking, he said, "Because if they had shown up asking for a dwoozle-widget, Sisko or Kira or somebody would have asked what it looked like, and as soon as they said it was in a Cardassian strongbox, O'Brien would have steered them to Quark's Place."

"Unless the Lonat captain put it in the box." It was a feeble possibility, and Quark knew it as well as Odo. A locked Cardassian box was worth much less than jewelry from the Gamma quadrant; why not just sell it as is? Quark could have found a buyer in ten minutes willing to pay 500,000 bars of gold-pressed latinum for Gamma jewelry . . . especially since it was obviously a device of some sort.

"Don't you think Dr. Bashir or Chief O'Brien would have said something about an unknown, alien device they had just scanned?" asked Quark. Odo just grunted.

"Of course," mused the Ferengi, "the same P and L would apply to *any* unknown device, even if it had nothing to do with me."

"And if they wanted a *known* device," added Odo, "we could have simply replicated one for them. I hate to admit it, Quark, but I think you're right. And they didn't want money, or they would have taken your latinum, or at least something of value.

"That leaves only one choice: The invaders were looking for a *person,* somebody in particular."

"Great. That only narrows it down to about five hundred and seventy-five people, eh Odo? A brilliantly concise deduction."

"We have one other piece of evidence you're overlooking, Constable Quark."

"Yes . . . ?" asked Quark, suspiciously.

"They searched the entire station and killed all but two people on board . . . and they didn't find who they were looking for. Either they were wildly misinformed— and they seem to have been quite sure—or the person they wanted was one of us."

Dax looked up, blinking. She had been monitoring the audio on Chief O'Brien, heard his exclamation—"You murdering bastards"—then silence.

She quickly swiveled in her chair and ordered the computer to locate O'Brien. The computer ground on for many seconds before the answer finally appeared on the monitor: CHIEF MILES O'BRIEN IS NOT ABOARD DS9.

"Benjamin," she said, "I think we have a problem."

Sisko looked up from his own station at the operations table, where he continually monitored the progress of the invaders and the damage they had caused to DS9 so far.

"I . . ." Dax paused, not sure whether it was just another false alarm. "O'Brien's signal disappeared again." She looked up at the commander. "I have a feeling this time—I think it's the real thing."

Sisko considered for a moment. "Has the ship done anything recently?"

"Not for ninety minutes," she answered, "which was the last time I batted away a bomb. It's been virtually dead, almost as if—"

"As if its only purpose was to occupy us while the invader team boarded and got a toehold. Any thoughts on what 'the other one like us' might mean, old man?"

Jadzia Dax closed her eyes, rubbing her temples. She felt dead: dead tired, dead in thought; when she caught her reflection in a metal surface, she saw that even her spots had faded to near-invisibility.

I even feel *like an "old man" today,* she thought.

She opened her eyes. "They think we're holding one of them captive." *Duh. Dazzle the kid with your brilliance, why don't you?*

Sisko said nothing; he leaned on his console and maintained a discreet silence, waiting for something a bit deeper.

"But they don't know how or why."

"They do seem a bit fuzzy on the incident," agreed the commander. "So where did they get the information? Did someone tell them we're holding one of them captive?"

"Doesn't parse. Unless the source was extremely reliable, I can't imagine an intelligent culture launching a dangerous attack on the basis of hearsay evidence. They're not *that* far advanced over us; for all they knew, we might have had 'planet-buster' bombs aboard. They exist; we just don't have them here."

Sisko stroked his chin; for the ten thousandth time, Dax remarked silently on the "leadership image" of her young protégé. Benjamin looked and acted more like a great leader than any other person she had met, Trill or monospecies. His bursts of passion were becoming fewer and sparser as he grew out of childhood.

I wish Trill could be permanently implanted in humans, Dax thought for the ten thousand and first time; *Benjamin would make a wonderful Trill.*

While the commander pondered, Dax ran a level-one diagnostic check on the computer; it had been behaving oddly, running very slow and sometimes giving nonsense answers. As she feared, the destruction caused by the invaders was taking its toll: memory banks, circuits, and data sensors all over the station had been damaged or destroyed, and the computer's brain was overloading. Systems that critically depended on the computer were shutting down—sometimes quietly, sometimes with a bang.

If O'Brien were here, she thought, then killed the rest of the wish. As long as she was wishing, why not just wish the invaders right back to the Gamma quadrant?

"If the source *were* extremely reliable," said Sisko, "then presumably he would know we were not holding one of them captive. We've certainly received no visitors from the Gamma quadrant, and the only people we're holding are known Federation members . . . petty criminals and one attempted rape.

"Changing the subject," he added, "has anyone located Odo, old man?"

Dax shook her head. "Same as O'Brien: he is not aboard DS-Nine. Benjamin, I hate to say it, but I think O'Brien is dead. I've already sent a medevac crew to tunnel two to see what's happened and report. But if O'Brien were conscious, he would have found a way to tell us.

"And, Benjamin, I have more bad news. The computer system is shutting down left and right. At this point, I would have to declare it unreliable. If there's another bomb attack, you'd better bat them away manually."

Sisko felt a familiar tightening in his gut. *It's happening again . . . it's all happening again.* These invaders were like the Borg: relentless killing machines. And they already controlled a significant fraction of his station.

He put his hand on Dax's shoulder. "Please, when you have the time, could you . . . ?" He could not easily articulate his fear.

No matter; Dax understood. Dax always understood. When he—*she* had a moment, she would check to see where Jake was, if Sisko's son was still "aboard the station."

"And Odo?" he asked.

"Frankly, I doubt that Odo is dead. But he is clearly incapacitated by some means, or he, too, would have found a way to contact us. Quark was listed as missing around the same time we noticed Odo's absence; they may be together, or it may be a coincidence."

Commander Sisko's mind was still processing the earlier part of the conversation; he had the ability to work many problems in parallel, finding lateral connections between them. "Odo and possibly Quark disappear. Almost exactly a day later, the station is attacked by visitors from the Gamma quadrant who claim we're holding one of them hostage. These two facts are related, Lieutenant. Find out who was the last person to see Odo or Quark. I want to know what the devil they were doing."

He took a deep breath, calming himself. The hairs on the nape of Dax's neck rose; through long association with the commander, she knew she would not enjoy hearing the next thing he had to say.

"Then as soon as that's done, I want you—I want you out in the field. You're the only other person on the station who can jury-rig phasers into grenades."

I don't notice you *volunteering,* she thought angrily. She immediately checked herself, spots blushing deep vermilion.

Of course Sisko had not volunteered for combat; he was the commanding officer. His place was here, in Ops. Duty, not cowardice, kept him at the nerve center.

Curzon Dax would never even have thought that, Jadzia Dax corrected herself. Suddenly, a shiver crept up her spine. A horrible image popped into her head: Sisko, slowly dying from the extremities inward as the station was destroyed.

She looked at the ragged commander, standing stiffly at a useless command console, and she shuddered. *Your hours are sand, Ben Sisko. They're drifting through the hourglass; and when the last grain falls, you die.*

"The phaser grenades haven't worked too well," she said quietly. Her gut tightened; it had been a long time since Dax had actually fought in person-to-person combat.

"They're the best we've got, old man." He gave Dax's shoulder a final, affectionate squeeze, then returned to O'Brien's station to monitor the battle.

Dr. Julian Bashir, medical officer of Deep Space 9, stood over the body of his latest patient, desperately trying to help the woman without getting any of her blood on his clothes or hands—not because of squeamishness or fastidiousness, though he was normally the most well groomed person on Deep Space 9; rather, the patients were being trucked into the medical facility so quickly that he had no time to change clothes or even wash up between one patient and the next. Bashir did not want to contaminate one casualty with the blood of another.

The infirmary resembled a horrific parody of a Denarian flophouse, with dead, dying, and merely mortally wounded patients lying on every flat surface available, leaving only narrow footpaths for Bashir and his nurse. Blood covered the normally gleaming white deck, making the floor slick.

Bashir had set up emergency surgery lights over the operating table, since the illumination was erratic; in their hellish, blue-white glare, he examined the most recent patient, a Bajoran woman he did not recognize, fortunately.

He probed gently with the field scalpel, feeling the

interior dimensions of the wound through the forcefield held in his delicate surgeon's fingers.

Bajoran anatomy . . . heart is here, *primary lung lobe, secondary lobe, liver, post-liver . . .* The damage was almost unimaginable. From what he could tell, when the projectiles fired by the invaders entered a body, they began to tumble, bouncing around inside the person's abdominal cavity like a ball bearing shaken in a cylinder.

"My God," he breathed, "no wonder we use phasers."

With time and care, the woman would live. Almost all the damage was repairable, given sufficient time and attention. At this moment, Dr. Bashir had neither.

Triage time, he decided. "Sorry, Nurse. Too much damage. Next patient." His stomach ached from having passed so many casual death sentences that day; but the highest calling of his profession—"Above all else, do no harm"—prevented him from giving treatment in difficult cases when it would mean a dozen others died from lack of even minimal care.

He jabbed his communicator. "Bashir here," he said, then blinked; who had called him? He could not even remember.

"When was the last time you saw Odo? Or Quark?"

"What?" He was already examining another patient. Julian Bashir smiled; this one was a boy, but he had only a minor chest wound; this time he could do something, he could be a real doctor.

"Julian, this is important." A familiar voice . . . *Jadzia's* voice! Yes, it would be important then.

"Quark? I, um, saw him about a day ago. Yes, yesterday at twelve hundred. He had some sort of box he wanted me to scan."

"What about Odo?"

"Odo was with him. In fact, I think it was Odo who insisted the box be scanned; said it was from the Gamma quadrant, might be dangerous."

There was a pause, and Bashir returned to his patient. *Human . . . heart, lungs here.* He repaired the damage,

115

leaving minor vascular work for a nurse or attendant to finish up—ordinarily, he could have lost his license for that; but under the circumstances, it was vital.

He completely forgot he was in a conversation with the lovely Lieutenant Dax until she spoke again.

"The box?"

"What?"

"The box was from the Gamma quadrant?"

"Something *in* the box. Some Gamma device; it was pretty low power, didn't seem dangerous."

"I wonder. Julian, could you do me a favor?"

"Of course."

"Let me leave a channel open; you just keep thinking about the box and whatever was inside it. Anything else you think of about Quark or Odo, just say it out loud. I'll be monitoring."

"I would be honored," he said. He turned to his nurse, Chief Broome: "Next patient, please."

A new voice entered the link: "And if the invaders come to the infirmary to interrogate you," said Commander Sisko, "see if you can get them to talk, explain why they're doing this and what they want. But don't put yourself in harm's way, Doctor."

"Believe me, I won't."

"We need you too much. There are going to be a lot more casualties."

Chief John Broome, transferred from the Ordover system just in time to see the station destroyed, floated in the next patient on a gurney, parked her in front of Dr. Bashir. The doctor gasped, stared for a moment: she was a young latinum prospector named Ashley Grayson; Bashir had taken her to dinner at the Replimat and a DS9 Spacelings production of *The King in Yellow* just two nights ago.

For an instant he stared, frozen; his stomach contracted into a painful ball. His mind insisted upon superimposing her image from the tryst over her wounded body on the gurney.

Even near death, her face was regal, trusting. *I'll save you!* he thought.

Then professionalism regained control, and he began to probe. *Human . . . heart, spleen, C6 and C7, upper carapace . . .* He lowered his eyes. "Sorry, Ashley," he whispered; "too much damage, Ensign. Next—next patient, please."

After a few moments, he realized that Lieutenant Dax must have signed off; he had not heard her, not said goodbye.

He had not quite said goodbye to Ashley, either. Julian blinked, felt a tear for the first time since the crisis began. Until now, Bashir had quite simply been too bloody busy to grieve.

"Goodbye, Ms. Grayson," he said, bowing slightly; "you were a gracious lady to the end."

Time passed, an hour or more. Bashir looked at his chronometer: 2302. He decided to steal a few seconds to begin recording his medical log, documenting the number of deaths and injuries in the melee.

The med-lab door slid open, and Bashir absently looked up from the monitor to see how many more patients were being deposited.

Two strange people stood at the door, dressed in gray-black armor, their faces obscured by reflective "bubble" helmets.

Julian stared, puzzled. "May I help you?" he asked.

A flat, mechanical voice answered, doubtless a Universal Translator of some strange design: "This is the medical lab."

"Yes . . ."

"You are the officer of medical matters."

"Yes."

The two soldiers entered the lab. As soon as Julian saw their projectile rifles, he realized who and *what* they were.

Dax spoke to Sisko. "The last person to talk to Odo and Quark that I can find is Julian Bashir, twelve hundred yesterday. Shortly before they disappeared, they brought a box to Julian for a bioscan. Julian said the box contained an unknown device from the Gamma quadrant.

"The last person to see Odo and Quark, without talking to them, was Riga Anda, Ensign Kropotkian's wife. At twelve-thirty, she was having a quiet drink in Quark's Place, if you can believe that, when Odo and Quark entered and went immediately up to Quark's office."

"Can Rom confirm that?" asked Sisko. "Did he see them leave?"

"Rom is dead."

For a moment, they both fell silent, listening to the remaining militia report the progress of battle. It was bad; they had been pushed out of a pie wedge of the habitat ring surrounding tunnel two, and the invaders were trying to blow the emergency airlocks open with high explosives.

Dax looked speculatively at the phaser sequencer. "Benjamin, what would happen if we fired the array at our own habitat ring? We might just be able to nick it."

"I've been thinking about that. If this station were Federation, I would have ordered it immediately. But the Cardassians always favored sheer, centralized mass over structural modularity; there's a very good chance that the entire station would disintegrate."

"If it comes to that, you might bear it in mind."

"It might come to that, old man. But not just yet. Next question: Why haven't they come up here yet, to Ops? If they want to conquer the station, this is the place to do it."

"Then maybe they don't want to conquer the station. Maybe they don't care. Count your blessings, Benjamin. They don't want DS-Nine; they don't have enough time for a complete takeover job. They just want their comrade. They're fanning out from the Promenade, poking their noses into every nook and cranny."

Dax looked wistfully at the sequencer, continued her analysis. "Quark finds, buys, or steals a sealed box containing an unknown device from the Gamma quadrant. Odo is worried enough that he has Julian make a bioscan; if we ever find O'Brien and he's alive, we can ask if they took it to him, too.

"Then they return to Quark's, go up to the office, and disappear.

"A day later, the invaders show up looking for somebody, the 'other one' like them. They insist we're holding him. They begin a room-by-room search, killing everyone they run across. This can't be a coincidence, Benjamin."

"Not likely."

Suddenly, Dax felt a wave of anger explode from her friend. Sisko momentarily lost control, smashed his hand into the science console. *"Damn it!* What in God's name did they *do?* What the hell did they find?"

Immediately abashed, he folded his arms, withdrew into himself.

Dax considered. "My guess? I would say that whatever the device was, it included some sort of subspace transponder, something with an identifiable signal. Something that should always have been kept with this person the invaders are looking for."

Sisko looked up at the monitor, his face lighting up. "Yes . . . yes! Old man, that's it! That device put out a subspace signal that said 'Here I am.' No wonder they don't believe us when we say we don't have him. The physical evidence indicates we *do.*"

Dax rose, stared slowly around Ops; she felt a firm conviction that it was the last time she would see the clunky, Cardassian operations table, the jail-like commander's office, or O'Brien's systems core, probably the cleanest spot on the entire station.

"I'd better get moving, Commander," she said, voice catching in her throat. "Lieutenant Tara said the militia has only a few grenades left."

Dax paused; a lump of unexpressed emotion welled in her throat. It was probably the last time she would see Ben Sisko as well.

"By the way, sir, there's a bag of grenades on my chair, just for you. And the invader ship is still out there, but it hasn't budged. Are you sure you can—?"

Sisko smiled grimly. "I can, even without the computer. I was handling phasers and shields before you were born. Half of you, anyway."

"I've also been monitoring Dr. Bashir," she added, driven by the compulsion to convey every last bit of information now, before she left and did not return; "Transfer it to your console speaker?"

Sisko nodded absently. "Turn it low; I'm monitoring practically the entire station."

Dax rose, walked around the table. She fought down the impulse to hug Sisko goodbye: *You'd want me to be strong as I mount the gallows,* thought Dax.

The Trill strode to the ladder, spoke without looking back: "Fight well until I get back," she said. She began the long climb down to level six and one of the weapons lockers, but she could not resist a quick peek as her head cleared the hatchway.

The commander's head was bowed, and he made a point of not watching her leave.

Lieutenant Jadzia Dax pressed her lips together; *I won't make it harder on you,* she thought resolutely. She continued the climb without saying goodbye.

Major Kira Nerys crouched in a large vent, holding herself absolutely still as a squad of invaders marched by. Tunnel two had become an invader stronghold, a communications conduit between their Promenade platoon and their habitat platoon.

Kira waited, watching for her chance.

She had been hiding in the vent for nearly an hour. Groups of invaders had passed her position eleven times in that hour; any one of them could have seen her merely by turning its head and actually looking at the grille—

she was clearly visible behind it. But nobody had looked. Why should they? What defender would be insane enough to penetrate the nucleus of their forces?

Suddenly, she stiffened. Footsteps approached. She listened closely, finally heard what she had waited for all this time: the footsteps of a *single* invader.

She risked a quick peek as it walked by: single invader, rifle slung over its shoulder, ammunition drum attached to its back, carrying a Federation tricorder.

Flashback, Shakaar underground. Comes a Cardassian. He's got something I need very desperately. . . .

She opened the grate; it squeaked slightly, but the invader ignored it. She glanced quickly to her right; the others were so far up the tunnel she could barely see them.

To the left, the tunnel disappeared into blackness; the invaders had shot up a junction node, plunging the tunnel and part of the habitat ring into total darkness. The invaders probably used infrared. Kira realized she had to move quickly.

She swung out of her cramped hiding place, scuttled quietly up behind the invader.

At the last moment, it felt a presence, started to turn; Kira caught it in an awkward posture, shoulders half turned toward its back. She grabbed its arms, wrapped her leg around its, and the force of her tackle drove it to the ground, Kira on top of it.

One second—just one . . .

The phaser grenade already in her right hand was set to one second. She thumbed the Arm button, jammed the grenade underneath the invader's chest, and yanked her arm free.

Its body armor shielded her from the blast. They both were thrown backward and up a meter or more. Kira climbed shakily to her knees, staggered to her feet; the invader pulled itself into a fetal position, lying on its side, knees up, arms wrapped around its gut.

Kira stared in amazement: *The bastard's still alive!* She

waited a moment, but it did not get up. She exhaled sharply, unaware until that moment that she had been holding her breath.

O'Brien, I could kiss you, she thought, *except Keiko would kill me. Prophets, I forgot.*

Quickly, before it could recover, Kira unstrapped its ammo pack and slung it over her arm, picked up its rifle, and ran for the vent. She finally had a weapon that even the invaders would have to respect!

Now, at last, she could begin rounding up civilians, preferably children, to evacuate via runabout.

Kira Nerys, anti-Cardassian saboteur or Bajoran freedom-fighter, depending which side one had been on, squirmed through the tight burrow toward tunnel three, trying to figure out how to load the rifle and work the trigger.

Terrible images popped unbidden into her head—not the carnage she had just seen, but visions of years past, crawling through different corridors, fighting a different, implacable foe.

Same blood, different costume, she thought.

CHAPTER
9

PLEASE, SIRAS, make it work—Holy Siras, make these damned things work! Dax jogged along tunnel three, a fifteen-kilogram bag of new-made phaser grenades draped over one aching shoulder.

Her breath came raggedly; sweat dripped down her face and chest. Still, she smiled: *Curzon Dax would have plopped to the ground gasping halfway back.* Jadzia Dax was a dance fiend.

The long tunnel was deserted, its soft, normal glow causing shivers to crawl up and down her spine. The war had bypassed tunnel three, and the false vision of normalcy pervading the happy little corridor was more horrifying than a pile of dead bodies.

Of course, Curzon Dax probably would have had a better idea of strategy, and probably knew more about explosives than Jadzia Dax did. *I am that which I am—now,* she thought.

She slowed to a walk, shifted the bag yet again to the other shoulder. Ahead was the airlock door, sealed shut. The militia had cleverly shut them all, forcing the invaders to blast their way through every few meters.

Now what?

She scanned with her tricorder: nothing; but of course, the invaders had done something to damp out the tricorders, apparently figuring out that the crew was tracking them. Listening at the door was silly—it was a double-doored, vacuum-sealed airlock; but she did it anyway, heard nothing.

"Well, I hope that here goes nothing." Dax pulled out a grenade. "Emergency override, airlock thirty-seven, Jadzia Dax."

The door slid open; she winced, prepared to feel a hundred metal pellets puncture her body.

The corridor was empty.

She breezed through, slapped the fast-close control pad; the door rolled shut again. *I am in the land of Turill ga'Lia, the final battle of the Children of Lia,* she decided. In one well-known Trill myth, small, spritelike gods fought the enormous but slow-witted giants at the final battle, killing everyone on both sides except one male and one female, one of each race—of course, there were endless arguments about which sex was represented by the big, stupid giant.

She skulked cautiously in the direction of tunnel two. After about ten meters, she came to another airlock.

The tricorder still showed nothing, but Jadzia Dax heard clickings and scrapings from the bulkheads. Something was there.

She touched her communicator. "Excuse me, are there any invaders between airlocks thirty-eight and thirty-nine?"

A voice responded almost instantly. "War zone; get out unless you're armed." During the brief communication, Dax heard multiple gunshot noises and phaser blasts.

"Dax from Ops," she said; "grenades. I'm coming through."

Before she could say a word to pass the airlock, however, it slid open. The instant the seal was cracked, Dax winced at a cacophony louder than she had ever heard before, assaulting her ears like a pair of knitting needles shoved deep. She gritted her teeth and dropped to all fours, crawling forward behind the hasty barricades.

Most of the militia members seemed frightened by the invaders' firearms; none had any experience with weapons that made a loud report and banged against barriers with explosive impact.

But the last remnants of the second company held. They retreated slowly, airlock by airlock, making the invaders fight for every meter of ground.

The militia was using the "Bata" method, firing their phasers into the ceiling above the invaders and the floor beneath them, raining rubble upon their heads and trying to drop them down levels. The invaders had to advance slowly, laying torn bulkheads across the holes and digging themselves out when necessary.

There were still too many deaths and woundings; but since the defenders had changed tactics, there had been no more interrogation-executions. They died on their feet, not their knees.

A militia sergeant put his hand on Dax's back; a Bajoran rank insignia was drawn directly on his shirt with some kind of ink, another throwback.

"I bring you weapons of mass destruction," said Dax, mock-heroically.

He stared at her as if she were a goddess. Dax decided he was both cute and smart enough to recognize her true status of divinity.

"Here," she said, handing him the workout bag stuffed full of phaser grenades. She kept two for herself, their clips hooked in her hip pockets. "Now I've got to get out of here and make more."

"Can't we replicate these?" asked the sergeant.

"Sure," said Dax, "if you think completely uncharged phaser grenades will do you any good."

"Can't you override that?"

She revised downward her estimate of his intelligence. "You can't replicate pure energy, um, Sergeant."

Dax quickly withdrew before he could say anything more. She had no time to chat, even with a hunk; she had explosives to manufacture.

Now I know how Kira feels, she thought.

She returned through airlock thirty-nine, and it closed instantly behind her.

As she walked, something tickled the back of her brain. Something about replicating phasers.

Even before O'Brien had explained it to them, Dax knew it would not work; the replicators could not replicate a charged phaser because they could not actually create energy; all they could do was rearrange molecules.

The only way they could create "energy," of a sort, was to create chemicals that could then interact, like hydrochloric acid and lye.

Or like . . .

Dax froze, flooded with the sudden brilliance of a supernova.

Or like *gunpowder,* she realized.

Gods, she thought, *you may not be able to replicate a charged phaser . . . but you* could *replicate a loaded gun!*

She slapped her communicator so hard she almost knocked it off her shirt. "Benjamin, I've got it! I've got it!"

"Got what?" queried Sisko's gravelly but still-controlled voice.

"Benjamin, we can't replicate a phaser grenade, but we *can* replicate an arsenal of firearms! We can arm this militia with something that'll actually *work* against the invaders!"

Silence for a moment; Dax held her breath, praying that Sisko would not think of some critical objection that would render her plan useless.

"Old man," said the commander, awed, "you are a genius."

"I've been telling you that for decades," she said. "Quick, patch me into the computer; I need to download some specs." While Sisko programmed the computer for a data-dump download through the comm link, Dax removed her communicator and slid it into the input slot on her tricorder. She readied the tricorder to receive the data.

"Ready," said Commander Sisko.

"Computer," said Dax, "what is the most powerful, hand-held, chemically propelled projectile weapon you have in your library?"

After a moment, the leaden, broken voice responded. "The Klingon GarTadGar-Eleven, also known as the Klingon 'windowpane.'"

Dax whistled; she once saw a history holo of one of the early Klingon wars of succession, where they used the earlier-model GTG-4; even the toned-down version was powerful enough to punch through a "crawling fortress."

"Download full specifications," she ordered.

"Access is restricted to—"

"Emergency override, Lieutenant Jadzia Dax."

"Download in progress." After a second, the computer added, "Download complete."

"Wish me luck, Benjamin. Dax out."

"Good luck, old man."

She flipped the tricorder over, popped out the data clip. She clutched it in her hand and sprinted down the corridor, looking for a replicator.

She found one less than five meters along; the faceplate dangled loosely by one corner and sparks shot from the reception bin. Fiber-optic cables were torn out. Clearly, the replicator had taken a direct hit from a bomb of some sort.

"Damn it!" swore Dax, feeling immediately chagrined; at her age, she should be able to control her emotions. She jogged farther, came to a sealed airlock door.

Licking her dry lips, she used her emergency override to open the door. The corridor was empty.

She jogged along, found another replicator; this one looked intact.

Fingers fumbling, she tried to press the data clip into

the clip slot, instead dropped it on the floor. "Easy, girl," she told herself. "Only the body is young; the mind is not afraid." Jadzia Dax picked up the data clip, tried again; this time, it popped in properly.

The replicators used a subset of the computer library, only containing molecular specifications for items that were customarily replicated. In particular, most dangerous items could *not* be replicated without supplying both an appropriate security clearance and the full specs.

"Lieutenant Jadzia Dax," she told the replicator, "security override." She selected the clip as the input source, selected the bundle named "Klingon GTG-11," and pressed the replicate button.

The replicator made a very odd noise. An object phased into existence in the bin . . . it was nothing but a horribly twisted hunk of metal.

Feeling a horrible suspicion, Dax tried it again; the metal piece was different this time, but just as useless. Clearly, the replicator was simply creating random structures.

She pried the data clip out, skittered over to a second replicator. She repeated the procedure with the same result.

Dax stared at the precious data clip, useless if the replicators had been damaged.

"It can't be. It *can't* be—it's too good an idea, blast it."

She looked at the next airlock door; conceivably, only the replicators in this section were damaged. Perhaps somewhere on the ship, there was a working replicator. She only needed one.

Dax popped the data clip out, ran to the door. "Lieutenant Jadzia Dax," she said; "emergency override, airlock thirty-five."

The door slid open. Dax started to walk into the corridor; then she stopped dead, staring in disbelief.

Whoops . . .

A strike team of five invaders had flanked the militia. They were coming along the corridor, blowing airlocks as they came.

At first, she did not know whether they had seen her. She slowly edged backward. Then one of the invaders raised his rifle and fired a shot.

Dax ducked the moment he raised his gun, and the bullet tore a chunk out of the bulkhead where her chest had just been. She spun and pelted back up the corridor, hearing their booted feet close behind her.

She skidded to a halt, staring at the now-closed door of airlock thirty-six. No time for an override.

There was a door on her left; she charged full speed, smashed through it before the computer even had the chance to signal the potential occupant of the apartment that he, she, or it had a visitor.

Quark walked unsteadily, eyes unfocused. *Too much. Just too much. . . .*

The thought that all this could very well be his fault ate at his mind, numbed him. His voice was subdued; he had lost much of his normal Ferengi fire.

It's not my fault. I wasn't even here! I was frozen with—it—for three days, while all this happened. The explanation did not even convince Quark himself.

He stared forward along the corridor. The habitat ring was warped and buckled by the heat of massed phasers and invader explosives, as if a giant had come along and hammered it into a roller coaster. All of the lights were out in this section due to the shot-up junction node, and acrid smoke still hung stale in the air . . . as it would forever without recirculators.

As he shined his flash farther up, the light vanished in the hazy gloom. Quark swallowed: *anything* might be out there—an abyss to fall in, an ice-brittle deck to fall through, or even a renegade, slavering invader with nineteen legs and poison-dripping tusks, ready to chew off the Ferengi's ears.

He stepped on a large, flat piece of wood, once an expensive Bajoran table inlaid with tigerstone, probably left over from the Cardassian occupation. It held firm for the first few steps, then rotated treacherously.

Quark flapped his arms, teetered on one foot over a pile of sharp-looking glass shards.

Odo's arm shot out more than three meters, caught the Ferengi by the collar, and yanked him back to solid deck.

"Hm. Thank you," said Quark, distractedly. He looked down at yet another dead body. But this time, something seemed different, wrong.

It took several beats before he realized what; no bullet holes. "Odo," said Quark, "take a look at this."

The constable looked the body up and down before the discrepancy dawned on him as well. He took hold of the woman's shoulder, flipped her over onto her front like a sack of grain . . . no bullet holes on that side either.

"So what killed her?" asked the Ferengi.

"I don't know. This is odd. Her face and limbs seem contorted, as if she were in excruciating pain. But I don't see any marks at all." He let the body fall back to the deck, stood dismissively. "No time to worry about it. She probably has a wound we can't detect without medical equipment."

"Maybe . . ." began Quark, trailed into silence.

"Yes?"

The Ferengi looked up at Odo. "Do you think she died because she was *fated* to die? Was the entire station condemned because I delved into things that Ferengi were not meant to know?"

Odo stared at him. "A long time ago, I told Dr. Bashir that the most horrible hell I could imagine was being stuck with an unrepentant Quark on a dead station forever."

"You did?"

"I remember it distinctly. I remember everything I say distinctly. This was shortly after the aphasia plague had afflicted the station. I said to Dr. Bashir, 'At least you would be dead; for me, trapped here with Quark, the nightmare would have just begun.'' I have since revised my opinion."

"You have? That's nice of you to—"

"The *worst* hell is being trapped on a dead station with a guilt-ridden, *remorseful* Quark.

"So for the sake of my sanity, Quark, will you *please* revert to your normal, old, annoying, irritating, but slightly more interesting self?"

Quark glared at the constable, lifted his upper lip in a Ferengi type-eleven sneer. "Per your request, I shall try to be a bit less ethical."

"Thank you. I don't like to see patterns upended."

Quark snorted, stormed down the habitat ring corridor.

They were still on level fifteen, still had not found any other survivors. "I doubt Nog would stay on this level," suggested Quark; "looks like the epicenter of the war. Nog has enough of the Ferengi instinct for self-preservation—"

"Ferengi cowardice."

"Call it what you will, but the Ferengi have survived in the galactic community for four hundred years, prospering by trade with Klingons, Romulans, Cardassians, Stroptophans—"

"Strop—what?"

"—and even humans without ever fighting a war. And do you know why?"

"The Ferengi cringe?"

"Who asked you? No, because the Ferengi, among all the civilized races—"

"I'll let that one pass."

"—*the Ferengi,* among all civilized races, know how to turn any circumstance into a profitable deal. It's a racial trait, like philanthropy in humans and insufferable arrogance in . . . in whatever *your* race might be called. No, there is no way that Nog would end up involved in the combat. His good sense would lead him to the deepest, darkest hole in DS-Nine, taking Jake with him. We have to go deeper."

"In the first place," said Odo wearily, "we don't even know whether Nog survived the attack, though I admit we haven't found his body. Second, have you noticed that there *are no* intact turbolifts or climbshafts in this section? I've been looking for them.

"Third, I told you before that our primary task is to determine what happened, then find a working run-about, get outside the communications shield, and call the Federation and Bajor."

"To quote a famous human philosopher, 'Ask not what you can do for your country; ask rather what you can do for yourself.'"

"Who said *that?*"

"Oh, I can't remember every slightest detail, Odo. Leona Boesky or President Henry Ford, one of the founders of Earth economics. We study other worlds' great economists in business school, you know."

They walked past a door knocked off its hinges. The Ferengi glanced inside, continued walking. "But what Leona Boesky meant was . . ."

Quark stopped, staring straight ahead, face turning distinctly yellow.

"What is it? What's wrong, Quark?"

"I . . . I don't know. Did you glance inside that room we just passed?"

"No."

"I think you should."

Odo stared at Quark; the Ferengi was acting odd, even for a Ferengi. Puzzled, the constable retraced his steps, glanced inside the room, and at once understood what had affected Quark.

"I'm afraid you weren't hallucinating, Quark," he said. "It is she."

Reluctantly, knowing what he had seen but hoping to delay confirmation just a few more seconds, Quark returned to the door. He looked inside.

Jadzia Dax sat on the floor, leaning back against the outer bulkhead. Her eyes were closed, hands lying limp on the deck at her sides. Two large bullet holes marred the perfect beauty of her lovely face, one in her cheek, the other in her forehead, directly above her eyes.

An enigmatic smile painted her full lips, red even in death. The enticing spots along her neck, normally dark brown, were now bone white.

She looked carefully arranged, as if she had carefully sat herself down against the wall to die facing the open door. But that was absurd; the forehead center-shot would have pierced her brain to the stem, killing her instantly. Either she was already sitting there when she was shot, or somebody had arranged her in a macabre simulation of serenity.

But it was exactly how Quark would have expected Jadzia Dax's body to be found: elegant, composed, at peace.

Odo entered the room, Quark at his heels. The Ferengi approached her body and crouched low to look one last time in her perfect face.

He was startled by an exclamation from normally implacable Odo: "I was right!"

Quark turned, saw something that almost made him forget Dax entirely.

Lying on its face against the inner bulkhead, where it could not be seen from the corridor, was the very first body of a dead invader they had yet seen.

Quark turned back to Dax, understanding her cryptic smile. Lieutenant Jadzia Dax had figured out a way to kill an invader.

Nice timing, Dax, the Trill chastised herself. She stared left, right, like a hunted animal. The deserted apartment might as well have been a cage—there were no other exits.

If she could only get to a working replicator, cram in her data clip, and make a Klingon "windowpane," she could take out the entire invader team!

Then the pain hit. The nerves in her arm screamed in agony, but she managed to stifle the sound in her throat. She could not even slightly move her left arm, where she had smashed through the door.

It's broken, she thought inanely. The pain throbbed

worse than anything she could remember feeling before in her life, though Curzon Dax had been both phasered and knifed.

She looked around the room; there was one replicator.

Dax started to run to it; but before she got even halfway, she felt a presence loom behind her. The hairs on the nape of her neck stood straight, and she felt her spots flush deep vermilion. She turned slowly, palming the two phaser grenades she had held out, holding them behind her back.

The invader stood in the doorway, still as a stone, its rifle pointed at her face. She waited, but it said nothing. In a moment, it was joined by a slightly smaller version of itself . . . same body armor, helmet, same cut of cloth; but the second invader had a hand-sized version of the firearm in its right hand.

Dax knew what the inquisitor was going to ask before it spoke; chills still marched up and down her spine as she heard her death sentence: "Where is the other one like us."

"We want to help you," she improvised, fighting back tears at the pain; "help you find the other one like you." She edged toward the replicator.

The inquisitor stared, motionless. Unlike every other race of beings Dax had ever seen, the invaders became literally *motionless* when they stopped moving; there were no tiny, involuntary twitches of the leg or arm muscles, no rocking back and forth from one foot to the other. Even its chest froze—no visible pulse or respirations. The inquisitor just *froze* as if it had seen a Gorgon in the ancient human mythology.

She wondered: Could it be *communicating* with the others? She took the opportunity to move a bit closer to the replicator, ready the data clip in her fingers.

It spoke. The effect was so sudden, so much like a statue come to life, that Dax jumped. "You know where the other one is."

She assumed the words were meant as a question, despite the flat intonation. "I can figure it out. But I need more information. How did you find out that the other one was here?"

Again the inquisitor paused. Her questions seemed to throw its rhythm off, confuse it. The pain in her arm beat a new agony with every beat of her pulse. She took another step. *Almost there . . .*

"We received the signal," it said at last.

Good girl, Dax! You nailed it. "What did the signal say? It might tell me where the other one is now if I knew where it was then."

"It was the signal."

"Did it say in what part of the station it was at that moment?"

"It was the signal. Where is the other one."

"Is the signal produced by a device? We might locate the other one by finding the signaling device."

The inquisitor froze for a long time. Evidently it was considering how much to tell her; either that, or it simply was not used to being the questionee, rather than the questioner. *Communing; definitely communing.*

Dax took the final two sideways steps; she stood next to the replicator, trying to figure out how to jam in the data clip, select the input source, and replicate a "windowpane," all before the invader fired its rifle.

"Yes," it finally said.

"A device small enough to hold in one hand?"

"Yes. Where is the device."

Progress . . . "It was in the medical lab, and it was in Quark's Place. Quark's Place is the large, three-story facility on the Promenade, where you first beamed in. I can lead you there. Let me lead you; we can find this device together. But I'm very hungry; I can't think unless I intake some food."

The inquisitor answered immediately, ignoring her last statement. "Did you see this device."

For a moment, Dax dithered between the truth and a plausible lie. "Yes," she said at last. "Do you mind if I obtain some food from this device?" She indicated the replicator.

"What does the device look like."

Dax was confused for a moment until she realized the invader meant the signaling device, not the replicator.

Cardassian crawlfish, she thought; how would she know what it looked like? But she had to answer. "It's—about the size of my hand, with a hand grip, smooth like your helmet—"

She knew instantly she had said one thing too many. She thought of the old story that Sisko had told her when she was a "he," Curzon Dax:

Abraham Lincoln, a middle-period president of Earth, or some part of Earth, was a lawyer early in his career. He once defended a man accused of biting off his opponent's ear in a barroom fight.

There was one witness. Lincoln asked the man, "Did you see the fight?"

"No, sir," said the witness.

"Did you see my client attack Mr. Jenkins?"

"No, sir."

"Did you see my client bite Mr. Jenkins's ear?"

"No, sir."

"Well then, and think very hard about this question, *did you see my client bite Mr. Jenkins's ear off?*"

The witness looked Lincoln in the eye: "No, sir," he repeated.

At that moment, Lincoln had him. He could have sat down, having completely destroyed the man as a witness. But instead, the great Abraham Lincoln made one of the few mistakes in his career.

He asked one question too many.

"Then how in tarnation," he thundered to the witness, "do you know that my client *did* bite Mr. Jenkins's ear off?"

"Because I saw him spit it out afterward," came the devastating reply.

The device was smooth, like your helmet . . . Ding, wrong, Lieutenant. But thank you for playing.

"I'm sorry," said Dax, "my mind must be going. I meant to say it was angled—"

The inquisitor calmly raised his hand firearm. Dax whirled to the replicator, jammed in the data clip. She heard a gunshot behind her, and the replicator control pad exploded into a wreckage of metal, plastiglass, and bright blue electrical discharge.

She turned back to face the invader, knowing she had lost the gamble. Jadzia Dax felt a strangely delicious peace descend upon her; she knew she was about to die, and that there was nothing she could do about it.

But she was not afraid. "I'd prefer it in the front," she said, smiling mysteriously.

The explosion from the barrel filled her ears, echoed like the deep rumble of the fusion reactors. In slow motion, Dax felt a tremendous hammer-blow against her face. Her head felt like it had caved in under the impact.

For an instant that stretched to eternity, Dax rocked back, balanced on her heels. Then she slowly fell, gravity a gently, bright-painted rainbow. The pain in her arm and shoulder vanished, replaced by a delicious, foggy shroud.

Blackness. I should see blackness. Instead, every color of the prism of light swirled around her vision, though red predominated: orange; orange-red, the hair color of humans from certain parts of Ireland; ocher.

All the old human names floated through her mind in the last seconds. Benjamin was a wonderful observer of nuances of hue: the lively flame red; cocola red, though nobody knew what "cocola" was; cherry red; cardinal red; carnation red; crimson.

Blood red, and the darker reds—ruby, damask, burnt crimson, iron red, claret red, scarlet, copper.

Deepening at last into the lowest frequencies . . . magenta, maroon, vermilion, and infrared. The last color stretched on and on, like life—never quite ending . . . the waves lengthened until their wavelength was infinite, energy approaching zero but never quite reaching it.

Jadzia Dax's wavelength approached zero, then hesitated. A tiny fluctuation remained, a faint whisper of coherent frequency somewhere above zero.

The colors faded into the infrared; she could not see anymore. But a piece of her remained, felt the lifeless body surrounding her.

Merciful Mother, thought Dax—not Jadzia Dax or Curzon Dax, but for the first time, in quite a while, just *Dax; Jadzia's brain is dead, but I am still alive in her chest!*

Dax considered the situation. The host body, Jadzia, was brain-dead; but the rest of her body was workable, except for a broken arm and dislocated shoulder. The Trill implant Dax, the "worm," was still alive.

And still connected . . . True; Jadzia's nervous system had grown into the worm, intertwined with Dax until they truly were one entity. Now, with Jadzia's brain off-line, Dax wondered if it could still move her body.

It experimented; the arm lifted, albeit jerkily. The eyelids fluttered open, and Dax could see (blurry; it could not bring the two eyes into focus on the same object).

The inquisitor, satisfied at his handiwork, had turned around, was leaving through the smashed door.

Dax tried to raise Jadzia's left arm; it would not work, the shattered bone, torn muscle, and separated tendons too damaged to move.

But the right arm worked . . . and it still held one of the two phaser grenades.

Dax raised Jadzia's arm; every manipulation required conscious contraction or relaxation of every applicable muscle. Dax made the thumb press the 1, for one second, then press the Arm button. It pulled Jadzia's arm back like a catapult and let fly the grenade.

The grenade struck the inquisitor in the back at the exact instant it exploded. The security woman Dax had heard through the comm link with O'Brien was right, thick brogue and all: they *did* have "muckle-mare armor tae fore than aft."

The inquisitor was blown forward against the inner bulkhead by the force of the explosion. It did not get up again.

The second invader, still facing Dax, survived the explosion . . . barely. It climbed to its feet, staggered back into the room. Jadzia's eyesight dimmed as even the autonomic functions began to shut down. The invader crouched by the inquisitor, examined its body. At last, it rose, turned to Jadzia and Dax, and fired another round into Jadzia's head.

The rifle shot struck lower, with much more force than the inquisitor's pistol shot, obliterating the limbic system that controlled heart, lungs, and other autonomic functions. Dax lost all control of Jadzia's body, and Jadzia's eyes closed. Dax could no longer see.

The infrared deepened, the frequency dropping. The wavelength approached infinity asymptotically as the frequency dropped to zero.

I did it was Dax's last thought, though it no longer remembered what exactly it had done.

CHAPTER
10

"I KNOW THEM," repeated Odo as he fumbled with the invader's helmet latches; "I *know* this race!" After several moments, he managed to pull the black bubble off the creature's head.

Inside was a vaguely reptilian face covered by soft, springy, cactuslike spines. A casual observer might mistake it for fur, until touching it.

The fur-spines were coated with a brownish sap, which might have been excreted by the long, well-muscled tongue that lolled out of the invader's mouth. The sap had hardened into a tacky, resinous shellac after drying in the still air for two days.

The creature's eyes were huge and perfectly circular with a vertical slit between the eyelids, rather than horizontal, as in humans, Cardassians, Klingons, and most other humanoid races.

"Who are they?" asked Quark from across the room. For some reason, he felt dread at the thought of approaching the creature . . . not that he was afraid it would suddenly spring back to life and kill him; rather, he felt a premonition that it would somehow *talk to him,* imparting some dreadful secret that Quark did not want to know.

"They have no name," said Odo, rising and inspecting the invader's hand firearm. "They are the most secretive race known, and the only people I've ever heard refer to them are Cardassians. I don't think anyone else has met them, which is just as well."

"What do you mean, they don't have a name?"

"I mean they don't tell anyone who they are. They don't make treaties, trade agreements, or friends. They don't talk to other races. The Cardassians call them the *Bekkir,* but that's just a Cardassian animal similar to an Earth badger or a Ferengi digfish—it digs a hole and hides, and only attacks those who venture too near.

"Gul Dukat told me that the Cardassians attempted to make common cause with them against the Klingons a hundred years or so ago, but the Bekkir destroyed the three Cardassian ships sent as emissaries, and the Cardassians decided to leave them alone."

"How strangely un-Cardassian," said Quark. "I would have expected a punitive expedition. I'm disappointed."

"They live in the Gamma quadrant, too far for an effective campaign. This was pre-wormhole, remember. Anyway, nobody knows how many of them there are or how powerful their technology is. The Bekkir are extreme xenophobes, fearing and despising all other races that have ever contacted them. Nobody knows anything about them."

"Well," said Quark, "we know something now. We know they can come tens of thousands of light-years to attack a space station."

"That is curious. According to Cardassian lore—and much of this could be myth—there are only two ways to provoke an attack by Bekkir: to attempt to find out their home system, or to hold one of them captive."

Odo and Quark simultaneously looked at each other, immediately grasping the obvious. Odo spoke first. "So *something* made them think a Bekkir was being held on

DS-Nine. Now, I wonder what that something could be, eh Quark?''

Without warning, Odo turned his arms into flexible, snakelike appendages that whipped out, coiled around the Ferengi, and dragged him closer. Quark struggled and squawked, lunging for freedom, trying to keep far away from the Bekkir body.

As Odo dragged Quark closer, the commander saw a glow beneath the Bekkir, centering on his arm, which was pinned under his back. Bringing Quark into near contact with the Bekkir, he saw the glow flare brilliantly . . . something on the Bekkir's wrist reacted vividly to Quark's presence.

Or more likely to the time bubble device that Quark still carried.

"Spill it, Quark," said the constable; "drop it into my hand. Now." He uncoiled one arm, shrank it back to normal.

Quark cringed in perfect Ferengi form. Using the classic "dead rat" grip, he removed the device and placed it into Odo's hand. "Take it," he said, making a face as though the device were a piece of offal picked up from the ground.

Odo let go of the Ferengi, who backed away, elbows tucked to his sides, hands raised with the palms outward, head turned aside in a thoroughly submissive fashion, pulled down as far into the shoulders as it would go. Quark would have described it as Ferengi cringe number five, *I express great shame for my stupidity and throw myself on your mercy; please don't kill and eat me.*

Odo pulled the Bekkir's arm from underneath its body, held the device up to a wristband. The band flared bright red, sent a slight electrical shock through the Bekkir's arm that caused Odo to yank his own hand away.

Odo glared back at Quark. The Ferengi had shifted to the most extreme cringe of all, on his knees, body prostrated before Odo, hands straight out in front of him with fingers spread wide, face hidden against the deck

(number sixty-three: *Please make my death as quick and efficient as possible, avoiding needless suffering on my part. I suggest a quick knife-thrust between the third and fourth cervical vertebrae.*)

"Oh, get up, you scrabbling coward. Nobody's going to kill you."

Quark merely whimpered.

Odo sighed. "I'm not even going to lock you up."

The Ferengi cautiously peeked over his outstretched hands. "You're not?"

Odo sat on the floor, resting his hands on his knees, as he had seen humans do when at their ease. In fact, he was starting to feel tired; in just a few hours, Odo would have to revert to liquid and "sleep" for a period of time.

It had been awful to revert to his natural form in front of Ambassador Lwaxana Troi; it was unthinkable to do so in front of *Quark,* of all people. But how could he avoid it? There was no possible way he could hold out until help arrived, even from Bajor.

"I've been thinking about your case ever since you activated the Bekkir device." Quark immediately dropped back into cringe number sixty-three again, but Odo ignored him and continued. "Is it really your responsibility? Can I hold you to blame?

"True, it is now clear that your actions caused the Bekkir to imagine we were holding one of them captive, which led to this search-and-destroy mission. But there is a great principle of justice—*justice*—that you can only hold someone responsible for results reasonably inferable from his actions.

"If a Ferengi leans against a wall, and because of poor construction the wall falls down, you don't arrest the Ferengi; you arrest the owner who didn't maintain his building."

Quark finally stopped whimpering as he began to realize that Odo might possibly let him off the fishhook.

The constable sniffed. The next sentence went against all his conscious opinions about Quark, arising instead out of his innate sense of absolute right and wrong.

"I cannot find it within me to blame you for the Bekkir's attack when there is a much more obvious culprit available: the Bekkir themselves. Had they only talked to Commander Sisko, told him *why* they thought a Bekkir was imprisoned, he would surely have asked among his senior officers and Ops crew. When he did, O'Brien and Dr. Bashir would have told him about the device that I had them scan; and there would have been no reason for the Bekkir to murder five hundred and seventy-one people.

"Being the only law-enforcement official present, thereby constituting a justice committee of one member, I hereby find the defendant Not Guilty by reason of stupidity, unforeseeable result, and the Ferengi's natural, monkeylike curiosity.

"Get up, Quark; you're a free man again—God help us all."

Major Kira Nerys held up her hand; behind her, the column of children and a few adults stopped, frightened. She checked the time: 2715—no wonder she felt exhausted; she had been fighting continuously for more than fifteen hours.

Kira blinked, and she was back in the Shakaar; Cardassians had invaded Bajor again. They were coming!

She shook her head, clearing the cobwebs; there were no Cardassians . . . it was even worse: tireless, remorseless killing machines, worse than the Borg, though on a smaller scale.

She put her finger to her lips to emphasize silence, held up two fingers, and pointed forward, past the intersection at which she waited. The first two children dashed across, as silently as they could. The invaders at the other end of the corridor did not notice.

Kira signaled for the next two children, then the next. In all, twelve children scuttled past the occupied corridor: eight Bajorans, two humans, a Betazoid, and a little Vulcan girl.

144

The two Bajoran runabout pilots Kira had rounded up were not so silent; one slipped, her shoes making a squeak on the polished deck. The invaders heard them and turned.

Kira caught the first one with a dead-center shot in its chest, using the captured rifle. The bullet cracked through the armor as if it were papier-mâché, apparently killing the occupant instantly.

The moment it fell, it flared brilliant red. Kira turned her face away; when she looked back, the invader body had vanished, leaving behind nothing but its heat-twisted armor.

Strange, she thought; *the bullets didn't do that to us.*

Kira Nerys crossed the corridor and waited at the intersection, crouched low with her rifle just peeking around the corner. Her invader counterpart dropped to its belly and began plinking at her.

Kira did not waste ammunition, knowing it was an impossible shot. Instead, she withdrew behind her column, all of them heading for access ladder twelve leading up to the service bay, where the runabout *Orinoco* waited.

She only ventured ten meters down the corridor, however, then hovered, hugging the bulkhead and aiming low at the intersection she had just left.

As Kira predicted, the cautious invader crawled all the way to the intersection, lay flat on its stomach, and eased its bubble head past the corner.

It saw her just as she saw it. The invader only froze for an instant; but an instant was long enough. Kira Nerys fired two rounds into the invader's face. The helmet shattered, exposing a ruddy brown, furry, reptilian face, now splattered with black blood. The invader convulsed as if suffering a grand mal seizure, then fell still.

A second later, it, too, melted into a bubbly goo.

Kira nodded, finally understanding: it was not the bullets that caused the meltdown; it was a security mechanism designed not to allow intact invader bodies to fall into enemy hands, where they might be dissected, their weaknesses probed.

Kira backed up until she bumped into her column. "Move it, move it!" she commanded.

They stealthily followed two more turns along the sterile, almost antiseptic corridors of level fifteen between tunnels one and three.

The invaders held the rest of the upper level of the habitat ring, but the sporadic fighting had dropped down to level eighteen, as the few remaining militia defenders tried a last attempt to outflank the invaders by burrowing under.

Kira cursed silently that the invaders seemed to be growing more technologically innovative by the hour: now they had extended the transporter lock-on signal damping field so that Ops could not even beam people *to* a pad, where the coordinates were known to the angstrom. This prevented the logical evacuation method: beam the kids one by one directly to the runabout.

Instead, they had to hoof it, right through the combat zone, then climb a ladder into the service bay and load up. It was a rescue fraught with peril.

Kira tapped her communicator. "Kira," she whispered; "just below target, sir. Cycle the *Orinoco*."

Sisko's voice drifted back, soft and distant, as if he spoke from a tiny room. "Ready, Major."

"Who's left?"

"You and I are the only senior crew."

"Dax?"

"She doesn't answer her hail."

"I got a gun. One of theirs."

"Excellent."

"I found out they can be killed. When you kill them, they melt down."

"Lieutenant Dax had a brilliant idea: replicating gunpowder firearms."

"I thought O'Brien said that wouldn't work?"

"He was talking about phasers, energy weapons. I mean the chemical kind of firearms, like you have. I can't get any of the replicators up here working; they're just turning out random metal. How would you feel about trying to replicate your gun?"

"Um, what do you mean, random metal?"

"Twisted hunks of porous, metallic compound," said Commander Sisko. "Formless, as if the pattern generator had been destroyed."

Kira thought for a moment. "Wouldn't the replicator have to take this gun apart and re-create it before it would have the specs stored?"

"Yes," said Sisko. "That's why I asked whether you wanted to risk it. Can you get another gun if that one is wrecked?"

"Damn! Wish I'd known earlier; I might have been able to. But not now; there's no one around here."

"If you get an opportunity . . . it could be our best chance, Major."

"Aye, sir. Next bastard I kill I'll grab its gun and shove it in a replicator. What about the chief? Can't he fix the pattern generator?"

"O'Brien is dead; a militia sergeant spotted what's left of him in an air vent. Security is gone; the militia will fight to the last but have no hope of victory."

She closed her eyes, let the weariness seep through her flesh. *So many battles; so many hopeless causes. You take what small victories you can, live to fight again on better ground.* "These are all the kids I could find, sir. I, um, I couldn't locate Jake."

"I know. You would have told me."

"Or Nog. They're probably together . . . probably hidden in some deep hole. Maybe the invaders won't find them."

There was a long silence. When Sisko spoke, his voice was as flat and emotionless as the invaders' themselves. It gave Kira the creeps.

"It makes no difference, Major. This station is lost, and my duty is clear. I cannot allow the invader strike team to leave here alive."

A knife of ice jabbed Kira's heart. *Can't let them leave*

alive? He can't mean—"Sir, if I can get out past the communications shield, we can call for help."

"From Bajor? What will they send, Major Kira? A starship? Can Bajor send me a starship and Federation troops to retake Deep Space Nine?"

She clenched her teeth. They both knew that Bajor had no military vessels capable of fighting the invader ship, and the nearest Federation starship was at least two days away. The station would be lost long before then. For that matter, the invaders might even attack Bajor itself next.

The attack from the wormhole *might* just presage a general invasion of Federation space from the Gamma quadrant; the Federation could not allow even such a remote outpost as Deep Space 9 to fall without inflicting unacceptable casualties on the enemy. Otherwise, it was like hanging a neon sign: FREE EATS! COME AND GET IT!

Sisko was right; there was only one decision he could make.

Thank the prophets I'm not in command, she thought. "Sir, let me get this group packed off in the *Orinoco*, then I'll round up another batch and ship them off on the *Rio Grande*. And I promise to find Jake."

"Better be aboard that one yourself, Major."

"I understand, sir."

"Warn Bajor they might have to defend themselves if more ships come through the wormhole."

"Yes, sir."

"Inform me when the runabout's away. Out."

For a few seconds, Kira digested the conversation. She could rescue this batch of kids, and another group of kids or civilians, but then Sisko would have no choice but to destroy the station—and himself with it, undoubtedly, to make sure none of the invaders escaped.

Maybe I should stay behind too, she wondered, *make room for one more civilian.*

No; it was impossible. Somebody had to apprise Bajor of the threat—somebody with enough credibility to make them *believe* the warning, which meant a Bajoran military officer . . . which meant Major Kira, who, despite being nicknamed "Major Pain-in-the-ass" by the provisional government, was certainly not considered an alarmist.

Even so, Bajor would not likely respond favorably to the message "Good luck; you're all doomed by a bunch of bubbleheads shooting ancient, gunpowder weapons."

But what else could they do? Like everyone else in the civilized quadrants, the Bajoran military machine was deployed to defend against armadas of ships firing disruptors or phasers or photon torpedoes. Nobody had fought a gunpowder-commando war in centuries!

The invaders were not primitive; they obviously had warp drive, transporters, and armor that *shielded* against particle-beam weaponry. Their military evolution had followed a different track, however: rather than dump projectile weapons, as had every other civilized race, they refined them, turned them into immensely efficient killing machines.

She pinched herself. *Stop musing, gal; time to act!*

"Are you rested?" she asked. The children nodded silently. The Bajoran kids were used to disruptions of this sort, and they took it upon themselves to calm and care for the other kids. "Let's go."

Kira went up the ladder first, followed by the female pilot with the squeaky shoe, the parade of children, and the backup pilot.

They had almost reached the service bay when a single shot exploded beneath them. The backup pilot dropped heavily, dead before he struck the deck.

Kira swore angrily, forgetting the children; if they heard, they were too frightened to care.

She leaned way off the ladder, dangling by one foot and hand, urging the kids past her, up into the service bay. The position left her utterly vulnerable to attack from below; she could not aim and fire the invader gun with one hand.

She could, however, fire from the hip; she would not likely hit anyone, but she could slow them down. Kira blindly fired a steady drumbeat of shots down the ladderway, one every two or three seconds to conserve ammunition. Above her, the last of the children cleared the hatch into the service bay.

"Lock the door," she shouted to the pilot.

The woman stared. "What?"

"Lock shut the damned door, you pinhead!" She saw a quick movement below, laced a couple of rounds into the crack of the corridor, all she could see from her vantage. "The door to the rest of the habitat ring—lock it shut so you don't get ambushed while you're taking off!"

The Bajoran pilot's face brightened; she got it and ran off toward the door while Kira fired in the general direction of anything that moved.

Major Kira Nerys climbed the ladder into the service bay, lay on her stomach, peering down into the gloom. She set her torch on the opposite side of the hatch, sticking it onto the metal so it shined straight down the ladder: anybody coming up would necessarily have to look directly into the bright flash.

She waited, heart pounding, breath ragged.

Prophets, I can't believe it. It's all going to end. Now.

I won't leave this room alive. She smiled sardonically. *Sorry, Commander; I suppose I won't be able to replicate that gun for you.*

The kids dashed across the bay to the runabout, opened the door by themselves and piled in. Their silent, pinched faces looked back at Kira.

She silently shook her head. A tear wet her cheek.

"Goodbye," she mouthed silently, turned attention back to the ladderway.

A bubblehead moved cautiously into the light. This time, Kira could use both hands. She aimed, fired, and its helmet shattered in an explosion of black blood and prickly flesh. It fell heavily, flared brilliant red, and turned into a slag heap.

She jerked away from the opening as the invaders returned fire, furious at the death of their comrade; she could actually hear cracks as the bullets streaked supersonically past her head, making mini-sonic booms.

The fusillade stopped. She waited a few seconds, shouldered her rifle while still away from the hatch, then whirled around, already firing down the ladderway before she could even see them.

She caught the first bubblehead in its chest, knocking it off the ladder. It fell into the one below, and both crashed noisily to the deck.

The invader she had shot did not flare; instead, it softly and suddenly vanished away, like a Boojum from *The Hunting of the Snark.*

She fired two more wild rounds before finally acquiring a target, the second invader from the ladder, who was just scrambling to its feet. She splattered the creature's helmet, and it flared and melted satisfactorily.

She developed a theory: the invaders' armor protected their bodies from anything but a dead-on hit; the only definitely fatal shot was a head shot. When they died, they melted down; when they were merely wounded, they vanished.

A loud rumble caught her off guard. She yanked her rifle up out of the ladderway, whirled around only to discover it was the runabout firing its engines at full throttle *in the service bay,* lifting off without wasting time by riding the elevator up to the launching pad.

Kira snapped back, but no more bubbleheads polluted the ladderway.

Something flew up at Kira, hitting her in the nose. She blinked with surprise; it was a black cylinder, as wide and thick as her fist, made of some sort of metal. Before even consciously realizing what it was, she kicked it back down the hatch and threw herself to the side.

The cylinder exploded violently. Even outside the direct concussion cone, the shock knocked her off her knees onto her rear. She scrambled up, saw another black cylinder incoming.

Kira batted it back with the butt of the rifle, remembering the game of cosmic "baseball" she had played with the invader ship. *Sisko, you would love this,* she thought as she smacked a third grenade back at the bubbleheads even before the second blew up; but the third grenade erupted directly below her, not off to the side like the others.

The force caught her full in the face and upper body, flinging her back away from the hatch into the service bay. Stunned, Kira rolled back and forth, feebly trying to get off her back and onto her knees again. The runabout was just clearing the deck between the service bay and launchpad, rotating to face outward.

She watched it as it passed through the launchpad, fired impulse engines again, and disappeared behind the lip of the deck hatch.

Launching—have to tell Sisko it's launching . . .

Kira pawed at her communicator, but was still too shaky to make her hand work correctly.

She gritted her teeth, bore down hard, and *forced* her groping fingers to find the communicator. "Kira," she gasped, "run—runa—launch . . ."

Gasping, she rolled to her knees just as the first black-bubbled head popped up the hatch. By luck, her rifle was lying at her side, pointed roughly in the right direction.

Grabbing it, she pushed it forward until the muzzle almost touched the black globe, fired a round into the invader's face.

It dropped out of sight before she could see whether it slagged; but this time, another bubblehead chucked a grenade through the hatch in Kira's direction.

Sisko should put me on a baseball team, she thought, batting the grenade away, into a corner of the service bay.

She fell to her belly, arms laced over her head, as the grenade exploded. It rolled her over twice, but she was actually less disoriented than she had been after the last one.

She crouched, rifle pointed at the hatch, waiting to either fire a round or stick another grenade. *I can do this for the rest of my life, you bastards!*

CHAPTER
11

Odo STARED AT the third Bekkir bloodstain he had seen. Quark had found the puddle at the intersection of a corridor. From the angle of the spattered blood, Odo could easily tell the direction from which the shot had come.

Yet again, pieces of twisted, melted armor surrounded the blood, as if, after dying, the Bekkir had been fried with some intense heat that left nothing behind.

"Looks like somebody was retreating," said Quark, "shooting them with their own guns."

Odo nodded. "Probably just one gun, and not much ammunition. Clever. Very clever. Defensive armor evolves at the same pace as offensive weapons: the only gun likely to be able to penetrate Bekkir armor is a Bekkir gun. Hard to tell, since the Bekkir have apparently destroyed the bodies."

"Sounds like the gruesome sort of thing that a Bajoran major would think of," said Quark, sounding simultaneously impressed and disapproving.

"Or Commander Sisko," agreed Odo. "The civilians appear to have been as unsuccessful as the security team.

An experienced soldier might think of incapacitating a Bekkir and taking its rifle."

"So is Kira still alive? Or maybe Sisko?"

"I doubt it," said Odo. "If they were alive, conscious, and still on the station, they'd be in Ops, repairing the damage."

Odo continued down the corridor, backtracking the shot telemetry. He climbed or vaulted over heaped rubble, collapsed bulkheads and overheads, crouched and wriggled through tenuous, fragile "tunnels" formed by fallen debris. He did not change his shape; his energy was running low, and every change taxed him tremendously. He would have to change to his natural state in few enough hours as it was, and he intended to be in a place of relative safety—and privacy from Quark, if possible.

The Ferengi, for his own part, labored to keep up . . . frightened that he would be crushed by a metallic cave-in, but more afraid of being left alone and lost in the twisted shards of what was once DS9. Quark was not an athlete, but he did a credible job of following the constable.

They passed several spots where the cold stars of Bajor leered through gaping mouths in the skin of the station; only the stationwide atmospheric shield kept DS9 pressurized.

With the fusion power plants down, the shield, too, would soon fail, forcing them to don pressure suits.

"More blood," said Odo in a small, tired-sounding voice. He examined two more puddles of black blood and pink flesh that was probably Bekkir brain tissue; again, twisted heaps of liquefied armor lay scattered nearby.

"I detect a pattern," said Odo, examining the armor. "When a Bekkir dies, an automatic incendiary device consumes the body, destroying any evidence that might yield clues about their race.

"The Bekkir that Dax killed didn't burn."

"I've thought of that. The same explosion that killed

him probably destroyed the burn-mechanism—a stroke of good fortune for us. These others were simply shot, leaving the incendiaries intact."

"Oh." Quark simply watched, impassive. He had already seen too much blood to care one way or the other about more any deaths, friend or foe. He knew there were 571 corpses on DS9 at that moment—572, counting the Bekkir Dax had killed—but it seemed to him as if they had already seen twice that many.

He knew it was not true, just his fear and disgust. But it *was* true that a number of the corpses were completely unmarked . . . though each was as twisted and contorted as the unmarked corpse they found by tunnel two, looking as if it had died of an epileptic seizure.

They all died violently—but how?

The enigma nearly made Quark believe in divine retribution. Had the remote outpost somehow offended the gods of commerce, incurring supernatural wrath? If so, then they walked as the only living beings on a ghost station.

"Blast radius," mumbled Odo, turning slowly to scan the room. The constable was right: on the deck, the overhead, among the remnants of machinery and furniture, the appurtenances of life for the living, they saw a clear explosion pattern, everything extending away from a common point.

Rather, several points. Odo carefully traced the streaks backward, as if finding the "perspective point" in a painting, and found not one but at least three, possibly four distinct "ground zeros."

"And look," added the constable, "here is a piece of another Bekkir's greaves—unburned. This time, the explosion was significantly more powerful, leaving no other trace; but again, the incendiary device was obviously destroyed."

Odo's face suddenly lit up. "Quark, do you know where we are?"

The Ferengi stared in hopeless confusion. The overhead itself had collapsed inward, not rupturing, but bulging inward like a surreal inverted mountain. It looked as if something tremendous had crashed into it, a huge fist hammering the ceiling into concavity.

A tiny hole in the overhead let them see a bit into the room above. Quark could see the side of something white, could not make out any more details.

"I don't have the slightest idea where we are, Odo," said Quark, peevishly.

"You should. You've been here many times. Or rather, *there.*" He pointed up, into the room above. "A runabout service bay is directly above us," he clarified; "number three, I believe. There used to be an access ladder here, somewhere, but it's gone. Probably destroyed by the explosive devices."

"There's something up there," said Quark, squinting upward; "something on the other side of the ceiling. Can we get up there to look?"

He looked down; Odo was rummaging in the wreckage, found a long piece of tubing that almost reached the ceiling. "If you can climb this pole, you can," said the constable.

"What? Climb that ridiculous thing? Odo, you're a shapechanger, blast you! Why don't you just elongate or turn into a snake or something and have a look?"

Odo frowned. "I'm not an entertainment for the rubes, Quark. I don't change form merely for your momentary convenience. Climb, or stay below and hold it steady."

Quark considered: Odo looked human-sized, but he massed closer to two hundred kilos, as Quark had found out to his regret in the early days on the station, when he once tried to tackle the constable. Holding a greasy pipe steady while such a giant climbed it would be much more work than climbing the same greasy pipe. The Ferengi volunteered to climb.

Odo clutched it in a steel grip, squatting so that Quark could use him as a stool to get partway up.

Reluctantly, Quark began to climb.

* * *

Commander Sisko sat at the operations table, alone in Ops, impatiently waiting for Kira's signal that the runabout was about to launch. His finger hovered over the photon torpedo fire-control button.

In a mere sixteen hours, the wink of a galactic eye, Benjamin Sisko had fallen from commander of a Starfleet deep-space station to one of a few survivors on a shattered hulk.

Although the invader ship had been for all intents dead for many hours, he intended to take no chances: just before the *Orinoco* launched, Sisko planned to fire a barrage of torpedoes programmed to detonate close to the ship, between it and launching pad three. He hoped to provide cover for the launch of the runabout, allowing it to get outside the communications shield long enough to broadcast a warning.

At maximum warp, the *Thule* or the *Clifford Simak* could be at the station in twenty-eight hours; either was probably powerful enough to contain the invasion to DS9, especially if Benjamin Sisko's plan worked.

He watched the flickering monitors, seeing two views of the invader ship simultaneously. Silent tears welled in his eyes; the same monitors also showed such terrible damage to the station that Sisko felt as if he himself had been ripped and gutted.

Blasts had peeled back the skin of DS9 like an onion. Entire sections were shredded into a twisted artifact, a mockery of his first command.

I run a tight cenotaph, he thought inanely; *floating tomb, deep-space crypt, city of the dead.* In their way, these invaders were as remorselessly destructive as the Borg, who, under the command of "Locutus of Borg"— otherwise known as Jean-Luc Picard of the *Enterprise*— had murdered Sisko's wife, Jennifer.

He activated the communicator; at least the invaders had not managed to block out that system. "Sisko to Major Kira; apprise me."

No answer. "Computer, emergency override, open the channel."

All the displays in Ops dimmed, nearly went out. Sisko held his breath; the computer had been heavily damaged in the fighting. It automatically rerouted its logic clips to avoid damage; but there was so much carnage that each command felt like an invitation to disaster.

At last, the displays returned, and a choppy voice with gaps and holes said what sounded like "ch-n-l t-bl-sh." *Channel established.*

Sisko heard a deep popping noise, so loud it drowned out all other sounds. "Kira, answer me—what's happening? Do you need assistance?"

Assistance? From whom?

Still no answer. Either Kira was not paying attention, or the loud popping—probably the chemical gun she had liberated—had deafened her, and she could not even hear his hail.

Just then a deep explosion echoed in Ops, followed by static from the audio feed.

One of the monitors flickered. Sisko turned his head, not quite quickly enough to see what had happened.

A moment later, on the other monitor, he saw what the flicker had been. The *Orinoco* had already launched.

"What the hell—!" Commander Sisko immediately fired the preset torpedo-barrage.

In a slow-motion nightmare, he saw the *Orinoco* streak directly away from the station, saw some sort of sensor array on the invader ship rotate, tracking the runabout.

"Come on," he pleaded with the lumbering torpedoes, "now! Do it now! Explode, *explode!*"

His anger out of control, he pounded again and again on the console as the dumb torpedoes, unequipped by nature to realize that the situation had changed, rigidly followed their program, *Sisko's* program.

For an instant, the "firehose" gun extended from the invader ship, fired another stream of extraordinarily fast projectiles toward the runabout; then the torpedoes exploded, one of them detonating close enough to the unshielded rail gun to obliterate it.

The projectiles themselves were not touched, however.

Traveling several kilometers per second, they were just fast enough to remain outside the blast radius.

They struck the aft of the runabout in a glancing blow, shearing through one of the impulse pods and damaging the other. The little craft spun dizzyingly out of control.

Horrified, Sisko watched helplessly as the pilot fought to steer the crippled runabout. Then, miraculously, he or she seemed to get the *Orinoco* under a vague sort of control . . . but instead of continuing on past the invader ship, out past the communications shield, the pilot turned the runabout around and headed back toward DS9.

"No!" shouted Sisko at the monitor. He stared in amazement as the pilot, apparently confused, headed directly toward the launching pad from which the craft had come, accelerating.

Two more grenades, more than Kira Nerys could bat aside. Out of the corner of her eye, she saw one roll just a few meters away, and she braced for impact.

She blinked, found herself across the service bay, upside down against a bulkhead. She saw another grenade explode silently, felt the buffet but did not hear anything.

I'm deaf, she thought dispassionately.

She looked down, past her right foot. The roof of the service bay had been blown apart, leaving a clear view up to the launching pad, thence through the terminal to space itself.

She glanced up at the miserable, worthless hatch in the service-bay floor. A bubblehead was just popping out of the hole, like a Bajoran *bicket* about to raid the garden. It joined the other invader already crouched in the service bay.

They did not see her; the last grenade had blown her so far away that they had lost track of where she was.

Major Kira rolled upright and tried to stand, but collapsed instantly. Looking down, she saw that her left leg ended just below her kneecap. Fortunately, the same concussion that had torn free her leg had nearly sealed the wound.

Guess I'll get to see how good dear Dr. Julian really is.

Kira stayed low, scanning the room. She located the invader rifle, ten meters away along the bulkhead.

She crawled slowly, wondering that she felt nothing in her leg. In fact, she could swear she still felt the leg itself, felt her boot scraping along the deck, felt each individual rivet as her nonexistent toes scraped across it. She even had traction.

She reached the rifle just as the searching bubbleheads spotted her. They knelt to fire, but Kira grabbed the gun, rolled across her back, and fired an offhand shot.

She raised her eyebrows in astonishment as it struck one of the kneeling invaders in the throat; it fell backward, clutching at its neck and writhing in pain.

Couldn't do that again in the next thousand years of my life, she concluded. An instant later, the invader feebly pawed at its chest, shimmered, and vanished.

The second invader aimed carefully, squeezed off a round that took Kira squarely in the stomach.

She felt a sledgehammer pound her in the gut. An unbearable pressure exploded up her throat. Kira's left side began to tremble uncontrollably.

She rolled to her left, felt terrific pain just below her rib cage. By laying the rifle across her breasts, she steadied it enough to aim another shot, taking number two in its face. The invader flash-burned.

She waited in profound silence, not even hearing her own ragged breath; no more bubbleheads boiled out of the hatch. Either they had fled—not likely—or Major Kira Nerys of Shakaar had killed them all.

After a moment, she dropped the rifle. She lifted a weak, nearly dead hand to her communicator.

She could not hear her own voice, not even echoing in her own bone cavities; she could not tell whether she spoke aloud or merely thought the words.

"Kira," she mouthed; "runabout—away. . . ." A wave of dizziness overcame her; she let her head sink back, looking up at the stars. She saw the invader ship, saw bright flashes: Sisko's torpedoes; she had warned him of the launch in time.

"Dying," she gasped, praying to the prophets that she was speaking aloud, and that her communicator had not been damaged. "Transport—Bashir—*now.*"

Kira saw a tiny pinpoint of light through the peeled-back ceiling, like a bright star moving erratically across the sky.

Sisko was trying to lock on to her. The invaders had set up a field that blocked the transporter; but O'Brien would find a way around it. Odo could hold the bad guys off until they could transport her to Dr. Bashir's sickbay.

Dax knelt beside Kira, stroked her hair. *Don't worry,* said the Trill; *just hang on. You feel that? It's the transporter beam locking on to you.* The bright spark grew brighter, larger.

Someone was holding her hand. Kira could not move her head, but she saw it was the old Kai Opaka, returned from the Gamma quadrant in time to rescue the little major girl. But was she still Kai? Kira could not remember.

Are you still there, Jadzia? asked Kira. *Where is the transporter? Hasn't O'Brien fixed it yet?*

He's in the classroom with Keiko right now, said her friend, *learning how to repair the damage.* But for some odd reason, Keiko kept repeating the Bajoran alphabet, over and over, while the operations chief took careful notes.

Guys, she said, *fun's fun, but you'd better hurry. I see the prophets coming with their bright lantern of truth, and I have to be up and out of here before they get here or they'll take me home with them.*

Abruptly, Kira realized that the light was really a Bajoran torchship, docking at the launching pad, come to take her home to Mother.

Mother patted her hand, but she was also Dax. *Curiouser and curiouser,* said the science officer, quoting her favorite Earth book, *Alice in Wonderland.*

Nerys smiled. The prophets had come, riding a hot runabout. They settled, settled. She saw them loom large in the launching terminal.

Larger.

Larger. . . .

Two days after his only home is destroyed by armor-plated aliens, Quark shimmies gracefully up a pole. . . .

Quark clutched the pole with a death grip, both arms wrapped around it so hard they locked in a cramp. His eyes crossed and uncrossed.

"Go ahead," insisted Odo; "what's the matter with you?"

"So high . . . so far to fall . . ."

Odo rolled his eyes. "Quark, you loogan, you're less than your own, diminutive height off the deck!"

It was true; the dizzying drop below the Ferengi seized him with vertigo. "Oh," he moaned pitifully, "oh . . . ooooooooooooh . . ."

"Just get *up* there and stop *whining.*" The constable shoved Quark's rump viciously, propelling the Ferengi up the slick pole at a terrifying velocity. Quark slid off the fore end of the pole, still climbing. He stopped, started to plummet back; reflexively, he shot his arms out, catching the edges of the hatch.

He dangled thus over the precipice, swinging back and forth, too frightened to move either up or down.

"That will do," observed Odo. "Now squirm up through the hatch and find something to let down to me. I doubt you can hold me on the pole."

Quark squealed, managed to heave one elbow over the lip; but there he stuck.

"Now, don't you make me come up there," warned the constable.

"You sound like my mother," accused Quark.

"You had a mother? What an odd thought . . . Quark as a juvenile delinquent."

By fierce squirming and leg kicking, the Ferengi squeezed both elbows through the hatch, humped up and over the edge onto the deck. He extracted his legs, then stared in horror at his beautiful, verdant green jacket, number sixteen.

It was absolutely ruined, the double-breasted front now a one-and-a-half-breasted set of dangling rags.

"My suit!" he wailed. "Look what you've done to my suit!"

"Is it ruined? Good, then you won't mind using it as a rope to haul me up."

"You'll pay for this! You and the rest of the blasted Federation! I'll *sue!*"

"Don't be ridiculous, Quark," sneered Odo; "where are you going to find a lawyer to take your case in trade for three free spins at Dabo?"

Annoyed, the Ferengi smoothed his coat with what dignity he could muster, turned decisively away from the hatch—and froze in astonishment. He finally got a good look at the white object he had seen from below.

The wreckage of a runabout hulked in the service bay, having smashed entirely through the launching-pad level above. The gash it left behind looked straight out to open space.

The impact of the runabout was so great, it had buckled the heavily reinforced deck of the service bay, causing the bizarre "inverted mountain" effect when seen from the room below.

"Astonishing," he whispered. The runabout had crashed right through one level and into the one below.

The name *Orinoco* was clearly visible on the side of the craft; it was definitely one of their own.

Without warning, Odo's head bobbed up through the hatch, almost between Quark's feet. The Ferengi yelped, leapt backward in panic, windmilling his arms. The constable's expression of irritation at having to waste energy shapechanging died immediately when he saw the runabout.

Without a word, Odo slithered up through the opening, retracting to normal size. He walked around the wreckage, surveying it. "It's quite a sight," he said at last.

"Ah. So that's your professional opinion as a peace officer and trained observer."

Puzzled, Odo went back around aft the runabout, looked curiously at the rear. Then he looked all around the room, finally shaking his head. "There's a huge piece missing. The left impulse engine is completely gone. Of course, that would explain the loss of stability that led to the crash—"

"Ack," said Quark from inside the runabout. He emerged a paler pink than Odo had ever seen him display before.

"Survivors?" asked the constable. Quark stared incredulously, slapped his hand to his mouth and ran to a corner of the room.

Odo followed curiously. "I believe it's an evolutionary behavior," he helpfully explained, "designed to purge the stomach in preparation for fight or flight. Though why you choose to do it now is beyond me, since neither action would be appropriate. And you appear to have ruined what's left of your suit."

"Thank you very much, Odo. I hope someday, when you're in your liquid state, a dog laps you up."

"I've never understood why orange Ferengi wear green suits anyway."

"I am not orange! I'm pink, you color-blind cretin."

Odo leaned through a gash in the side of the *Orinoco* to see what had upset Quark. Inside, he saw the remains of a number of children and a female Bajoran pilot, in the condition one would expect after such a violent accident, but nothing that would explain Quark's regurgitation.

He shrugged, standing up again. As he did, he noticed the Ferengi doubled over, arms wrapped around gut; but Quark was staring curiously at something beneath the runabout.

Odo bent low to examine it: it was a booted foot.

The two of them spent nearly an hour excavating, tearing pieces off the craft, and shifting it to finally unearth the impromptu tomb. The body was pummeled meat, almost unrecognizable. Then at once, Quark said, "It's her" in a small voice.

"Her who?"

"Major Kira."

Odo inspected the body. "How can you possibly tell who it is? The face is . . . well, you know."

"Never you mind! I, um, recognize her. Trust me—it's definitely Kira Nerys."

Odo gazed with sadness on the remains of the one person on DS9 who nearly understood him, the other outsider. He looked back at Quark; the Ferengi had removed his jacket, stood waiting with a grave look.

"May I?" he asked.

Odo nodded, and Quark gently laid his coat over the body, covering the face and upper torso. One of her legs was missing, probably destroyed when the runabout fell atop her.

Strange, thought Odo, *I feel I should say something.* What was it Bajorans said? "Go with the prophets, Kira Nerys. Find a place where there are no Cardassians, and the children can play outside, in the sun."

Odo stood, looked across the room toward the open service-bay door. Near the door, a strange bundle caught his eye.

He strolled closer, visually examined it. "Quark," he asked, "were you over here?"

"No. You know I just came up the hatch, and I'm still here."

"Come here and look at this."

Nervous at what he might find, Quark tiptoed carefully over to where Odo squatted. At the shapechanger's feet lay the body of a child, probably thrown from the runabout in the crash. It was laid out straight, covered with an emergency blanket from a medikit.

"So? It's another body. Probably from the *Orinoco,* like the rest of them in there."

"Yes, but Quark—I didn't cover it up." Odo looked sharply at the Ferengi. "Somebody else has been here . . . *recently.*"

"You mean . . . you mean someone did survive? Someone besides us?"

Odo nodded. "There is no other explanation. The Bekkir would never undertake such funerary concerns for another species; they apparently don't even have any consideration for their own dead, except for frying them to leave no trace."

The constable squatted down, pondered the covered body. "No, Quark, the only rational conclusion is that we are not alone on DS-Nine."

CHAPTER
12

QUARK AND ODO followed the trail of carefully arranged bodies around the habitat ring to tunnel one, then down the tunnel back to the core section.

Whoever the person was, he or she was thorough; the bodies were covered whenever possible, and if not, they were laid out respectfully, legs straight and arms crossed over their chests: a human custom.

After passing nearly thirty such macabre death scenes, they had ventured deep into the bowels of the core. The lights were out here too, and the only illumination was from the small flashes they carried.

The body-trail led inexorably upward, and eventually, Odo and Quark found themselves back on the upper Promenade level, but on the other side from Quark's Place.

"We never saw this side," said the Ferengi.

"I remember," said Odo; he sounded even wearier and more tired. He stumbled as he walked. "We followed Jake's trail to tunnel two, then across to the habitat ring."

Quark stopped the constable with a hand on his arm,

pointed at the bulkhead. "Looks like we picked it up again."

Odo shone his torch on the spot the Ferengi indicated. There on the wall, illuminated by the eerie blue light of the flash, was a sigil:

J.S. 47234.3 →

The arrow pointed right along the Promenade.

"Jake Sisko," said Quark.

"Yes, yes, I got it."

"Stardate yesterday. Isn't the infirmary in that direction?"

Odo nodded. "That makes sense; Jake would want to get to the infirmary to see if Bashir were alive, or if not, to gain access to the medical equipment."

They carefully worked their way among the crumbled ruins of the Promenade, dodging deadfalls and shattered storefronts. It was the aftermath of a war zone, with all the unexpected dangers of Facility Durut Kun after the Cardassians torpedoed it or Dresden after the firebombing.

At last, they climbed over the last mountain of rubble, finally reached the infirmary, offices of Dr. Julian Bashir, Lieutenant (j.g.).

The door was jammed shut. Odo tried to open it, but was too weak. The two of them braced and worked it halfway open, enough to slip inside.

"Well, I guess we can assume Jake didn't make it in here," said Odo; "he couldn't have thrown the door."

There had been no bomb blasts or major damage to Bashir's infirmary. It was a small suite of four rooms, including waiting room, outpatient rooms one and two, and surgery.

They shone their lights around the office. There was blood on the floor, far more than one would expect from the relatively light destruction. A man's body was slumped over the medical table. "Treating patients?"

asked Quark, pulling his feet out of a puddle of partially dried blood. His boots made a sucking noise.

"Undoubtedly."

"That—um, I mean *he*—he was a medic, I presume."

Odo followed Quark's eyes, recognized the burly man with the beard as a medical tech. "Yes, Chief Broome; just transferred from the *Neil Armstrong* starbase in Ordover."

"Another one with no bullet holes, no blood."

"Well, perhaps some of the blood on the floor is his."

"From where? There's not a wound on him. Odo, this is creepy . . . how much do you know about ghosts and gods?"

Odo made a disgusted noise, turned his back on the superstitious Ferengi. He shined his flash systematically around the infirmary. "Ah. Found him."

Dr. Bashir was quite dead, sitting on a stool, back propped up by his own desk. A circular bullet hole graced his forehead, between his eyes. The wound had bled copiously, caking Bashir's face.

Behind him, a personal medical log input screen flashed off and on: *Recording, await input. Recording, await input.*

The medical log had a separate power unit, not connected to the station systems. Struck by a notion, Odo leaned over the log. "Terminate input," he said.

Immediately the monitor changed: *Log recorded. Review? Y N*

"Yes," said Odo. The machine blanked for a moment while it found the beginning of the entry. Then it began to play back. Quark and Odo stared, grotesquely fascinated, as the tense, agitated image of Bashir appeared on the screen.

It was 2302; eleven hours after the terrifying attack began. Eleven hours of the most horrific duty of all for Julian Bashir: combat triage, deciding who would die, who would live another few, miserable hours.

For a minute and a half, Dr. Bashir tersely recorded his medical log entry, detailing the casualties from the Gamma invasion. It was the most upsetting thing he had ever done—not because he thought he would be slain himself, though he knew that was a distinct possibility, but because there was nothing he could do about the situation.

All his phenomenal medical skills could not bring people back to life or cure multiple projectile wounds . . . not when every hour brought twenty or thirty more patients.

Wounds such as these required considerably more time than two minutes per patient.

The med-lab door slid open. Bashir absently looked up from his log entry, wondering how many more patients were being launched his way.

Outside the door, he saw two soldiers attired in armor with black "bubble" helmets covering their heads. "May I help you?" he asked, confused.

A flat, mechanical Universal Translator voice answered: "This is the medical lab."

"Yes."

"You are the officer of medical matters."

"Yes."

The two invaders entered the lab. When Julian saw their rifles, he realized who and what they were. He stood, forgetting to terminate his log entry, and leaned backward as far as he could, until his shoulders were almost touching the monitor/videocam.

"What—what do you want?"

"Where is the other one like us."

Bashir was about to answer that he did not know, when he remembered the commander's orders: *If they interrogate you, keep them talking; find out why they're attacking the station.* "Would he have been brought here?" asked Julian instead.

The inquisitor paused, considered.

* * *

Odo waved his hand at the monitor. "Move your body, Doctor!" he griped at the display, which showed only Dr. Bashir's back; the good doctor had backed up so far, he covered the videocam that might have shown what was happening.

"I don't think he can hear you," muttered Quark, stealing a glance at Bashir's body against the wall. Shouting at the monitor was shouting two days into the past.

"The other was distressed and may have been injured. An injured captive would be taken here."

It took Bashir a moment to realize the last statement was actually a question. "Y-yes," he agreed; "if he were injured, he would be taken here. Would he have still been wearing the armor?"

Again, the inquisitor paused. "The armor may have been removed upon capture. The other wore a device."

"A device? What did it look like?"

Bashir stood a little straighter, straining his mind to think of something else reasonable to ask, something to establish a dialogue, maybe save his life. He shifted slightly away from his desk, rubbing his chin pensively.

The invader flexed its hand, retrieved a peculiar device from somewhere; Bashir could not tell where. It held up the device for the doctor to see.

Superficially, it resembled nothing so much as a huge, ornate belt buckle.

In the infirmary, Quark looked studiously away from the image on the monitor, feeling his ears burn red. The device the Bekkir held up was identical to the one that Quark had activated.

"Yes, yes," said Odo, more to himself than the Ferengi, "but what *is* it? Why is it so important?"

The Bekkir's voice was flat, tinny. It sounded more like a machine than did the computer itself, quiet and without inflection.

* * *

"What does the device do?" asked Bashir.

Instead of answering, the invader retreated intransigently to its earlier line: "Where is the other one like us."

Bashir thought furiously, more alive than at any time since his final exams for the medical board. *Diagnose the situation,* he told himself; *use your talents . . . treat it as a medical problem!*

Step one: find the symptoms.

"So you—you believe the 'other one' is here because you received a signal from him using that device, yes?" The worst part about patients was that they always believed they were better able to diagnose themselves than the doctor; you always had to focus in on the exact symptom set they manifested—*not* on their interpretation of the symptoms.

"Yes," said the invader.

"Was it a voice message, or an automatic signal?"

This time, the invader paused for a long time. Bashir realized it was not just formulating the answer; it was deciding whether the doctor had a "need to know" the information. It was weighing the risks and benefits.

But the station was nearly captured. Julian had followed Sisko's updates as best he could; the doctor could not state exactly where the invaders were or how many DS9 defenders had been killed, but he did know the battle was lost; Sisko still hoped to win the war by delaying them long enough that a starship could arrive.

The invaders knew that they had won the battle; thus the inquisitor did not worry about revealing information to Dr. Bashir.

"The signal is automatic when activated."

"Then you don't actually know that the other one was ever here." Bashir's lips were so dry, he could barely speak. He avoided licking them; it might be an offensive gesture to the invaders. "For example, what if somebody else got ahold of this device—somehow. Say the Cardassians stole it, and somebody else bought it from them and brought it here. It might be activated by someone, ah, not related to you at all."

"Yes," agreed the invader. It did not seem distressed at the possibility. "This will be known soon."

"Why? What do you mean, will be known? How can you tell who activated the device?"

No pause at all this time; Bashir felt a hole opening in the pit of his stomach . . . perhaps the invader felt no concern about telling him because it had no intention of allowing the doctor to live—not after obtaining whatever information it needed.

"We will stay until the other one reappears."

"Reappears? From where?"

Quark looked at Odo. The constable appeared totally puzzled. "Freeze log playback," said Quark. He puzzled to himself, "What did the Bekkir mean, when the other one reappears?"

Quark paced up and down the small room, tugging at his ear. *Something—where is it?—deeper . . . yes!*

"Odo," he said, "something's been gnawing my ears for hours now, and I just figured out what it is. When I—uh, that is, when the device activated, what happened?"

"From our perspective? There was a timeless interval of disorientation, followed by a discontinuity."

"When we returned to normal, three days had elapsed. What did you say happened to us?"

"Static-time field. We were frozen for three days, with no passage of internal time."

"But think about it, Odo. What would that look like from the outside?"

The constable stood, pulled at his chin, stretching it out of shape. "I hadn't thought about that. I would presume it would look like a totally black globe—no photons escaping."

"Or maybe a perfect mirror, if the surrounding photon waves reflected from the impenetrable time barrier.

Either way, it would be rather noticeable, wouldn't you say?"

"One would think so."

"Of course it would! Even if nobody noticed *your* absence, I'm sure the disappearance of the most prominent Ferengi citizen of Deep Space Nine would cause a frantic search . . . beginning in Quark's Place. What would you think if somebody went missing, and in his office, you found a huge, impenetrable, mirrored globe?"

"I would think there might be some connection," conceded Odo.

"Hah! You'd test it with every known sensor you had. O'Brien would figure out a way to weigh it, and Lieutenant Dax would guess that it was a static-time field. Even if nobody could turn it off, they would set up an array of equipment around it. My office would have looked like Ops! Did you see any equipment in there?"

"Well . . ."

"And what about the Bekkir? Surely *they* know how to detect the field and turn it off, even if we couldn't. Why didn't we pop back into the real world surrounded by a platoon of the spiny creeps?"

"Hm."

"'Hm' is an understatement. It makes no logical sense at all. So we *could not possibly* have been in a 'time-stasis field.'"

Odo thought the logical train through from beginning to end, twice, sure that there must be a flaw. Quark the logician? It was absurd. But he could find no hole.

"But that means," said Odo, "that instead of being frozen in time for three days, we simply *jumped forward* three days. Some sort of a quantum—"

"Exactly. And that must be what the Bekkir meant . . . he meant they would wait until we reappeared, three days after activating the distress signal."

Odo smiled grimly. "Which leaves one puzzling little mystery: Why aren't they here now?"

Odo took over, staring at the frozen image of the Bekkir, still questioning Dr. Bashir. Even the shapeshifter felt a strange dread, looking from Bashir trying to save himself by clever repartee to Bashir lying dead.

"You activate the device, sending a distress signal to the Bekkir while simultaneously catapulting us three days into the future.

"The Bekkir receive the signal, presume it is one of their own people taken captive. They follow the signal through the wormhole to DS9.

"They invade the station, presuming he will appear again in three days. Wait, something's wrong here. . . . They systematically search the station, questioning and killing everyone here, asking where the other Bekkir is . . . that's it! Quark, don't you see what's wrong with this construction?"

The Ferengi nodded. It was obvious, even to him. "If they know we're not going to reappear for three days, then why are they asking where the other one is, rather than where he *was* when he sent the distress signal?"

"Unless," mused Odo, "the Bekkir have some way of reversing the time-projection effect . . . of . . ."

They stared at each other with a wild surmise, tried to speak simultaneously.

"Back! We can go—"

"There *must* be some way of returning to—"

They fell silent, turned back breathlessly to the monitor. "Resume playback," said Odo.

"If an animal returns instead of the other one like us, it will be destroyed and the device recovered. You saw the device."

"Yes," said Bashir slowly. He tried to predict the effect of various scenarios on the invader, but xenopsychology was not his specialty. *I think I know damned well who activated that device,* he realized.

"The device was in possession of one like us."

Bashir hesitated, aware that his next answer could be his last. *Do they want to hear yes or no?*

If he said no, and the Bekkir believed him, then there

was no reason to continue killing anyone. They could simply wait until Quark "reappeared," whatever that meant, take the device, and leave.

On the other hand, given their obvious xenophobia— "If an *animal* returns instead of the other one like us," the invader had said—they might well decide to kill the rest of them anyway, just to avoid problems, possible retaliation.

On the third hand, if he said no, and they did not believe him, they would expect an invader to reappear. In that case, they needed to pacify the station to protect the "other one" before it reappeared.

The invader also might kill Bashir himself, who would have proven himself an unreliable source.

If he said yes, the same possibilities obtained, depending whether they believed him or not. On the fourth hand, though, "pacifying" the station might not necessarily mean killing everyone. If they were convinced that DS9 had somehow captured one of the invaders, they might be concerned enough about *how* they had done it to be willing to accept a compromise—a truce.

The few people still left alive might be spared.

Only a second or two had passed while the possibilities raced through Bashir's mind. He decided on his answer. "Yes. The device was in the possession of one like you when I saw it."

The invader digested this piece of data, obviously trying to decide whether Bashir told the truth or lied through his teeth.

"No other animal says it saw another one like us."

"They didn't. We kept him hidden."

"The other one is here now."

"No. He vanished." His eyes flicked to the chronometer display in the corner of the medical log monitor, subtracted back to when Quark and Odo first brought the device to be scanned, which was 1200 the previous day. "About thirty-nine hours ago."

"The other one was here when it vanished."

"No. He was hidden. In a secret place."

"You know where this secret place is."

"Yes."

"Others know where the other one was when it vanished."

Yes? Or no? When someone points a weapon at you and
asks you a question, you tell him whatever you think he
expects to hear.

"Um, yes. Others know."

"The Commander Siss-Ko of this place knows."

"Yes."

The instant the word escaped his cracked lips, Bashir
knew it was a terrible mistake. Others allegedly knew
where the "other one" had been when it vanished.

Thus, Bashir became expendable.

"But I'm the only—" he began as the inquisitor raised
his hand weapon.

Odo and Quark watched the two-day-old execution,
spellbound. The Ferengi desperately wished he could
turn his head away, not see the gun raised to Bashir's
forehead, hear the explosion, see the doctor collapse
backward, a small geyser erupting from his skull.

No love was wasted between Quark and Julian Bashir;
it was Bashir who threatened to tell Dax and Kira about
Quark's entirely innocent, playful holosex program using
their images. It was Bashir who had threatened to shut
down Quark's Place for "health-code violations" on
more than one occasion—doubtless in cahoots with
Odo.

Still, the Ferengi had no desire to see the young pup die
so brutally, shot down as casually as a farmer might kill a
Ferengi digfish found among the crops.

For some reason, however, he could neither look away
nor even shut his eyes; some part of him he never knew
existed forced him to watch, record the final seconds of
the doctor's life.

When it was over, the Bekkir lowered its firearm and
departed the room without a backward glance, chittering
to its comrade.

Quark continued to stare at the monitor. The medical log entry continued, as he knew it would for the next two days, up until the point where Quark and Odo entered the infirmary and turned it off.

"Terminate playback," said a subdued Quark.

"Somebody should remember him," Odo said.

"Dr. Bashir?" Quark asked in surprise. "I don't recall you two getting along."

Odo looked at the Ferengi with a deadly glare, almost causing Quark to back up a step. "It doesn't matter," said the constable; "*nobody* should die like that, murdered as you or I might squash an insect. I want to remember him *and* I want a copy of that log for evidence."

Quark stared. "You want *evidence?* How about the entire, butchered station—isn't that enough?"

"Quark, even if I were the *only* survivor of the raid, I would *still* be chief of Security; my job is to collect all important evidence. You'll thank me for it later, since it makes it slightly harder for Starfleet or Bajor to accuse you as the natural suspect."

Odo pulled a data clip from a pile on the desk and snapped it into place. It took Bashir's medical computer several seconds to download the log to the data clip, since it was much slower than the station computer would have been, had it not been destroyed. Then Odo removed the clip and pocketed it.

All at once, the Ferengi's ears curled back. At first, he did not understand the reaction, thought it was rational fear when confronted by invaders who would not even deal.

Then he understood . . . *something was behind him.*

Quark spun abruptly, intending to dive to the floor and let whatever watched him shoot Odo instead of himself.

Instead, he found himself crouched, useless phaser in his hand, pointed at—

Jake Sisko stood in the med-lab doorway, staring at them as if they were ghosts. Molly O'Brien clutched his hand, silent and white as death.

CHAPTER
13

"ARE YOU . . ." Jake began. He started over, apparently confused about who they were. "You don't want to know where the other one is?"

"Jake," said Odo, "don't you recognize me? Are you injured?"

Jake Sisko stared from Odo to Quark, back again. "Odo?" he asked.

The constable dropped to his haunches, made himself slightly smaller, despite his aching tiredness. He had read somewhere that human children can be frightened by large adults. "Jake, it's very clever of you to survive this long. I'm proud of you."

"No," said the boy, shaking his head. Molly grabbed his legs, hid behind them, and Jake put his hand protectively on her head . . . just as a father would.

"Yes. You did well." Odo had also read that children who survived disasters that killed their parents often felt terrible guilt for surviving, even when they had nothing to do with the calamity. "I knew your father very well, and he would be—"

Odo fell silent; Jake's eyes had glazed over. He turned,

wandered down the corridor, leading Molly. He seemed to have completely forgotten that Odo and Quark existed.

Odo began to follow, but a surprisingly strong grip pulled him back. Quark said quietly into Odo's ear, "I don't think you should mention Commander Sisko just now to the boy."

"Why? Surely he must realize—"

"Humans are not like Ferengi. They sometimes have a hard time accepting reality. N-Nog told me that Jake sometimes pretended his mother was still alive, and he had talked to her earlier that day."

Quark looked truly stricken, and Odo was about to ask what the problem was when he suddenly realized: if Nog still lived, he would have found Jake by now. Quark had finally accepted that his nephew was dead. It was a crushing blow to the Ferengi.

True to his description, the Ferengi held up well. His face was as pale as a pie crust, not pink at all. Odo guessed this meant Quark's blood was pooling in his abdominal area . . . he was in mild shock. But he said nothing, followed quickly after the constable as they both hurried after Jake and Molly.

Odo caught up with the boy halfway down the corridor. Jake stared at him as if seeing him for the first time.

Perhaps he is, thought Odo. *Maybe he's erased the last few moments from memory, to avoid thinking about his father.* It was a bad sign: how could Odo get the boy to tell them what had happened, where the Bekkir were now, if he could not bring himself to remember?

"Odo!" said Jake. "And Quark. How did you two survive? And where were you? People were looking all over the place for you. Some people even thought—no, never mind."

"What?" asked Odo. "Some people what?"

"Where were you?"

Odo quickly sketched the events of the last subjective day to Jake; but he altered the story somewhat, telling the boy that the device activated itself without help from anyone. Quark said nothing; but on his face, Odo saw an expression that was as close as a Ferengi ever got to gratitude.

It annoyed the constable. He had altered the story for a reason, not to save face for Quark. He needed the boy's absolute trust, which would be impossible if Jake thought either Odo or Quark was responsible for the attack on the station and Sisko's death.

"A distress signal?"

"Apparently so. When they received it, the Bekkir decided that we were holding one of them hostage and demanded his release, killing all who could not answer.

"But that brings up an interesting question, Jake. Perhaps you can help me with this."

"What?"

"Surely the Bekkir would know how far into the future the device projects itself. Why didn't they simply wait two more days until we reappeared? Where did they go, and why?"

Quark was the first to see Jake's eyes begin to drift again. Quickly, before the boy could fade away, he asked his own question. "Jake, you never told us how you managed to save Molly. We followed your trail from Keiko's schoolroom to where you tried to get to Ops, then to tunnel number two. But we lost you. Was Nog—" Quark swallowed. "Was Nog with you then? What happened to him?"

Jake blinked, returned to reality. "Oh. He . . . well, let me start back at the school, two days ago, about twelve-thirty. . . ."

Jake fumbled frantically at the access hatch. Bolted shut! The bogeymen were interrogating Mrs. O'Brien.

They were going to kill her.

He started to tug on the hatch, hoping to rip it right off the wall, when a hand pulled him back.

Nog snarled wickedly, handed Jake a spanner he had probably filched from Mrs. O'Brien's husband.

With the wrench, Jake quickly unbolted the grille,

pulled it silently off the hatch. Nog shimmied through first; Jake was just about to follow when he remembered that Mrs. O'Brien had brought her little girl, Molly, to class that day for show-and-tell.

Molly! Jake spun around on his knees, ducked down further, and scanned the floor for a pair of tiny feet. He stretched his arm out, grateful that he had inherited a long, lanky build from his dad, and pinched the little girl to get her to look down.

The toddler squatted, stared at Jake with wide, solemn eyes. He put his finger to his lips, then gestured her forward.

Molly hesitated, looked back at Mommy; but Mommy was talking with the bad man, and Molly was scared. She remembered Jake. She had seen him before. He was not a stranger.

Mommy always said stay away from strangers, but Jake was a friend. His daddy was Mommy's boss.

Mommy was frightened—Molly could tell—and mommies *never* got frightened. That scared Molly most of all. She got down to her hands and knees and crawled under the desk, went where Jake pointed. She made no sound; she knew something was awfully wrong, and she had to be a perfect little angel.

Jake made her crawl into a dark hole, and she was scared again. But he crawled in right behind her.

Then Molly heard the gunshots. She screamed, a high-pitched, piercing yowl, and scrabbled down the burrow as fast as her skinny little legs could take her.

Jake looked back over his shoulder as Molly disappeared down the rabbit hole, saw the soldier grab Mrs. O'Brien. Jake stopped, almost turned around to jump the guy; but then he thought about Dad, how he always said you should think with your human brain, not your reptile brain. Dad always felt like an idiot when he let his temper take control.

Abruptly, Jake realized the invader could see him. They stared at each other for a beat. The soldier raised his weapon.

Mrs. O'Brien bent low and tackled the invader, lifting it clean off its feet. Jake was impressed; Mrs. O'Brien was smaller than Jake was.

Then he understood. She was sacrificing herself to save Jake and Nog—and Molly.

At once, he knew where his duty lay. He spun around, dived into the hatch after the little girl. Molly waited uncertainly in the tunnel, looking back over her shoulder. She looked like she wanted to go back to her mother.

Just then, they heard the gunshots, and Molly beetled off so quickly that Jake was soon left in her dust. Of course, she and Nog had an unfair advantage: they both were short, with little legs that did not bump and bang the tunnel sides every time they crawled a step.

Suddenly, an explosion ripped the schoolroom behind them. Jake was knocked forward by the shock wave, collapsing on top of Molly.

"Get off! Get off!" she screamed, worming out from underneath him. His back ached, felt like he had been kicked by a mule . . . an unpleasant experience he had actually had once on a farm.

They crawled and crawled, then stopped and rested. Nobody wanted to talk; Jake kept glancing back over his shoulder, expecting to hear the scrabbling of a gray-booted, black-helmeted murderer close at their heels.

They resumed their flight, crawling for another hour before Nog stopped suddenly, causing Molly to rear-end him. Jake, looking back over his shoulder, ploughed into the pair, bowling both over.

Molly was the first to disentangle herself. "You clumsy *doji!*"

"Dodger?" he asked, trying to figure out what she had called him. He and Nog unscrambled themselves. "What did you stop for?" he asked his Ferengi friend.

"Intersection," said Nog, rolling his eyes. "This is the way we should go." He pointed at a ladder leading down.

Jake shook his head. "No, we need to go *up*. Up to Ops."

Nog was adamant. "We should get out of the core. We

can get down to level fifteen here and get out to the habitat ring."

"Ops! Dad'll know what to do."

Nog sat, rested his hands on his knees, watching down the tunnel they had just crawled. "If your father can do anything, he's doing it already. The last thing he needs is you hanging around Ops, distracting him."

"But what good is going to the habitat ring? Don't you think they'll come there, too?"

"Yes, but *later!* It'll take them hours to pacify the entire core section, and that's hours in which we might beat them. Let's get out to the habitat ring, find a nice, deep hole, and wait this thing out."

Now Jake folded his arms. He could out-stubborn anyone, even a Ferengi. "And how do you know they're not already in the habitat ring?"

Nog scowled, chewing a fingernail with his sharp, pointy teeth. "Well . . ."

"In any case, I think we should tell Mr. O'Brien what happened to his wife."

"*You* can tell him that, if you want. Me, I would like to keep on living."

"Look, I think he'd want to know, Nog. And . . . and we can ask my dad what to do. If he says we should go out to the habitat ring, well, we can get there a hell of a lot faster using the transporter, right?"

Nog curled his lip. He hated losing an argument. He waved Jake forward. "Your wish is our command, O great, exalted leader."

"Well, you don't have to get sarcastic about it," muttered Jake, taking point.

He led them the other way, to a different ladder leading up. They climbed two levels, until they found another passage leading inward, toward the inner core. Jake remembered seeing a tube the last time he was in Ops; it stretched straight through the inner core, many levels down. Far below, he saw that it ended at a closed hatch.

If I can just figure out what that hatch looks like from this side, we're home free.

Every so often, they would stop, sit quietly, and listen. They still heard the tumult of battle, faint and far off. The noise carried through the metal bulkheads themselves, sounding weird and tinny, like a holovision turned way down.

Molly had not said a word since she called Jake a dodger. She looked pale, as if she had begun to realize that her mother was probably dead. When they stopped to listen, Jake held her hand; it was what his father would have done, were he present.

The lights flickered, dimmed. Then they came up again. Jake continued to crawl, feeling more urgently than ever that his father needed him, though he could not say why. Then all at once, the lights failed completely.

Jake paused for a moment, Molly and Nog piling up behind him. Then he continued forward, feeling his way along the floor cautiously.

He nearly cracked his head open on a huge, metal post sticking down from the ceiling. His skull made a deep *bong*, reverberated through his teeth. Jake sat back, rubbing his tender forehead with one hand and exploring the obstruction with the other.

It was a cylinder, about a meter in diameter. On the bottom, about waist-height off the tunnel floor, was a small wheel, like a manual hatch screw.

The hatch!

Clearing his throat, Jake said aloud, "Computer . . . open the hatch."

A soft voice answered: "Authorization, please."

"Jake Sisko—this is an emergency! We have to get to Ops."

"You are not authorized to access this ladderway," said the computer.

"Um, emergency override."

"You are not authorized to issue an emergency override."

"Patch me through to Dad, now!"

"Specify person to be contacted."

Jake slammed his fist into the cylinder, was rewarded

with an aching knuckle. He calmed himself, remembering his father. "Patch me through to Commander Benjamin Sisko, you idiot box."

"Communications are secure. Authorization, please."

"Computer, this is an *absolute emergency!*"

"Communications are secure. Authorization, please."

"Emergency communications override!"

The computer answered, and a disgusted Jake spoke the words along with it. "You are not authorized to issue an emergency override."

He rolled his own eyes, invisible in the dark. "All right, Nog. You win. We can't get in."

"I didn't think you would."

"Why didn't you *say* anything then?"

"Hah. Would you have believed me, a mere Ferengi?"

"So now where do we go? Which way to the habitat ring?"

Nog chuckled nastily. "After me, O great, exalted follower." He pushed past, led them farther down the pitch-dark tunnel.

Nog lay flat and still in the shaft, watching the corridor outside the ventilation grille with sharp Ferengi eyes. Jake desperately wanted to ask his friend what he saw, what was out there; but his brief, whispered query elicited only a furious glare and a silent finger to lips.

A moment later, a squad of invaders quick-timed down the corridor; Jake caught a brief glimpse of their shiny black armor, gray gloves and boots, mirror-black helmets over Nog's shoulder as they passed.

He put his arm around Molly, making sure she stayed quiet.

One invader looked directly into the ventilation shaft. The kids froze, not daring even to breathe. But if it saw anything, it did not register; the invader squad jogged on by, none raising the alarm.

After a few minutes of silence, during which Jake fidgeted like a restless puppy while the Ferengi remained as still as a sleeping crocodile, Nog cautiously gestured them forward.

"How do we get the grate off?" he asked Jake.

"Is it clear?"

Nog nodded, his huge, sensitive ears flexing slightly as he listened to sounds no human could hear. "Nobody around. Got any ideas?"

Jake squirmed around, then suddenly lashed out with both feet, catching the grate square. It popped off its moorings with a dreadful clang, tumbled to the ground, spinning and ringing like a huge Ferengi gold coin.

Nog gasped. Jake leaped out into the corridor. His friend followed; then Jake reached in and helped Molly O'Brien out.

"Humans!" said Nog, making it sound like a curse. "We coming back here?"

"Of course not."

Jake picked up the grate, tossed it back into the shaft. "Let's get the hell out of here."

"Why?" asked the Ferengi. "If the invaders are all deaf, dumb, and blind, we'll be fine right here."

Jake rolled his eyes, and Nog led them stealthily down the corridor. Back in the ventilation shaft, Nog had led them to a narrow "chimney" dropping down four levels to level fifteen, where the connecting tunnels led from the core section to the habitat ring. He showed Jake how to press his back against one wall, feet against the opposite, and squirm slowly down the chimney. Nog had gone first, followed by Jake, with Molly riding in Jake's lap.

Now Nog led them around the corridor toward tunnel two, stopping every few steps to listen.

Suddenly, Nog hesitated, staring at something on the deck. It took Jake a few moments to realize what he looked at: it was a dead body.

"Uncle Jake," said Molly, "is that man taking a nap?"

"Shh," said Jake, "don't wake him. Let's go." Taking her firmly by the hand, he led the way toward the tunnel. Nog followed, still staring back at the body.

Jake refused to look back, tried to push thoughts of his mother out of his head. The body lay in a pool of blood, just like—

Another one. Wincing, Jake kept his eyes focused on the middle distance, led Molly around the corpse using his peripheral vision.

Soon the bodies were so thick, he *had* to look down to avoid stepping on one or tripping. He felt like an old-fashioned football player, training by hopping from tire to tire.

The level-fifteen lighting was sporadic, flickering between dim and nonexistent. In the brief, lightning flashes of illumination, Jake saw that Molly's face was pale. Young as she was, no more than two or three, she obviously figured out that all these people were not "sleeping."

Jake had seen dead bodies before, but never anything like this. They clogged the corridor, nearly all facing back in the direction the kids had come from.

Jake stopped, stepped close to Nog to whisper. "I don't like this. It looks like they died defending the corridor from invaders going the same way *we're* going. What if we run into them?"

The Ferengi nodded. "I know. I can hear them up ahead, about fifty meters. But the tunnel entrance is just up a little farther."

Jake followed, nearly lost. He had never taken the connecting tunnel on foot, only in a turbolift. And of course, he simply got on the turbolift somewhere else and announced, "Habitat ring, section nine"; he never actually watched where it went.

Nog suddenly stopped next to a sealed hatch, as big as the airlocks leading out to the docking pylons, though not as massive.

The hatch was thrown closed, and there were few dead bodies near it. Apparently, the defenders had been retreating so quickly at that point that they did not even bother trying to open the connecting tunnel.

Ahead, even Jake heard gunfire and faint screams. Nog carefully examined the airlock door.

"Good," he said, "still sealed. The invaders haven't figured out how to get there yet."

"You know," said Jake, "I don't think they know much about the station at all . . . you'd think they would have beamed straight to Ops, killed everyone, and taken over."

Nog shrugged. "They don't think much of us. Maybe they don't consider us dangerous enough to develop a strategy against us."

The hatch was locked, of course. Like the Ops access, it refused to open for the boys, apparently not being impressed that Jake was the son of the station commander.

"Don't worry," said Nog. He grinned crookedly, which of course is the only way a Ferengi *can* grin, and produced a cylinder made of bright green, translucent plastic. "I filched this from Uncle Quark."

"What is it?"

"It's some sort of security override. Supposed to open doors."

Jake stared angrily. "Then why didn't you tell me about it when we were trying to get up to Ops?"

"You—"

"And if you say 'You didn't ask,' I'll pop you one in your ears!"

Nog jumped backward. "I, uh, that is, it's just a level-one security override. Actually, I stole it from Father, and Uncle Quark doesn't let him keep any of the others. To get into Ops, you'd need a level-four override."

"How does it work?"

Nog smirked. "Simple, for a Ferengi. You just slide it in here." He slid the cylinder into a slot on the door. The slot was much bigger than the cylinder, obviously made for something else entirely, and Nog did not seem sure how to arrange the green tube in the hole. "Then you—I guess you twist it, like *this.*"

He spun the tube. It stopped. Nothing happened.

He glowered in confusion, tugging his ear in a mannerism that Jake had seen Quark use many times.

Not expecting any results, Jake whimsically said, "Hatch open."

With a hiss, the door rolled back out of the way.

"Right, like that," said Nog. He extracted his cylinder, and they slipped through as the door rolled shut. Jake tested it; it had locked itself again.

"Safe at last," he breathed, wiping sweat from his forehead. The long, cool connecting tunnel to the habitat ring lay before them. There were no more bodies; the invaders were locked safely outside.

In great agitation, Quark grabbed Jake's arm, not gently. "Nog—what happened to Nog?"

Jake pulled back, angry and frightened at the same time. "It's hard to remember," he said tensely. That was obviously false; whatever had happened to the Ferengi boy had happened less than two days before.

Before a problem could develop, Constable Odo pulled Quark's hand free, separated the two. Neither was a match for Odo in size or mass, so both grew silent.

"Sorry," said the Ferengi; "I need to know what happened to my nephew, and you were taking forever."

"Well, you'll just have to wait," retorted Jake. "Molly needs tending, and she's more important right now."

She stood in the middle of the floor, sucking her thumb and shaking all over. "It's okay, Molly," said Jake in a soothing voice. "Uncle Quark's just upset, like we all are. Let me check your pants."

Molly obediently came over to Jake, stood quietly while he snuck a quick peek in her diapers. "You've been doing very good, Molly," he said; "I'm impressed. You keep it up, and we'll have you back in your regular pants tomorrow."

She took his hand, gripped one of Jake's fingers in each hand with a death grip.

"She was kind of scared right after—after *it* happened," he confided to Quark and Odo. "She sort of forgot her toilet training for a day or so. I found some diapers in Mrs. O'Brien's quarters. But she's done really good all day today; I think she's ready to go back to pants."

"This is absolutely fascinating," sneered Quark. But he said it quietly enough that Jake could pretend he did not hear.

"Up," demanded Molly. Jake picked her up, held her in his arms. She stared solemnly at Quark. *"Gaijin,"* she declared, nodding.

"No," said Jake, "that's Uncle Quark. He's Nog's uncle, too."

"Gaijin. He's an old gnome, like Rumplestiltskin."

"Oh, don't remind me," said Odo, agitated at the memory of the day when wishes were granted left and right.

Jake smiled. "Don't feel bad, Mr. Quark. She called me a dodger. I still don't know what she meant."

"Doji," corrected Molly.

"What's *doji* mean, honey?"

She solemnly pressed his nose. "You fell on top of me, Uncle Jake. You're a clumsy boy, a *doji."* The little girl hugged Jake happily.

"Is that what your mommy says?"

At the mention of Keiko O'Brien, Molly sniffed, wrapped her arms around Jake's neck, and hung on.

"We've got to find her some food, Odo. She hasn't eaten since last night. The replicators don't work; all they make are weird, metal sculptures."

"Sculptures?" demanded Odo.

At the mention of food, Quark suddenly realized how ravenous he himself was. Subjectively, it had been more than twenty-four hours since his own breakfast, four days ago.

But Odo was not listening. He stood absolutely still, forgetting even to simulate breathing. Quark stared;

something seemed wrong. Then he realized: Odo was concentrating so hard, he had allowed himself to begin sagging, especially the head and shoulders.

"Odo, pull yourself together," snapped the starving Ferengi. "It's disgusting."

"Eh? Oh, yes. I was just thinking. Jake," asked the constable, "do you remember what time it was when you heard Commander Sisko's evacuation order?"

"Hm . . . I was still in school, but we were almost done for the morning. I'd say it was about twelve-thirty."

"Quark and I reappeared in the office about ten-thirty this morning. How long has it been since we appeared, Quark?"

"The human is right. Why don't we find something to eat first? I always think better when my stomach is full."

"That's because your head is empty. I wouldn't have asked you if it weren't important, Quark! How long has it been?"

"Cops," snarled the Ferengi. He fished out an ornate pocket watch, scrutinized it. "It's zero-nine hundred now, and I think my watch read twelve-thirty when I looked at it right after we reappeared. Twenty-four and a half hours."

Odo thought deeply. "We moved about three days into the future; that would be eighty-four hours. But your watch was two hours faster than the chronometer in your office, so we actually moved eighty-two hours ahead, give or take a few minutes."

"So?"

"So the invaders attacked the station shortly before twelve-thirty the day after we vanished—twenty-eight hours, exactly one day after we disappeared. If we assume the Bekkir device *can* move us back in time, but only in eighty-two-hour chunks, then if we went back right now, we'd arrive back at, um—" He closed his eyes for a moment, subtracting. "—at about nine-thirty the morning of the attack."

Quark lowered his brows, trying to figure what Odo

was getting at. Suddenly he realized. "Odo—the attack wouldn't have begun yet!"

"That's right . . . if it happened, say, half an hour before Commander Sisko gave the order to evacuate the core section, then we would still have three hours to stop the attack."

"That means," said Quark, "we have three hours to figure out how to make this blasted thing go into reverse. Odo, if we can do that—we can erase this whole last three days! The attack never comes, nobody is killed!"

"*If,*" cautioned Odo, ticking off the problems on his fingers, "*if* we can figure out how to reverse the Bekkir device; *if* we can do it in the next three hours; and *if* we can talk the Bekkir out of attacking when we *do* get back."

Quark and Odo watched each other silently, each waiting for the other to make a suggestion.

CHAPTER
14

"WELL, UNLESS YOU'VE GOT some brilliant idea," said Odo, "this is just a philosophical discussion. Even if the Bekkir had a way to go back, which is itself pure speculation, *we* don't know how to do it."

Quark had the signaling device out and was studying it intently. "I think I may have an idea," he said quietly.

"What?" Odo snatched it away, staring at it himself. "How did you get this out of my pocket?"

"Don't bother staring," said Quark; "it takes the cleverness of a Ferengi to deduce what—"

"There," said the constable, pointing at a shallow slot zigzagging across one face. "Looks like there's a piece missing from there. I'll bet if we found that missing piece, we could jump back. So what was your idea, Quark?"

"Never mind," said the Ferengi, miffed.

"So where might it have come from? What else was in the Cardassian strongbox, Quark?"

He shook his head. "Everything else was normal, Cardassian artifacts. Nothing remotely shaped like that."

"Are you going to tell me you can distinctly remember every, single thing in that box, after just the briefest glimpse?"

"Of course."

"How?"

"I bought it. I can tell you every single thing I own, describe it, and put a value on it without a second thought. Any Ferengi can."

"Hm. Why am I not surprised?"

"One Cardassian icicle gem, value a hundred and twelve mills; one discharged disruptor, third dynasty, value two dimes; one—"

"All right, all right! So does the missing piece even exist?"

Quark strode back and forth in the infirmary, careful not to look toward the corner, where Bashir's desk sat . . . with Dr. Bashir laid out under a sheet.

"So if we assume it sends you back in time, what would they use it for?"

Odo was not listening. For an instant, he almost lost his form. He normally had to revert to his liquid state every sixteen hours. With tremendous willpower, he could hold out somewhat longer.

The longest he had ever held out was twenty-eight hours . . . and it had already been more than twenty-five.

At the end of his twenty-eight-hour record, Odo had broken down into his liquid state in the cupped dress of Ambassador Lwaxana Troi. Even that was humiliating enough. But *Quark?* That squeezing, wrenching, grasping, clutching, covetous, old Ferengi?

That Quark should see him like that was an abominable thought . . . but it might come to pass if they could not get back in the next three hours.

Of course, if it took longer than three hours, the attack would have already started; and many, many people would already be dead.

Exerting his will to the utmost, Odo regained control over his rebelling molecular structure. He was still Constable Odo—for a time.

"I'm sorry," he said weakly; "what was the question again?"

Quark repeated it, and Odo considered the problem. "It's clear why they want to jump *forward;* if a Bekkir finds itself in an untenable position, about to be killed— or worse, captured—it activates the field and vanishes. Appearing three days later probably means the danger has passed."

"So why go back again? You'd just be jumping right back into danger."

"Not necessarily. If the Bekkir activates the device, hides for a day, then jumps back, it's the equivalent of jumping only one day into the future. If you activate it and only wait for three hours before jumping back, it's the same as jumping three hours into the future. You see the possibilities?"

"Yes . . ." said the Ferengi. "Yes, I do. Suppose you're on your way to an auction and an overzealous constable waylays you. If you jumped three days ahead and stayed, you'd miss the auction. But if you jumped ahead, stayed a hour, then jumped right back, the constable would think you had vanished and would go away, leaving you free to attend the auction."

"A rather crude attempt at wit, Quark, but you have the general idea. The point here is that you would probably be in a terrible hurry when you jumped forward . . . but not when you jumped back. You'd be jumping from a safe place, so you could take your time.

"In fact," continued the constable, "you wouldn't *want* it to be easy to jump back, just in case your device fell into criminal hands. Eh, Quark?"

"Hah, hah, hah. A real laugh nova."

"Jumping forward poses no problems; as far as the universe is concerned, it's the equivalent of simply hiding in a really clever hiding place for eighty-two hours.

"But jumping back, Quark, now that the Bekkir would want to control. In fact, I would bet you—"

"That the missing piece is on the Bekkir, not on the

device!" finished Quark. "It's probably attached to the Bekkir armor itself, so even if you steal the device, like the Cardassians did, you wouldn't be able to use the time-reverse function unless you also got a Bekkir!"

"I *was* just about to say that, Quark. So where would we find a dead Bekkir with a functional time-reverse unit?"

The pair immediately looked at each other, remembering at the same instant. "The habitat ring!" said Quark.

"Near tunnel three, airlock thirty-nine," clarified Odo.

"A dead Bekkir," Quark explained to Jake. "Lieutenant Dax found a way to kill one . . . and unlike the ones that Major Kira killed, the self-destruct didn't activate."

Jake nodded but did not answer.

But what did *happen to Nog?* wondered Quark. *Will Jake ever be able to tell us? Will he even be able to face the memory himself?*

"Well, we had better get started," said Odo wearily; "it's a long trek back to the habitat ring."

"If you would prefer to stay here, human," said Quark, "we'd understand."

"No, Mr. Quark. I know a faster way to get there, where we won't have to see any—any sleeping people."

They began walking back the way they had come, Jake leading the way. "I wonder," said Quark, trying to hide the ache in his chest, "if you could tell me what finally happened to my nephew."

Jake sighed, shifted his surrogate daughter to his other arm. She stirred in her sleep, cried out once, then fell back into her deep slumber.

The hours stretched after the attack, and the fighting for the station grew fiercer and fiercer.

As Jake predicted, the invaders eventually discovered the connecting tunnels, and the war moved to the habitat ring. Jake, Nog, and Molly went "underground," diving into more of Nog's infamous ventilation shafts, conduits, tunnels, and crawlspaces.

"How did you find all these places?" asked Jake,

amazed, after Nog led them in a hair-raising crawl beneath a metal-mesh floor while heavily armored invaders marched over their heads. Only the darkness of the habitat ring, its power conduits blown up, saved them from being easily seen.

"What do you think I do on all those days I don't waste in the schoolroom?"

"I dunno. I figured you were working in Quark's Place."

Nog laughed, bared his pointy teeth. "Work? Ferengi don't work! We *trade!* Bargain, cajole, sell."

"Your father *works* for Quark. Doesn't he?"

Nog said nothing for a while, simply glowered. "Don't mention Rom," he finally said. "It was just an accident I was born. *I* was an accident. I should have been Uncle Quark's boy." He turned to Jake. "You know how Ferengi produce children, don't you?"

"No," said Jake, fascinated.

"Good."

"You—!" Exasperated, Jake began to crawl along beneath the floor mesh.

"Where do you think you're going?"

"Food," snapped Jake. "Or don't you plan to eat in the future?"

"Hm. I guess you're right, human."

"That's what Quark always calls me: human."

"Well you are one, aren't you?"

"I was just noticing how much like your uncle you are."

"Really?" asked Nog, his whole attitude changing. "You really think I'm like him? Well, you're very perceptive, for a human, that is. Very smart! I've noticed that myself . . . in fact, just the other day, Uncle Quark said . . ."

They reached a trapdoor leading up into a runabout service bay. Jake stared longingly at the *Rio Grande,* undoubtedly all fueled and ready to launch. "Um, Nog . . . you don't happen to know how to pilot a runabout, do you?"

The Ferengi slowly shook his head.

"Too bad," said Jake.

Nog sighed. They walked backward toward the door leading back to the main corridor, keeping the runabout in constant view until the last moment.

"Too bad," whispered Jake once more.

Reaching behind him, Nog punched the touchplate, opening the door. He stepped out into the corridor and froze.

Jake was about to ask what happened when he saw the expression on Nog's face. He did not need to ask then; he knew, even before he heard the approaching bootsteps, the terrible error that Nog had just made.

For a knife-edged moment, Nog's eyes flicked toward the service bay, the still-open trapdoor. But it was across the room. Then his eyes locked on Jake's.

In an instant, Jake Sisko saw straight into his friend's heart. Nog knew immediately that his mistake would cost him his life.

But it did not have to cost his friends their lives as well.

A human might have hesitated, waffled for the few seconds it would take for the invader to reach the doorway and look inside, to see what he was looking at. *After all,* the human rationalizer would say, *misery loves company. They're eventually going to be captured and killed anyway . . . why not go to my death with my friends at my side?*

The human might reject temptation; but the damage would already be done.

Nog, however, was a Ferengi; and when a Ferengi walked into a deal, he did not waste time deciding what he wanted: *he already knew.*

That was their whole secret at the bargaining table, why they so often came out on top of a deal. Before the other party even studied the game rules, the Ferengi already knew exactly what he needed out of the bargain.

Nog wasted not a moment thinking his action through; his final glance was a single word: *goodbye.*

He turned, bolted like a chased rabbit.

The Ferengi's rapid departure broke the spell that bound Jake to the spot. He knew immediately that there was no way for anyone to save Nog now—and his own choice was between following his Ferengi friend to death, thus rendering the sacrifice pointless, or using the chance Nog had bought him.

Instantly, Jake grabbed Molly and spun, placing his back to the bulkhead right next to the open doorway. He did not try for the trapdoor; he knew he would never make it in time.

The only chance to save himself and Molly was if the invader became so intent upon Nog that he did not bother looking inside the service bay. If he poked his head in even momentarily, he could not possibly miss seeing Jake and Molly.

Jake held his breath. The pelting bootsteps pounded closer, closer, then pounded on by without a pause. The invader continued to run down the corridor, taking only a momentary glance to its right as it passed the door.

Jake let his breath out in an explosive gasp, sucked in air. Close to fainting, he slung Molly under his arm like a pobbyball and dashed for the trapdoor.

He had taken only three steps when he heard a burst of gunfire, followed by Nog's voice, screaming for mercy.

There was no mercy to be had. One more gunshot followed, and Nog's voice fell silent.

Tears flowed freely down Jake's face. He cried as he had not since his mother died in the Borg attack. But he did not let the tears slow him down.

I still have you to think about, Molly. We're all we've got.

He dropped down the trap, placed the frightened little girl on the deck, then reached up and shut the trap just as the invader returned. It came into the service bay, directly above them, and prowled around, trying to figure out what Nog had been looking at before the invader . . .

At last, it returned to the doorway, stopped, and took one, last look. Jake had knelt down, wrapped his arms around Molly and put his hand over her mouth, just in case. The little girl still did not know exactly what had just happened . . . but she knew she was in danger, for she remained absolutely still, not uttering a peep.

The invader left, and the door hissed shut behind it. Jake wrinkled his nose, smelling the telltale odor of a very frightened toddler.

Quark sat on his haunches, staring yet again at Lieutenant Dax's enigmatic serenity; but he was thinking about Nog, and the very heroic, very un-Ferengi way he had died two days earlier.

"I suppose I already knew it," he said. "If Nog were alive, by this time, he would have come back to the club. He'd have been there when we reappeared, Odo."

"I know," said the constable, uncomfortably.

"You knew all along, didn't you?"

"I guessed. Telling you didn't seem—practical."

"You wanted me to still have hope. If I allowed myself to realize that the boy was dead, you worried I might have wanted to join him."

"No. Not that; I just wanted you clearheaded."

Quark looked narrowly at the constable. "You actually were considerate of me, Odo. Admit it."

"Practicality. That's all."

Quark closed his eyes. "Nog was like . . . oh, to six hells with it. You know all the standard things people say when they lose a relative. You must have heard it from plenty of others; you don't need to hear it from Quark, as well."

"Thank you. It would be . . . unsettling."

"And thank you, human, for telling me how my nephew died."

"It should have been me."

"Nog couldn't have cared for Molly the way you have. He's a good boy—*was* a good boy, but a Ferengi boy. Taking care of human infants is not exactly his trade."

"Well," said Odo, "here it is." He nudged the Bekkir corpse with his foot. Two meters away was a small pile of ash, surrounded by an indentation melted into the deckplate. Odo noted it with satisfaction: the incendiary device, blown clear by the same explosion that had shattered the Bekkir's armor and killed the creature.

Quark looked at the shapechanger. Odo's flesh rippled with the strain. *He's way overdue to return to his liquid state. How much longer can he hold out?*

It was a terrible thought: so close, then Odo turns into a puddle, leaving Quark all alone to figure out the solution in time.

The constable bent low over the Bekkir body, examining its belt. "Nothing . . . Quark, let me see that signaling device again."

Quark fished it out of his pocket, brought it to Odo. They both searched the Bekkir's armor for the missing piece.

"Wait," breathed Quark; he looked closely at the Bekkir's wrist assembly. There were many pieces, most of them blown off by the force of the explosion that had killed it. But three metal pieces were still attached to its wrist, and one of them . . .

"Hah! This is it." Triumphantly, Quark removed a tiny, silvered "jigsaw puzzle" piece. He held it aloft. "It fits, I know it does."

Odo put his hand out for the piece, but Quark held it away from him. "It's my device, and I found the piece— I'm going to plug it in!"

Odo looked daggers at the Ferengi, handed back the signaler. Holding it gingerly, as if afraid it might explode in his hands, Quark gently rotated the piece to its correct orientation, then pressed it into place, gritting his sharp teeth and turning his face away.

Nothing happened.

Quark waited and waited, finally exhaling sharply. He panted, not realizing he had been holding his breath.

"Well, it's in," said Odo; "now what?"

Quark tugged his ear. "Probably has to be activated, just like the first button."

Odo nodded. "That makes sense. All right, where is that Ferengi burglar's tool you had?"

"It's *not* a burglar tool! It's just a—just a piece of equipment used to . . ." He pondered; how to tell Constable Odo about his first job, in a way that Odo would not misunderstand? A Ferengi would have understood immediately.

"Right out of university, I worked for my father. Whenever he participated in a blind auction—that's where you don't know the contents of an item being sold."

"I figured that much out, Quark."

"At a blind auction, my job was to, ah, take a look inside the box and evaluate the contents. You see? Even back then, I was a valuable, trusted appraiser."

Odo snorted. "Yes, even back then, you were a burglar and fraud artist."

"You just don't understand the Ferengi way," complained Quark.

"But enough of this cheery discussion. Where is that thing you used to activate the Bekkir device in the first place?"

Quark closed his eyes, trying to visualize what he had done with it. Suddenly, he slapped his forehead with a resounding smack. "I know exactly where it is."

"Where?"

"The floor of my office. In, um, in Quark's Place. Back on the Promenade."

Odo sighed in exasperation. "Well, as I seem to keep saying, let's move. We've already used up half an hour of our precious three."

Dutifully, Quark trooped back toward the power conduit that paralleled tunnel three in the connecting bridge, the same route Jake had led them along earlier. The boy had been nearly right: they only found two dead bodies, both the unwounded, "epileptic seizure" type.

"Can't go that way," said Odo. "We can't get around the Promenade . . . remember? It's blocked. We have to go back along tunnel two, which means we have to pass the battlefield again."

Jake swallowed. He had either been there already, or else he had a vivid imagination for what the "battlefield" was.

"Can you make it?" asked the constable, looking down at the boy.

Jake nodded bravely.

Molly stirred, sat up in his arms, blinking confusedly. "Is it suppertime, Daddy?"

"Hush," said Jake, setting her down on the ground. "We've got some walking to do; then I'm going to pick you up and carry you, and I want you to close your eyes and not peek. Okay?"

Molly asked, "When do we get to eat, Uncle Jake?"

"No food yet, honey. Do you promise not to peek?"

She nodded. "Aye, sir."

"Then let's go." They started to walk, when Jake suddenly exclaimed, "Wait a minute—*Quark* activated the device?"

His incredulous tone of voice made the Ferengi wince. "It's a long story," he said.

"Good," said Jake coldly. "We've got a long walk."

CHAPTER
15

ODO AND QUARK stood several meters away from Jake and Molly, who eagerly ate the contents of a box of puffy (and somewhat stale) rice-flour candy they found in the O'Briens' quarters: *mochi*, Molly called it.

Quark's stomach rumbled ominously as he watched the voracious kids; but the one time he casually suggested that they should split the *mochi* three ways instead of two, Odo gave the Ferengi such a vicious glare that the suggestion was dropped immediately.

"We haven't much time left," said Quark, annoyed that they were allowing Jake and Molly (but not Quark) to feed their faces. "This little excursion up to the habitat ring has already taken half an hour, and it's at least an hour back, making our way along tunnel two."

"The hour and a half remaining should be adequate time to avert the attack."

"If they believe us."

"You they might not believe, Quark. But Commander Sisko knows that I, at least, am not subject to wild fantasies or delusions of grandeur. He and Major Kira will believe me, though they would, of course, simply dismiss you."

"Well . . . something else worries me. What if—"

"What if what? Speak up, Quark; this is no time for private musings."

"I don't like to speculate on the future; but a Ferengi always considers all possible outcomes."

"And?"

"All right, suppose this is the missing piece, and suppose I can find a way to activate it."

"Like you did for the distress signal itself, precipitating this entire catastrophe."

"Yes, yes." Quark dismissed his earlier foible with an agitated handwave. "But do you remember how the Bekkir died?"

"It appeared to have died from a phaser grenade thrown directly behind it. Had it been facing the blast, I suspect it would have been stunned, but alive."

"Right. Dax blew it up. So what happens if the blast that was strong enough to kill a Bekkir through its armor and rip the flash-burner off was *also* strong enough to damage the wrist key?"

Odo frowned, manipulated his chin like putty with his fingers—a mannerism that profoundly disturbed Quark for some reason. The Ferengi looked away, feeling queasy.

"Yes, I see your point. Regardless that all our deductions are spot-on, if the equipment is broken, it still won't work."

"Worse . . . it might catapult us forward instead of backward. Or backward a hundred years."

"I doubt it. The more complicated the device, the more likely any damage is to simply render it ineffective . . . I suspect it's like a biological system; the vast majority of mutations are fatal. Although that seems not to have held true in your case, Quark."

"Ho ho."

"Do you see any way to avoid the risk?" asked Odo.

"No," said Quark angrily, "and it makes me feel less of

a Ferengi. We're *always* supposed to be able to find the risk-free solution. Did I ever tell you why Ferengi are the most successful—"

"More times than I care to remember, Quark."

"The point is, if this piece doesn't work, where can we get another one—one that wasn't blown up by a phaser grenade or slagged by its own incendiary device?"

Odo stretched his chin down to chest level, like a young boy stretching his chewing gum out of his mouth. Now Quark was truly nauseated. "Young Jake may be our only hope, then," said the constable. "Perhaps he can finally bring himself to tell us what happened to the rest of the Bekkir . . . and to Commander Sisko."

Jake stood up, brushed Molly off. "Thanks, Odo. I feel a lot better now. Are you okay now, Molly?"

Molly nodded, mouth still full of *mochi*.

"Okay, I guess we can go. We should be able to find a power conduit running along tunnel two, if it's the same as tunnel one."

Quark was surprised to discover how much he remembered from their first trip out to the habitat ring; he knew where to step, which footholds were treacherous. Jake stared fixedly at Odo's back as the constable limped along, so close to exhaustion that he quivered with every step. Molly rode in Jake's arms, and true to her promise, she kept her face buried in the boy's shoulder. She was not stupid, knew what she would see if she did peek.

Now that he looked for it, Quark noted just how many bodies were unmarred by bullet holes, even here in the war zone. Many unmarked bodies lay atop bullet-riddled bodies, but never the reverse.

The Ferengi caught up to Odo. "I think the unmarked bodies died after the other ones," he said.

"Yes, I noticed that too. And virtually none of the unmarked bodies have weapons. I think they were the civilian survivors who came out after the wave of combat passed by. Something killed them all suddenly, and very painfully."

"Without leaving a single wound, except where they fell and hit their heads after death."

Odo extracted his mini-tricorder, examined one of the bodies. "No lacerations, no soft-tissue damage, no bone damage . . . but massive neural destruction. I don't know what did it . . . they almost seem to have been killed by electrical discharge, except there are no burns."

Quark nodded toward the boy, whispered, "I'll bet he could tell us."

After a few more meters, Odo spoke as disarmingly as he could. "So, Jake, do you have any idea where the Bekkir are now? Did they leave?"

The boy looked uncomfortable with the question. "They're all gone," he said.

"That's a bit vague, isn't it? Did they leave the station?"

"Not exactly."

"Are they dead? Well, I guess so. They're not here, are they?"

A horrible thought formed in Quark's mind as he listened to the exchange. "Odo," he said, "you don't think they could have—used their time devices, do you?"

"Hm. It's a possibility; it would account for their disappearance."

"I'm pretty sure most of them are dead," said Jake, still being evasive.

Odo hesitated a long time before asking his next question. But Jake seemed stronger than he had when they first met, and of course it would be hard to forget that Odo and Quark existed after such lengthy contact.

"Jake," said the constable, "what happened to your father?"

The boy said nothing, merely gripped Molly tighter as if she, too, might softly and suddenly vanish away.

Odo tried another tack. "Is there anyone else alive on the station that you've seen, besides us?" Of course, Odo already knew the answer to that question.

"No," said Jake decisively.

"Then your father must be—"

"He's not dead!" shouted the boy, then immediately soothed Molly, who had begun crying at the sound.

Odo ceased the interrogation, which was going nowhere anyway. *Later, later,* he decided.

The gloom was nearly absolute; even Odo's and Quark's electric torch barely cut through the oppressive darkness. The blackout was total in this part of the habitat ring, though there might still be flickering emergency illumination once they got past junction node ninety-seven toward the core section.

The blackness made the mountains of debris seem more looming, hulking. The only light came from the awe-inspiring starscape, shining like Bajoran pinpearls through the torn skin of DS9.

Ghosts danced at the very edge of the seeking light of Quark's torch as it twisted left, right, left, searching a path. *Easy,* thought the Ferengi, remembering the old adage "The dead don't deal."

At last, they pushed up and over the huge deadfall that had nearly stopped them on the way in; this time, Odo, trapped in a two-legged shape by exhaustion, barely made it over. They reached the mouth of tunnel two.

Dim illumination snaked around the edge of the blown airlock, dimmer than Quark remembered. Then his sensitive Ferengi ears heard a sound that made him stop, clutching Odo's rubbery arm: the hiss of escaping air.

Quark listened carefully, triangulating until he found the leak. Air escaped through one of the many holes torn through the station, near a joint where the tunnel joined the habitat ring. He raised his hand to the gap, felt it sucked up against the bulkhead.

"Odo," he said, "the atmospheric shield has failed. The station is dying the death of a thousand cuts, leaking air like a sieve."

The constable said nothing. He knew what it meant: if they could not jump back in time, they might all suffocate before the Federation got around to sending a ship to investigate the silence. And the Bajorans, too, might be in no great hurry to send a ship, since they only reluctantly tolerated the Federation presence on the station.

The tunnel itself was reasonably clear, compared with the site of the main battle at the airlock. They hurried along it to the core section, found an access ladder, and climbed up to level eleven. Jake and Quark took turns carrying Molly, who was too little to use the ladder; Odo was too weak from trying to maintain his form just one more hour.

The light on the Promenade flickered less often than it had, and when it did, the flashes were dimmer. The emergency backup batteries were nearly exhausted. Quark realized to his annoyance that had the station shields not stayed up as long as they did, they would have had far more power available for life-support and illumination. Alas, by the time the Ferengi turned them off, they had drained the station reserves.

They backtracked along the route he and Odo had taken in the first few minutes, when they began to realize the extent of the destruction. They tracked back along the main Promenade level, finally reaching their destination, the point they had started out from so many hours ago: Quark's Place.

Without the lights, the people, the cries of the Dabo croupier, and drunken revelry, the tavern looked little and dingy. Quark was disgusted by it; such a decrepit, old bar, a money pit into which he had poured the best drinks of his life.

Is this it? Is this what I've dealt for all these years, a squalid watering hole at the edge of the universe?

They passed inside, up the stairs. Inside the office, the Ferengi found everything as he had left it: desk, safe, strongbox, Klingon clock.

On the floor were the ear-pricker and tensor, exactly where he had dropped them after activating the device.

He stooped, picked them up. He extracted the belt buckle from his vest pocket, placed it gently on the table.

Quark thumbed on the ear-pricker, deftly probed the piece.

After a few moments, he looked up, mouth grim and ears flushing. "Nothing," he said in a strangled tone of voice; "there's no field, no resistance. The piece is dead, Odo."

Odo knelt down to eye level with Jake Sisko. "Son," he said, "I know that it's very painful. You lost your mother in a Borg attack, and now you must face up to what happened to your father.

"But we *must know* what happened . . . if Commander Sisko killed the Bekkir, we must find their bodies, if any survived their self-destruct devices. Otherwise, we will not be able to return and avert the attack.

"Jake," Odo continued, "if there is any chance at all that we can go back and stop the station from being obliterated, we need to take it. We need to know what happened."

For a long moment, Jake stared at the deck. Only his eyelids moved, blinking rapidly. He seemed lost in a trance.

Finally, he stirred, looked up. "I don't know how much I can remember. It's confusing."

"You must try, human." Quark still held both the Bekkir signaling device and his ear-pricker, as if helpless to put them down.

Jake stared into the middle distance, neither with Quark and Odo, nor back during the attack, but *in between* in memory-limbo.

"Molly and I hid in the air ducts and ventilation shafts. We never stayed in one spot for longer than thirty, forty minutes. Constantly kept moving so they couldn't get a fix on us.

"The Bekkir patrols were *everywhere*. God, Odo, they had us; they had DS-Nine under total control."

Jake covered his eyes with his hands. For a moment, Odo thought the boy was crying; then he realized Jake was simply trying to visualize how it was, two days and a thousand years ago.

"I thought about you. Both of you. You see, when you disappeared before the attack, some people figured that you had had something to do with it—that you planned it."

"What!" exploded Odo. He had always known the people on DS9 considered him an outsider, distrusting and even fearing him. But actually to believe he would plan such a brutal attack on his only home?

"Why?" he asked. "What possible motivation could I have? It violates every principle of justice I hold close."

"I know, Odo. But when everyone around you dies, you have to have a reason; any reason is better than no reason. That attack was like the hammer of God, killing everyone, good or bad. They—we needed something or someone to blame. Someone to point at."

"Who?" demanded the constable. "Who pointed at me?"

Jake shook his head.

"Who accused me? I insist you tell me!"

"No, sir."

"Why? Whoever it was, whichever friend or enemy turned against me, he or she is dead now."

Quark interrupted. "Dead here and now, Odo. Not back where we're going."

"Quark is right. How could you ever look them in the eye, knowing what they did in a universe that never even happened?"

"But they betrayed my trust!"

"No," said Jake; "if your plan works, they only might betray your trust. They haven't done it yet."

Odo looked around the derelict gaming hall, seeing what it was before and might be again. "You're right," he admitted with difficulty. "Please continue. I won't interrupt again."

"It was while Molly and I were hiding in the wreck of the other runabout, the *Orinoco*," resumed Jake, "that I heard my father's first shipwide broadcast since the evacuation order. . . ."

Sixteen hours from the moment his command began to die, Commander Benjamin Sisko watched in impotent horror as the *Orinoco* spun out of control, then oriented itself on the only familiar sight the pilot could see: the launching pad it had just left.

"*Orinoco*, veer away!" shouted Sisko into the comm link. Again, "*Orinoco*, you are on collision course with the station—pull starboard, ease off your starboard engine."

The pilot either did not hear or did not care, continued at full thrusters directly into the launching pad.

The *Orinoco* slammed into the pad at several hundred meters per second, ploughing right through the immensely tough pad material, a hybrid of metal and monomolecular filament two meters thick. The remains of the craft finally came to rest embedded in the service bay, the level below the launching pad.

There could not possibly be any survivors; nevertheless, Sisko spent many long minutes fruitlessly trying to contact Major Kira, the pilot, or anyone else in the area. He heard nothing, not even static; perhaps the invaders were blocking communicators too now.

A chill crept up his spine. Benjamin Sisko had the distinct feeling that the invaders had finally figured out where Ops was and were on their way up at that very moment.

He briefly considered remaining at the console, going down with the station. Then he remembered his primary duty: no invader must be suffered to leave DS9 alive.

He heard a strange popping. Staring around the room, he finally realized it came from his speaker, not Ops itself.

His stomach twisted; Dax had left that speaker tuned to the comm link with Dr. Bashir.

"Computer," said Sisko, "replay last five minutes of Bashir comm link." After a long hesitation, during which Sisko was half-convinced the entire system had finally died, it began playback of Julian Bashir's final moments.

When it was over, the commander rested his face in his hands. *I wish I had heard it as it happened,* he thought. Not that he could have done anything—the infirmary was eleven levels down, and Sisko could not possibly have left Ops anyway, not even to try to save the doctor.

It would have been more respectful, however, to hear Bashir's heroism as it happened, instead of listening to the instant replay. The fact that it was merely recorded, not heard, cheapened his death.

"I have nothing left," said Commander Sisko, tears openly streaking his cheeks.

He wiped his eyes, felt the bile settle in his gut like poison. At least Bashir's death served one purpose: it hardened Sisko to his own bloody task.

He ran to the access ladder, peered down its depths. He thought he detected shapes moving in the blackness; but it could also be his imagination. He pressed his ear against the cold, metal rungs of the ladder, hearing many tiny clicks and thumps; but were they made by invaders climbing up to seize Ops, or by the sporadic fighting that was all that remained of the defense of DS9?

It doesn't matter, he thought; *I have no more time. Must act immediately.*

Sisko did a slow, careful 360-degree scan of the entire room, looking for another method of escape besides the access ladder, which might be swarming with invaders just a few levels down.

He saw nothing he did not already know about. The only three ways to leave Ops were transporting, climbing down the ladder, or using the turbolifts.

The first was prevented by the invaders' damping field, the second by the imminent presence of armed invaders on the ladder, and the last by disruptions to power conduits, junction nodes, and the wrecked turbolifts.

A nascent thought tickled his brain: true, the turbolifts were disabled; but the turbolift *shafts* themselves might be clear. But how to get there?

He slung the last-ever bag of O'Brien Specials over his shoulder, hurried to the closed doors of the turbolift, and tried to pry them open by main force. They would not budge, having been built by Cardassians. *That's fine,* he thought; *all I have to do is outsmart a bunch of Cardassian civil engineers.*

He needed a lever. Sisko stared around, sweat beading on his forehead. Fortunately, Ops was still well lit, else he might have missed the long, slender maintenance panel that O'Brien seemed to keep permanently detached from its console in the systems-core pit below the main viewer.

Sisko squatted, leapt down nearly a whole level into the systems core. Racing against time, he grabbed up the panel, tucked it under his arm, and pelted for the stairs back up to Ops. Out of breath, he jammed the panel into the crack between the turbolift doors, levered it back.

The doors gave slightly; Sisko tugged harder, yielding another few centimeters.

He wrapped his arms around the panel lever, planted his feet against the side of the turbolift, and performed the greatest squat-thrust of his life . . . sideways.

The panel bent, but not before jamming the doors open twenty-five or thirty centimeters—barely enough to squeeze by. Too late, Sisko realized he needed something to prop the doors open so he could let go of them and scrape through.

He hooked an elbow around the left door, planted his boot against the right, and heaved again. The doors opened a bit wider, rewarding his efforts. The bag of phaser grenades caught on the door. Would it rip, leaving him weaponless?

By inching his way into the opening like a caterpillar, Sisko managed to get his back against the left door without tearing the cloth sack. From that position, he looked down into the shaft.

It was a long, hard drop, at least fifteen levels, plenty enough to kill a man. But there were ladder rungs just across the shaft . . . *if* he could get to them.

He reached up with his left hand, feeling for a handhold. He found the lip of the doorframe, just wide enough that he might be able to steady himself for a few seconds. Taking a deep breath, Sisko caught it with the fingers of his left hand, then twisted entirely inside the shaft.

The doors slammed shut with a resounding clang, nearly catching the phaser bag between them. The bent panel that he had used to lever them open spun down the shaft like a helicopter blade. He listened carefully, finally heard it strike bottom.

That is a long *way down,* he thought, stomach tightening. His hold on the doorframe was beginning to slip.

Clenching his teeth, the commander fixed his eyes on where he remembered the rungs being, despite the pitch blackness that made them invisible.

He let go of the doorframe, teetered precariously on three centimeters of "deck" just inside the doors. Then with a grace and surety he had not felt in years, he leapt outward, hands groping wildly for the rungs that he knew were there, on the other side of the turbolift shaft.

He slammed against the opposite wall, barely catching one rung in each hand. His feet slid from beneath him.

Sisko dangled from his hands in absolute blackness over a deep pit, sweaty palms growing greasy from the oil on the ladder rungs. His feet scrambled against the wall, desperately seeking something to stand on.

At last, one foot found a ladder rung, and he let out his breath, perching himself as well as could be expected. *Aside from that, a perfect landing,* he thought, lips pressed tight.

The grenade bag swung out of control. Miraculously, only one grenade dropped, tumbling down the shaft.

Sisko heard noises from behind the turbolift doors, in

Ops itself. He held himself absolutely still, neither moving nor making a sound.

The invaders had discovered Ops. All that separated Sisko from the enemy were the heavy doors of the turbolift. At any moment, they might decide to pry them apart and peer within.

CHAPTER
16

STANDING ON THE LADDER, unmoving, making no sound, was the second hardest thing Benjamin Sisko had ever done in his life.

Every animal instinct in his body told him to *move*, climb up or climb down, anything to get out of direct line of fire should the invaders decide to lace a few rounds through the turbolift doors.

But he knew that if he moved, they would hear him, open the doors, and take a look.

A herd of invaders entered Ops. Sisko listened as they moved around, searching, tearing the place apart. Every few seconds, he heard a brief spray of gunfire as they shot out equipment, instruments, controls.

Suddenly, from far below, he heard the explosion of the phaser grenade that had dropped. Apparently, the fall had activated the timer.

The invaders fell silent. The grenade had detonated many levels below; but to the invaders, it sounded as if it came from inside the turbolift shaft.

An invader began to pound on the heavy metal doors. *Climb! Now! Get out of here!*

Sisko remained absolutely still as his heart pounded at 180 beats per minute.

The pounding finally ceased, but it was followed by an even more alarming noise: clawed fingers trying to wedge themselves between the turbolift doors.

Frantically, Sisko groped behind him as silently as he could for the sack of phaser grenades, but his straining arm could not find the opening. He felt the bag, but could not bend his arm deeply enough to reach its mouth.

The commander considered unlooping the bag from around his neck and shoulder; but that would likely send the entire bag spinning down the shaft to explode uselessly, a dozen or more levels below.

He waited helplessly, arms growing leaden and fingers numb, while the invader tried to pry open the doors by brute strength.

At last it gave up, as if satisfied that a weaker human could not have opened them, either.

After more shuffling around, opening panels and peering within to see if anyone was hiding there, the invaders left as they had come, by the access ladder.

Now I can move, he thought wearily—then discovered he could not. His arms and legs would not obey his command.

Sisko had tensed his muscles so much, waiting for the doors to slide open and the bullets to fly, that they had cramped. Gritting his teeth against the pain, he forced his aching biceps to loosen, lowering himself enough to flex his leg muscles.

Moving up and down like that a few times, he finally worked out enough of the cramp that he was able to climb; but his hands remained numb. He had to look closely at each hand as it gripped a rung, for he could not feel them, and a slip would be fatal.

The dim light that filtered through the door cracks at each level was all the illumination he received in the shaft. He clumped down level after level, the bag of highly explosive, jury-rigged phasers swinging out, then smacking back against his rump. *I guess that's what they mean about blowing your ass off.* The thought amused him all the way down to the landing.

The "landing" was actually a ledge near where the turboshaft changed directions, moving from a vertical drop to horizontal travel. A short gap in the track framework allowed him to duck out and stand on the landing.

Sisko had tried to keep count of the number of door cracks he passed; he believed he was on level eight.

Below him, the turbolift track made a graceful, majestic turn to the horizontal, taking at least a full level to do so. *Enters the Promenade,* he thought. *If I follow the track, I'll spiral the Promenade from level nine to eleven, then continue to spiral down like DNA to level fifteen.*

After that point, there were alternative tracks the turbolift could follow, depending on whether it was bound for the lower core, the habitat ring, or the interior of the midcore.

Sisko stood on the narrow ledge next to the track, massaging his arms and legs and flexing feeling back into his hands. After a few minutes' rest, he ducked back inside the wire netting of the turbolift track. He touched it; the net was still cold, still capable of holding the superconducting charge that supported the mag-lev turbolift.

"Thing is still operable," he said aloud, happy to hear any human voice—even his own. Operable meant that it was possible that a turbolift could come screaming up or down the track while he was inside it . . . a messy end to a semibrilliant Starfleet career for one Benjamin Sisko, Esq.

"From punk kid to station commander to turbolift hood ornament. I like it." He smiled, a bit too grim, and started down the steps of the long curve to level nine and horizontal movement.

Commander Sisko slowly circumnavigated the upper Promenade as he never had before, walking the track as it looped entirely around the station, dropping to level ten in the process. He heard no sounds of fighting outside the shaft; either no one was left alive on the Promenade, or else the survivors were hiding rather than defending.

Makes sense, he thought, careful not to voice his thoughts aloud this time, so close to an invader stronghold; *by this point, anyone left must realize that there's nothing we can do that we didn't already try.*

Except one possibility, Sisko's last duty. But only the station commander could make such a choice.

Sorry, people. I couldn't protect you. He hugged himself, to stay warm inside the supercooled, superconducting turbolift mesh. He could not shake the horrible, gut-wrenching feeling of losing a command, despite the fact that there never was anything they could have done; DS9 had already lost the war the moment the invaders came out of the wormhole.

It was the *Saratoga* all over again.

On the *Saratoga,* Sisko had been first officer when the Borg attacked and annihilated the ship. Sisko's wife, Jennifer, had been killed in that attack.

Now Sisko was about to kill both himself and his only son, Jake, assuming Jake was still alive.

He can't be. Nobody is. I'm on a dead, broken station drifting lifeless and defenseless in space. He quickly pushed away his son's image: thoughts of his boy would only make it difficult, perhaps impossible, to carry the final task through.

Duty makes a harsh taskmaster. God called Abraham to sacrifice Isaac in Moriah. Now duty calls me to sacrifice Jake for the blasted Federation of Planets.

Commander Sisko clenched his teeth to avoid laughing hysterically, concentrated again on the long, looping walk down again to level eleven.

His lonely footsteps echoed from metal walls enclosing the net. Each time his boot struck the half-meter-wide causeway laid belatedly in the track, attached by Federation engineers after the Cardassians abandoned the station, he imagined it was the death knell of another invader.

They must not take the station cheaply, he said again and again to himself. The cost must be devastating; anything less might lead to a full-scale invasion of Federation space, an invasion Starfleet might not be able to stem.

"He went—down," said Jake, holding Molly and rocking slowly back and forth, reconstructing his father's last stand, two days ago.

"Down?" asked Odo. "Down into the lower core?"

Jake nodded, but would say nothing more.

Odo took the boy's shoulders, helped him rise. He noticed how Jake held the little girl. Molly had obviously become as important to him as he was to her; she was his "daughter" now, as well as a talisman against evil memories. Whenever Jake began to remember, he could always find something Molly needed.

I am looking at raw, evolutionary survival instinct, thought the shapeshifter in awe. *A young boy, barely more than child himself, becomes a father because a little girl* needs *him to be. Life takes care of life.*

Not for the first time, Odo felt terrible, aching loss at not even knowing who his own people *were,* let alone knowing whether they, too, would become fathers to care for sudden orphans.

We are just; it is in our natures. But are we merciful? Are we loving, or harsh authoritarians who would condemn a helpless toddler to death because it "wasn't our problem"?

A disturbing passage from the human bard Shakespeare had haunted Odo for more than a year, since O'Brien's wife, Keiko, had quoted it to the constable, pleading on behalf of young Jake:

In the course of justice, none of us
Should see salvation: we do pray for mercy;
And that same prayer doth teach us all to render
The deeds of mercy.

How would I, myself, act? Odo shuddered, the action causing his chaotic, rebelling structure to ripple like gelatin. He could not even answer the last question.

They slipped silently out of Quark's Place, unwilling to disrespect the dead with the normal noise of the living. Odo led them to an access ramp, but found it blocked by a fallen beam.

The metal I-beam weighed far more than Quark could lift. Odo might have been able, had he been fresh and rested; but the strain of holding his shape for nearly twenty-seven hours left him weak as Betazoid brickel.

"Now what?" asked the Ferengi. Quark had donned another coat in his office, looked even dandier than usual, inappropriate garb for such a somber occasion.

"There are other ramps," said Odo, his voice warbling as his vocal cords reformed, shifted. "But they are in parts of the Promenade that are blocked." He thought for a moment. "I believe I know how to proceed."

He turned, scanned the blue-flickering scene for a turbolift door. It was hard to tell exactly where he was in the desolation; everything looked so different. He spotted one, led them over.

"Ah," objected Quark, worried, "we're not going to try climbing down the turbolift shaft—are we?"

Odo tried to roll his eyes, but one turned completely around, stared into its own optic nerve. "The turbolift runs horizontally around the Promenade," he explained, turning away to fix his eyeball, "which you would know if you had bothered yourself to study the station that has been your home for years."

Quark glowered. "I didn't go rooting around in the mulching bins or waste disposal units either."

"Really? That's too bad; they're fascinating. And of course, your life depends upon them every day."

Odo popped open the control pad next to the turbolift, lifted the security latch on the door circuitry. He typed a quick password on the touchplate, and the doors slid slowly open, revealing the shaft.

The quadrumvirate stepped inside a wire mesh cage,

found a narrow walkway that gently sloped and curved to follow the bend of the Promenade itself. They turned left, descended in lazy circles below the Promenade, into the lower core.

They had to walk slowly in the blackness, their torches illuminating only a few meters of the catwalk. The walk was raised nearly half a meter above the mesh itself, and a wrong step could lead to a broken leg. Quark took point, walking slowly and staring with wide, Ferengi eyes that gathered more light than did a human's or Odo's. Jake took hold of Quark's belt with one hand, while the other held Molly's hand firmly. The little girl walked behind, followed by Odo, quivering with every step.

The constable felt bouyant, bouncy, which was a bad sign; it meant he was near to liquefying. *Must hold on,* he told himself firmly. *We need all of us in order to survive and find a working jigsaw piece.*

Quark coughed violently, felt himself gasping for air. He shivered in the cold. "Atmosphere's growing thin," he said. "Leaks in the hull."

"How long do we have?" asked Jake, also sounding out of breath. Molly simply panted.

"The rest of our lives," said the Ferengi.

They passed a turbolift door on level thirteen. Blue flashes from outside peeked through the crack, faintly illuminating the shaft inside. Quark stopped, stared at something scratched low on the catwalk, as if someone had sat for several minutes, idly marking with a pen-knife.

B.S. 47235.5 →

Jake stared. "That . . . that's my—"

Quark looked at the mark. "Benjamin Sisko?" he guessed. Jake nodded dumbly.

"The arrow points down the catwalk," said the Ferengi. "I guess we're following the commander's trail."

The boy finally found his voice. "It's a private joke," he said. "We watched an old, old video made from a moving photograph back in the nineteenth or twentieth century, *Journey to the Center of the Earth.* It was a stupid sci-fi video, but I kind of liked it."

"Yes?" asked Odo, wondering where the story was leading.

"There was a character, Arne Saknussen. He went deep under the surface of the Earth, marking his trail by writing A.S. and an arrow using candle soot.

"Dad and I joked about that all the time, saying the station was so confusing that we should carry candles and mark our way."

"So Commander Sisko *did* go down," mused the constable. "But to where? How deep did he go, and why?"

Jake took a deep breath, began to speak quietly.

Sisko jogged along the turbolift track, breathing hard; by his estimate, he had run nearly seven kilometers, dropping from the lower Promenade to level twenty-eight in the lower core as the track spiraled tighter and tighter.

First climbing, then walking the difficult track, he had averaged about two kilometers per hour: it was now zero-four hundred, four hours after the *Orinoco* had crashed into its own launching terminal, twenty hours after the invaders attacked the station.

He leaned on his knees, gasping for air. *Not as fit as you used to be,* he chastised himself. Alas, the commanding officer of the farthest Federation outpost had very little free time for physical training; what time he did have, he devoted to Jake.

When his respirations slowed, he sat on the catwalk, trying to figure a way out of his dilemma. *Assume Jake is alive. How do I warn him what I'm going to do without also warning the invaders?* While he sat, he scratched yet another mark on the metal mesh, just in case Jake later came looking for his father.

Sudden guilt nagged at Sisko's mind. He tried to push it down, but it was persistent: what right had he to sacrifice every other person on DS9 if he was not willing to sacrifice his own son?

I've already shown my complete commitment to the sacrifice, he argued; *I'm one of those who will die.*

So? Others might also choose to let their children live by dying themselves. Why should Jake be the lucky one?

But Jake can warn the Federation! He can tell them what happened.

So might any other survivor. Why should your own son live when the others die?

"Might." If Jake survives, I know *he'll warn Starfleet. I don't have to wonder.*

Self-serving rationalization! It's totally unfair to save Jake if everyone else dies.

Then the absurdity of the argument struck Sisko: the sacrifice had nothing to do with Jake—the station had to die so that the Federation and Bajor would live . . . so, since Sisko had already made that decision, why should Jake die needlessly?

Sisko would save them all if he could, every crew member and civilian on Deep Space 9. But he could not. He *might* be able to save his son, however.

"Self-serving" or not, cold as it might be, it was the only rational decision. Being the man he was, as soon as Sisko had resolved the ethical dilemma in his own mind, he set it aside, never to brood on it again.

The real problem was that Jake could only survive if he was shielded against electromagnetic pulse, which meant one of five places: Ops, the central axis of DS9, or one of the three phaser-fire control rooms between the top and bottom weapons sails. The invaders, however, could probably rig an EMP force shield, given enough time to prepare.

Thus, Sisko had to somehow warn his son to get to a shielded area—if Jake was still alive and conscious—*without* alerting the invaders in any way.

The turboshaft went no deeper into the station than level twenty-eight, as a quick-time hike farther along the track proved. It wound less than a quarter turn around the narrow level before ending abruptly at a crash barrier.

"We do the next seven levels the hard way," he said aloud.

Sisko backtracked to the level twenty-eight door, grabbed the interior control pad, and wrenched it open. There was a touchpad with number keys. He started to type in his security-override code, then froze.

If the invaders had found a way to tap into the station computer, then as soon as he typed his code, they would be alerted that a security override by Commander Sisko was in effect on level twenty-eight, turbolift door C. The invaders could be on his trail in ten minutes . . . one minute if they were smart enough to take the turbolift itself.

"No. I'll have to short-circuit the door optics," he decided; if that showed up as anything, it would be classified as miscellaneous damage and presumably go unnoticed.

He tried to trace the circuit diagram on the inside of the control-pad cover, but it was too dark to read. *There must be a flash around here,* he thought. *Surely it would occur to maintenance that a person might suddenly need one . . . for example, if he dropped his own down among the grillework.*

Sisko explored the area around the door, finally discovered a faint, flashing red light. Closing on it, hands outstretched and groping, he found a rechargeable torch.

He needed both hands free to jimmy the circuits, so he clamped the flash between cheek and shoulder, oriented it onto the control-pad circuit diagram by twisting his body like Quasimodo, the Hunchback of Notre Dame.

Carefully tracing the fibers, he pulled one loose, re-attached it against another. A spark leapt into his face; when he finished blinking, the door was open.

He hesitated, debating whether to leave the door open for a quick retreat. Then he shrugged; he was never coming back this way again. Sisko plucked the fiber-optic cable from its "hot-wired" position, slipped through the doorway before the doors could close.

He stood in a cold, antiseptic cargo bay that throbbed with power from the fusion reactors, a mere seven levels below. Commander Sisko shivered, wrapped his arms around himself; despite their proximity to the generators, the DS9 cargo bays were given only marginal heat to save power, just enough to prevent supplies from freezing or cracking from the extreme cold of sunless space, now that they were so distant from Bajor's star.

The circular room surrounded the wide, gravity-generating hub, leaving only a small torus for storage. The central hub contained a number of instruments and controls embedded in the bulkhead, which was made out of hull material. A thermometer directly opposite the turbolift door read -36 C [237 K].

"Man, I wish I hadn't hadn't seen that," said the commander; now he felt twice as cold.

Shivering violently as his body heat leaked away, Sisko slowly circled the hub, looking for communications equipment. Finally he found what he wanted: a hard-wired communications intercom leading straight to Ops.

The invaders had disrupted normal communicator traffic, but a hardwired connection could probably still get through to the computer.

"Computer," he said, speaking through clenched teeth to keep them from chattering; "Sisko, security override two-twenty-two-Q, transmission location classified and tied to my override."

He waited; the silence stretched endlessly. At last, the severely damaged computer processed his request.

"Ov-rd-cepted."

"Open shipwide intercom along hard channels." The hard channels, direct fiber-optic links between Ops and every speaker on the station, had been installed by the Cardassians in case normal communications were subject to monitoring by an enemy. To monitor fiber-optic channels, you needed to physically string sensors within half a meter of the cables.

Hard channels were also virtually impossible to sever; the invaders would have to slice each and every cable, since they ran in parallel, not series.

"Ch-nl-pen," said the computer; *channel open.*

Now, how do I warn Jake? Never mind; there was plenty to say before he had to think about Jake.

Sisko breathed deeply, carefully composing his message. At last, he began to speak.

"Attention, invaders," he said, speaking quietly and unemotionally. His words blared out of the cargo-bay loudspeakers and an instant later echoed down the turbolift track, causing a slight feedback. The damaged computer failed to compensate.

"Attention, invading forces. This is Commander Benjamin Sisko, commanding officer of the Bajoran and United Federation of Planets starbase Deep Space Nine."

He paused, hoping he had their attention by now. "I hereby formally surrender this station. I direct all Bajoran militia forces to lay down their arms. This is a direct order. Further defensive operations will be considered a criminal act under the Uniform Alliance Act of Balor Two."

He waited, smiling, letting the words sink in. *And now the game begins. . . .*

"As surety for safe conduct off Deep Space 9 for all crew and residents, and to ensure the cessation of hostilities on the part of the invading forces, I shall continue to hold my prisoner hostage. This prisoner was taken into custody fifty-six hours ago.

"We are holding the prisoner in a secret location, which we shall not disclose until all Bajoran and Federation personnel have left the station. I am now ready to negotiate safe passage and the terms of surrender.

"I await your presence in the reactor pod, level thirty-five, the lowest level in the station. You have thirty minutes to arrive. Since the turbolifts are inoperative, I suggest you begin immediately.

"If thirty minutes pass and you have not arrived, I shall execute the prisoner."

Sisko licked his lips; and now came the warning that he prayed Jake would understand. He glanced at the chronometer on his wrist, since the station clocks were controlled by the computer and inoperative: 0426. Jake —if he still lived—had until 0456 to get to safety. Sisko decided to wait until 0500, if he could manage.

Ever since the rise of Bajoran fundamentalism and the attack on the schoolroom, coinciding with the power play by the orthodox Vedek Winn against the progressive Vedek Bareil, Bajoran "Sunday schools" had sprung up on the station.

Sisko had decided that sending his own son to Bajoran religious classes would placate a lot of hard hearts; as well, a dose of spiritual values might do Jake good. Thus, he had insisted Jake attend the religious classes.

The commander spoke now clearly and distinctly: "In the name of the great god Susurrora, I pray a great enlightenment envelops us all, allowing us to settle this issue with no further blood spilt."

Please Jake, he prayed now, *tell me you actually studied your lessons. . . .*

If he had, he would recognize the curious reference to a Bajoran deity: "Susurrora" was the Bajoran god of the sun.

CHAPTER
17

JAKE SPOKE QUIETLY, trying to remember the exact timing after more than two days.

"Molly and I heard the surrender while we were holed up in a common storage space above the quarters in level sixteen, section twenty-three of the habitat ring, above Mrs. O'Brien's quarters.

"I was so astonished that I almost missed the final part of his message. When it finally penetrated, I thought at first that he had, you know, suffered some kind of nervous breakdown."

"I was not aware that Commander Sisko was a religious man," said Odo.

"He's not. I knew Dad couldn't possibly have suddenly converted to *sun worship*, which is so old-fashioned even in Bajor that only radical students and troublemakers practice it—or at least, that's what Teacher Janra says, and she's going to be a Vedek someday.

"I figured out it must be a code right away; but for a long time, I didn't know what the hell—what the *heck* he meant.

"It was scary, lying there in the dark, knowing Dad

was trying to tell me something important but not knowing what."

"Well," said Odo, voice needlessly harsh, "what *did* he mean? I'm sorry to be short-tempered, but we have very little time left. Did your father actually go down to level thirty-five, or did he stay where he was?"

"He—he—he went d-down. All the way down, to the very deepest pit of the station."

Odo nodded. "Come on, we've rested more than enough. You can finish the story as you walk, Jake, but we *must find those invader bodies.*"

They rose miserably. Quark, Jake, and even Molly felt sick and light-headed from the sparse atmosphere— "altitude sickness," Quark called it. Their vision tunneled, and they lost both peripheral and color. Every few steps, they had to stop and wheeze, even though they still followed the turbolift track downward.

"I thought of all the things that the sun god does," said Jake, pausing for a breath between every few words. "He makes the sun rise, climb the sky, then set; he rides to battle with a golden sword on a chain; he rules the heavens. But I couldn't think of anything that made sense. Then finally, I started thinking of the sun itself . . . and that's when I suddenly remembered the fusion generators."

Molly sat cross-legged in the crawlspace, visible only as a darker hulk in the gloom; the only illumination came from a small window currently looking at the Hunters, one of the three or four Bajoran constellations that Jake could recognize.

Jake watched the clock: 0429. His father had made the cryptic announcement three minutes ago, giving them still another twenty-seven minutes to figure out what he meant.

"Sun," said Jake, thinking aloud. His shoulders ached from crawling on hands and knees in the tiny attic space above section twenty-three. "Heat, light, UV light, cosmic radiation—what is he trying to tell us?"

Jake's nose told him that she had dirtied her pants from fear.

He nearly shouted at her, then realized she was a very little girl who had just seen her mother killed, and whose father was probably dead as well. Instead, he crawled over and sat next to her. When he got close, he saw she was also sucking her thumb, something he had not seen her do for a year.

"Molly," he asked, "does your mom still keep your old diapers, from back when you were little?" She nodded miserably. "Look, honey, I know you're a big girl, but it's all right if you put your diapers on again and—um, pretend to be little for a while. Okay?"

"Okay," she said, using a very little voice.

They crawled stealthily toward the trapdoor that led down to the O'Briens' quarters. Jake opened the door, leaned down to listen, then lowered Molly to the floor. He continued to run through everything he knew about the Bajoran sun.

A little dimmer than Sol; warmer; you can see the aurora from almost anywhere in the northern hemisphere. About suns in general: *Big and hot; surface temperature only about 3500 K; core is several million K; gigantic, continuous fusion explosion—*

He suddenly gasped as he dangled from the roof trap, so struck by the solution that he forgot to drop until his hands began to hurt. "Fusion . . . he's going to do something to the fusion reactors, Molly!"

Jake looked at his watch. The luminous display read 0435, twenty-one minutes left before his father did whatever he was going to do.

He told Molly to take off her soiled pants and underpants, while he searched the O'Briens' bedroom for diapers, feeling like a burglar. He found several boxes of diaper-shaped plastic things. He brought a box back, and Molly, wearing only a shirt now, confirmed that they were, indeed, her old diapers.

A pile of soft cloths soaked in something that smelled like disinfectant were included with the box. Holding his breath and fighting against the gag reflex, Jake cleaned up the little girl. He tried to keep his eyes averted, not wanting to see the inevitable by-products of a toddler's diet; but it was impossible, since he needed his eyes to see where to wipe.

After a few moments, while he tried to figure out how to configure the diaper itself, he realized the nausea had passed. It was not as bad as he thought it would be.

"My dad—he's Commander Sisko, your parents' boss, you know—my dad's going to do something to kill the bad guys."

Molly looked at Jake with eyes as big as saucers. "Can't he just talk to them? Mommy says talking is better than violins."

"Violence," corrected Jake, smiling.

He got Molly's diaper on, told her to get a new pair of pants from a pile her mother had prepared. "Molly, you can only talk to people who're willing to talk to *you*. If a big kid started hitting you, you'd be too busy saying 'ouch' to talk to him, wouldn't you?" Her shadowy face nodded in understanding. "First you have to stop him from hitting you. *Then* you can talk about why he did it, and how to keep him from doing it again.

"But this time, it looks like the only way to get the invaders to stop hitting is to kill them. It's sad, but they've already killed most of us, Molly. The only other choice is to give up and let them hit Bajor and Earth and everywhere else."

She said nothing about the invaders, merely presented herself with clean pants to Jake. He looked at his watch; thirteen minutes left.

"But I don't know what he's going to do. Something about the fusion reactors." *Would he blow them up, make the entire station explode?*

No, that made no sense . . . if that is what he was going to do, why bother warning Jake? He would die anyway. Why risk the invaders figuring it out too and somehow getting off the station or shielding themselves?

*It's something we can survive if we're smart enough—
that's why Dad warned me!*

Jake paced, furious with himself for not being able to
think. He kept looking at his watch: twelve minutes;
eleven and a half; eleven minutes left!

"Look, this is stupid," he said out loud. *I'm so scared, I
can't think. What does Dad always quote? "The fear of
death is the beginning of slavery."*

Jake began to breathe deeply, rhythmically; it was
what his father always did when he began to lose his
temper, give in to anger. *Maybe it works when you're
afraid, too,* Jake hoped.

It did help. Thoughts popped into his mind, ways that
a reactor could go wrong besides exploding and taking
the entire station with it.

"It wouldn't be nuclear particle radiation," he said;
"there's not enough in the whole generator to do much to
us . . . and in any case, that doesn't work instantly.
Light? No, that wouldn't do anything. Heat would only
affect the lower core, which would probably just melt and
seal itself off from the rest of the station. Wouldn't jump
across empty space, so it wouldn't affect the habitat ring,
and I *know* there's invaders here, too."

At once, Jake realized what his father was planning. He
smacked his head so hard he staggered himself. "A pulse!
A huge, electromagnetic pulse effect! It fries electronic
equipment that isn't specially shielded . . . maybe if it's
strong enough, it does the same thing to a body."

*Great. Now you know how you're going to die. What
exactly can you do in nine minutes to shield yourself, kid?*

"Shielding," he said, pacing back and forth. Molly
watched him, not saying a word. "I can't make a shield. I
don't know how, or what you use to block an
electromagnetic pulse, and we've only got a few minutes.
But there's got to be places on the station that are *already*
shielded."

Jake suddenly had a strange thought. He squatted
down, face-to-face with the little girl—the daughter of
the chief of operations, Miles O'Brien.

"Molly," said Jake, "did your daddy ever talk about shields?"

She nodded.

"Did he ever say what parts of the station have special shielding?" Molly turned her head, stared at him with eyes as big as millstones, but said nothing.

Too complicated a question, he decided. "Did your daddy ever talk to you about emergencies?" It was a good bet; the few times Jake had talked with Chief O'Brien, he seemed to be pretty compulsive about procedures and plans.

Molly nodded again.

Buoyed by success, Jake asked the most important question of all. "Did Daddy ever say *where you should go* if the station was attacked, and he wasn't with you?"

"He told Mommy," she said.

"Did you hear him talking?"

Molly nodded.

"Do you remember what he said?"

Molly nodded.

"What did he say?"

Molly pondered deeply, rubbing her chin in an eerily adultlike mannerism that she must have picked up from her father. "Said go to the weepy cells," she said.

"The—weepy cells?"

She nodded solemnly.

"Do you know where the weepy cells are?" She thought a moment, then shook her head.

Great. Now what?

"Weep," he said, rolling the word. "Weepy. Weep cells. Wapey salls. Sulls, sales, sills—sales, sails—*the weapons sails!*" Jake grabbed Molly's hands. "Molly, is that what he said? Go to the weapons sails?"

She nodded. "Weepy cells," she agreed.

"Come on, Molly, we have to run now!" Jake caught her up under his arm, bolted out of the O'Briens' quarters. He sprinted along the corridor, trying to remember where the weapons-sail towers were located.

When they first arrived on DS9, Commander Sisko

had insisted that his son study and memorize a station diagram. At the time, Jake objected; he already knew where the Promenade and Ops were. "Isn't that good enough?" he asked.

Now he was glad his father had sternly insisted. Jake stopped, heart pounding, and closed his eyes. He visualized the diagram of the habitat ring, level fourteen.

The weapons-sail towers were on the top and bottom of the ring, above level thirteen and below level seventeen.

"Up," he decided. He took a last glance at his watch: six minutes to doomsday.

Still holding Molly, he ran at a quick jog toward the access ladder at the edge of section twenty-two, praying he did not run into any invaders along the way.

He made it to the ladderwell door, but it did not open when he walked up to it; in fact, Jake bumped his nose, not being able to stop himself in time.

He started to swear, using words he had learned from Nog, when he remembered Molly and clamped his mouth shut.

"Gotta be an emergency open," he said, and began searching the side of the doorway for instructions.

Molly reached up, poked a large, red button with her little finger. The door slid slowly open.

Jake stared at her for a moment, then caught her hand and dashed through. *Of course. She goes along with O'Brien when he fixes things.*

"Can you climb a ladder?" he asked Molly. She nodded, but Jake was not entirely sure she really knew. "You go first, Molly; I'll be right behind you."

He lifted her high up the ladder; when she was attached, he began to climb up himself. Molly seemed to have the basic idea, but could only work it by stretching way up with one hand, finding the rung, then reaching up with her other hand to the same rung.

Jake felt a terrible tightness in his stomach: at the rate Molly was climbing, they would never make it to the shielded weapons sail in time.

Not for a single moment did he consider abandoning her and saving himself; Jake was his father's son, and saving himself at the expense of Molly's life was not in his genetic makeup.

He did debate trying to hold on to her with one hand while he climbed with the other; but the ladder rungs were too far apart, being built for Cardassian arms and legs, and he needed both hands himself to climb.

"Come on, Molly," he encouraged, as they laboriously climbed one rung, another rung, a third rung.

He looked at his watch twice, seeing the time leak away like air from a ruptured hull, before deciding it was only upsetting him: they would either make it, or they would not; staring at his watch would not change anything.

At last, Molly flopped over onto the deck of level thirteen. Jake charged up the remaining rungs, scooped the girl up in both arms, and sprinted down the corridor.

Jake skidded to a halt as he passed a small corridor branching off from the main one. He visualized the diagram . . . that was it—it had to be. There were no other branches in the vicinity.

He squeezed down the unmarked corridor, pushing Molly ahead of him, then rounded a corner and came to another door, much thicker and heavier than any he had seen on DS9.

The door was locked. There was no red button for Molly to push.

Stunned, Jake looked at his watch. Thirty seconds.

Twenty-nine.

Twenty-eight. . . .

Commander Sisko walked hurriedly around the central hub of the cargo hold, found the open hatch leading to the lower-core ladderway. Slinging the bag of phaser grenades over his shoulder and fixing it so it would not swing against his legs, he began the long, downward climb into the fusion reactor chamber itself.

The air was strangely still and cold, considering that he was descending into the hottest hell that intelligent beings had yet devised: the "spiked" reaction, in which small bits of antimatter were flung into the stellar-core furnace of hydrogen fusion, producing temperatures in excess of 3,000,000 K. The straight matter-antimatter reactions that drove starships, while far more energetic, were also more efficient at converting that energy to motion, thus producing less waste heat.

But one thing the two types of reaction shared: under certain circumstances, they could produce a solitary shock wave, a soliton, called an electromagnetic pulse.

An EMP shock wave explodes outward at light-speed like a fist of lightning, punching through any electronic or electrochemical system . . . even a living body, if the pulse was strong enough.

Only very heavy shielding would stop an EMP of the size that Sisko envisioned. The rest of the station and almost every duotronic and biological system within it would be *disrupted* . . . which in the case of anything with an electrocolloidal brain meant complete neurological scrambling—death.

The invaders' armor might partially shield them from the full effects, depending on how far away from the source they were; thus, the closer he could lure them, the better his chances.

Sisko grabbed the outside of the ladder with hands and feet, slid down it to the deck below, not caring that he was tearing up his hands. In a few minutes, it would not matter anyway.

Down decks he went. He knew they could not beat him to the fusion reactors: there was no way other than the route he took himself.

Ordinarily, nobody ventured into the reactor chamber itself, the lowest pit of Deep Space 9. The danger was too great; if the shields surrounding the reaction leaked even the slightest, anybody within a few meters would be bombarded with electromagnetic radiation that over the long term would cause irreversible brain damage.

Worse, when high-energy electrons struck the metal hull surrounding the reactors, they produced bursts of

X rays that could cause radiation sickness all by themselves.

In a normal case, to make repairs on the reactors, you first shut them down. A Federation-built ship or station would have many, many failsafes designed into the basic structure of the deck itself, preventing a foolish person from violating the integrity of the reactor room while the reaction was "hot."

Deep Space 9, however, was designed by Cardassians. Benjamin Sisko gambled everything that the Cardassian engineers had shown their usual disdain for safety features.

He dropped down, down into the black, frozen abyss of the unheated lower core. Level after level he descended, six in all, to finally stand on the deck of level thirty-four.

It vibrated with a bone-jarring, constant quake in which he could discern a consistent pulse; the two working reactors were slightly out of synch, interfering with each other's vibration to produce beats, like a very slightly out-of-tune guitar.

He bent, touched the deck with his lacerated palm. It was hot. The shielding was not working very well.

Can I do it from up here?

No; Sisko kicked the deckplates, realized they were too thick, would shield the reactors too well. He would have to actually climb down into the reactor well itself.

He smiled grimly. *At least I have one advantage denied old Shadrach, Meshach, and Abednego,* he thought; *the reactor force shield.*

The deckplates contained a single, gigantic trapdoor, not quite large enough to pass a runabout, but at least half that size. It was sealed by five screw lugs, each the diameter of a porthole.

Sisko grabbed the first lug with both hands, struggled it around a dozen times before he heard a satisfying click. He quickly repeated the action for the next four lugs.

He stopped, sat very quiet, very still. Faintly above his

head, he heard noises. The invaders had reached the end of the turbolift track, were descending the six ladders toward their rendezvous with fate.

"Got to move," he said. He stooped, grabbed hold of the middle lug, braced his legs and heaved.

Nothing. Sweating, he tried again; if he was not able to open the trapdoor, his entire plan was worthless.

This time, Sisko was able to raise the door a few centimeters; then he felt a tearing in his stomach, was forced to drop it shut again.

"Damn!" He stamped on the trap in hot fury, then stepped back, feeling foolish. It was not locked, just very heavy . . . built for Cardassian muscles, not human. If it had been locked, he would not have been able to even budge it.

Quick, quick, quick! Think of something, you idiot. The commander was acutely conscious of the invaders closing fast from above.

He wished he could have held off on the broadcast until he was already in the reaction well; unfortunately, the intercom fiber optics did not extend below level twenty-eight.

He felt the weight of the phaser-grenade bag. He squeezed it. "Thank you," he whispered.

Sisko extracted a single grenade, laid it on the deck right next to the central lug. He bent, strained every muscle in his back and legs to raise the massive door up—just high enough to kick the phaser grenade forward. It stopped against the crack; as he lowered the trapdoor again, it jammed on the phaser grenade.

Sisko dropped heavily to his knees, almost fainting from the exertion. He had never before lifted a weight even approaching that door . . . it must have weighed at least two hundred kilos! Every joint in his body screamed in agony.

Still on his knees, he programmed the grenade for three seconds, then activated it.

He quickly crawled behind the center hub, heard the

powerful explosion, followed by a deep clang. When he poked his head back, the trap had been blown open by the grenade.

The invaders paused when they heard the explosion. After a moment, he heard the bangs and clanks start up again . . . no more than two levels above his head.

Before he could change his mind, Ben Sisko lowered himself down the final badger hole, dropped stiffly to the deck: level thirty-five, the fusion reaction well itself . . . the utter terminus of DS9.

In front of him were reactors three, four, five, and six, all dead. According to O'Brien, they still had so many leaks and other problems that activating them might melt the entire station. He turned around toward reactors one and two.

He stared back and forth at the two hulking giants—tiny, fragile eggshell cups, each containing an exploding star.

CHAPTER
18

"LEVEL TWENTY-EIGHT," gasped Quark, seeing double; "end of the line. Everybody off."

He staggered drunkenly toward the turbolift door; it did not open, as it had not for Commander Sisko, two days earlier.

Odo was not affected by the diminished atmosphere, now down to about a third normal pressure; he was, however, so exhausted that he might as well have suffered from altitude sickness. His mind wandered, could not maintain concentration.

He fooled with the control pad for a few seconds before it occurred to him that he might get a better view if he shined his flash *into* the open box, rather than onto the floor at his feet.

Inside, he saw a single, dangling fiber-optic cable unattached to anything on one end. He blinked, concentrated on re-forming his facial features into "Odo."

"Quark," he barked, "you used to be a petty crook. How do I cross-circuit this thing to open the door?"

"I am *not* a crook," insisted the Ferengi. "We have— very strict—rules of conduct. I just—"

"Yes, I know; you just gathered information for your father before blind auctions. All right, let's see some of the information you gathered: *Where do I stick this blasted cable?*"

Quark resisted the obvious temptation, studied the diagram. The box was identical to several such in the more common parts of the station.

"Oh. No problem. Here." He slid the optic into a multi-input junction port in the door-open circuit, bypassing the entire security design. The door opened immediately, stayed open.

Jake stayed inside the turbolift track, afraid to enter the cargo hold.

"What is the matter, Jake?" asked Odo.

"I—I can't do it."

"Staying here won't change what happened."

"If I go in there, it'll all be real. He'll really be . . . you know. Like that."

"Jake, whatever happened, happened already. Commander Sisko cannot still be alive on DS-Nine."

"Well maybe he got off the station!"

Odo sighed, a practiced response. "Jake, you're chasing after click-beetles. Your father is either alive or dead already, and nothing you do now will change that fact."

"But it's not *really real* until I actually see it. Until then, *anything* could have happened. He might be alive now, before I know for sure, but not after I see his b-b-body."

Quark spoke up. He seemed more affected by the thin atmosphere than any of them, even Molly. "If your—father were here—would he stay here—or—or go to see?"

Jake did not respond; but he slowly walked into the cargo hold. He began to sweat almost immediately, noted with surprise that unlike the last three levels, level twenty-eight was quite hot.

Quark recovered somewhat in the hot air, which was distinctly more Ferengi-friendly. "On we go, ho ho, down to the bowels of DS-Nine!" He reeled toward the ladderway, singing a space chanty; Quark felt positively giddy, but could not remember why, or what they were down here to do.

Quark led them down the ladder, level by level. The air grew hotter, then so hot it bothered even him. Molly was having a terrible time adjusting to both the thin atmosphere and now the temperature, which ranged well above fifty degrees centigrade. Jake was drowning in sweat; but now that he had made up his mind to see the job through, he made no further protest.

Quark stared at Odo, then began to giggle uncontrollably. The constable was melting in the dry, deserty heat like a burning candle, pieces of his head dripping down his body until they were reabsorbed around his hips.

By the time they reached level thirty-two, the ladder was so hot that only Odo could hold it in his bare hands.

Quark took off his jacket, gazed lovingly at it. Then he began to tear it into strips, which he wrapped around the hands of Molly, Jake, and himself. Using the slight protection, they climbed down one more ladder to level thirty-three.

There they stuck; the heat coming out from the ladderwell was enough to give third-degree burns to anyone who tried to brave it, except of course for Odo. If the atmosphere were as dense as it should have been and contained sufficient oxygen, anything inflammable would have already burnt to a crisp.

Jake thought of the old Earth city of Dresden, firebombed in the Second or Third World War: the citizens had fled to bomb shelters at the beginning of the raid, but baked inside as their city burned to the ground above them. When the enemy soldiers opened the shelters, the superheated bodies inside, suddenly supplied with oxygen from the outer air, spontaneously burst into flames.

It was the one image he would never forget from Mrs. O'Brien's Earth-history section.

"I don't think we're going any deeper," he said. Certainly Molly was not.

Quark had moved to the outer edge of the room. He stared listlessly out the series of window ports that lined the outer bulkhead.

The station slowly rotated with respect to the surrounding stars, not quickly enough to make docking difficult, but enough to share the view of the wormhole, the single feature that attracted the most custom.

The wormhole rotated into view now, a faint dark patch only really visible when a ship came through.

Thirty-one hours after the attack began, it was about to end.

Commander Sisko pressed his back firmly against reactor two, watched the invaders pour down the ladderway. There were more than he imagined had even invaded the station: wave after wave came, until more than fifty invaders had climbed into the reactor well.

They occupied the other side of the chamber, surrounding and filling all the space between the other, cold reactors. For a moment, they watched Sisko through their shiny black helmets; the red and yellow flashing lights that would indicate reactor status to a trained observer bounced off the invaders' armor and helmets, becoming thousands of red and yellow eyes staring at Sisko.

He stared back, calmer than he had ever felt since Jennifer's death. Ben Sisko felt serene, something his old friend Curzon Dax had once predicted he would only feel on his deathbed.

As one motion, the invaders raised their rifles to point directly at his heart. The inquisitor stepped forward, asked his by now tiresome, inflectionless question: "Where is the other one like us."

"I am holding him prisoner," said Sisko. "He is in a safe place where you will not find him."

The inquisitor considered this answer. "What proof do you give that you are holding one of us prisoner."

"None. Take it or leave it." Sisko spoke crisply, with complete authority. In serenity, he found both peace and joy at being alive. He knew what other warriors had felt, true warriors, as they drove to the attack . . . the mark of a warrior was his willingness to live or die according to his beliefs; even choosing to die could be a blow for life.

If you could no longer *live* on your feet, it was better to die on them than to crawl on your belly. Benjamin smiled, knowing he had won. For the moment.

Future battles with the invaders would be the next generation's legacy. *Sorry, Jake; wish I could have given you a peaceful life instead.*

The inquisitor hesitated, unsure how to proceed. Finally, it appeared to accept the authenticity of Sisko's claim. For the moment.

"What do you require to release the captive."

Another invader squad descended the ladder. Sisko kept his eyes away from them, kept them on the inquisitor; but inside, he was leading a high-school yell: *Sisko, Sisko, he's our man . . . if he can't lure 'em, no one can!*

"First," he said, "what are you called? Who are you?"

"The ones who used to be here call us Bekkir."

Bekkir: a Cardassian type of badger. A nickname, not a name.

"What do you call yourselves?"

"What do you require to release the captive."

How many more can I coax down here? "How many of you are on my station?"

"What do you require to release the captive."

"I need to know how many of you there are."

The inquisitor stood absolutely still, neither breathing nor twitching. *It's communing,* Sisko realized; *it's talking with the other Bekkir, deciding how much information to reveal.*

Of course, it knows I'm going to die anyway.

Sisko glanced up at the instrument panel, sought among the dozens of displays—temperature, pressure, force-shield density—for the one he wanted. At last, his roving eyes found a chronometer.

Twenty-two minutes had passed since he made his broadcast.

I promised Jake thirty . . . I can't implement Sisko's Last Stand for eight more minutes.

The Bekkir interrogator came to a decision. "We are sixty-eight. Tell what the captive did forty-four hours ago."

Great. A test. "Forty-four hours ago," said the commander; "let me try to remember." He pushed back a little farther into the gap between the two working fusion reactors, keeping his hands behind him. He thought furiously. *Forty-four hours—twelve-thirty two days ago.*

Quark and Odo had found a strange, Gamma-quadrant artifact—a Bekkir signaling device. They obviously activated it, undoubtedly about forty-four hours ago.

That summoned the Bekkir . . . but at the same time, the pair vanished without a trace.

What had the Bekkir said before? During the interrogation of Dr. Bashir, the inquisitor said that the "other one" would have vanished, but would shortly reappear. On the other hand, they had begun looking for it immediately after beaming to DS9. Clearly, the "other one" would ordinarily return after a specified length of time, but could return earlier.

"Forty-four hours ago?" asked Sisko. "I think that was right around the time the captive escaped for a period."

"The captive escaped."

"Disappeared right from its cell. Damnedest thing I ever saw. One minute it was there, the next it was gone."

"Where was this cell."

Sisko began to remember the interrogation of Bashir with crystal clarity. "In a secret place," he said.

"Have you seen the captive since."

"Oh yes. It reappeared about twenty hours after it left . . . right back in the same secret place."

The inquisitor and a number of other Bekkir froze, communing as excitedly as Bekkir could commune. "What condition was the captive in upon returning," asked the questioner.

"Badly injured," said Sisko. "It was in terrible shape, but it's still alive."

He looked at the chronometer: two more minutes.

The Bekkir had another town meeting. "You will lead us to this secret place," said the inquisitor.

"Like hell," said Sisko, still serene, at peace. "You have not met all my demands." He did a quick bubblehead count. There were about fifty Bekkir in the reactor well; assuming it was telling the truth about the force that had invaded the station, that left about fifteen to twenty Bekkir still at large.

It was not good enough, but it would have to be.

"What do you require to release the captive."

The guns were all still leveled at his chest, but nobody had fired yet. Ben Sisko had done it . . . if he could just hang on for another minute and a half.

He strained his brain . . . what else could he demand? A wicked thought struck him. "Reparations," he said.

"What reparations."

"I demand we calculate the value of each person you killed in gold-pressed latinum, and you pay this bounty to Bajor and the United Federation of Planets."

"Animals are of no value," said the inquisitor succinctly.

"*My* animals *are* of value."

"You will lead us to the secret place or you will die."

"How long do I have to make a decision?" asked Sisko.

"You are allowed thirty seconds."

For thirty seconds, Commander Benjamin Sisko scowled, studying the deckplates. Every few seconds, he glanced at the chronometer.

The time limit expired, and he was still forty-five seconds away from Jake's "safe time."

Assuming Jake figured it out. Hell, assuming Jake is even still alive!

The drama had played on long enough; the commander wearied of playacting. He pursed his lips. "All right, I'll lead you there. But I just want to know one, last question." He licked his lips. "Suppose you were in love with a queen, and the king found out. And suppose he set you down in an arena in front of two doors, and told you that behind one of the doors was a beautiful lady, the most beautiful courtesan in the entire kingdom . . . but behind the *other* door was a hungry, slavering tiger. The trouble is, you don't know which door leads to which fate.

"Now you look up at the queen, and by a secret sign she indicates you should open the left door.

"My question is, did she indicate the door with the courtesan, thus handing you over into the arms of another woman? Or did she indicate the door leading to the tiger, deciding she would rather see you dead than with another?

"In other words, if you open the door she indicated, does it lead to the lady or the tiger?"

The Bekkir inquisitor stood absolutely still, as did every other Bekkir in the chamber. Despite the total lack of external cues, Sisko could *feel* the rage and contempt that exuded from the massed invaders from the Gamma quadrant.

"Animals are of no value," reiterated the inquisitor, apparently realizing that it had been *had.*

Sisko smiled, glanced at the chronometer. *Time, son. I hope you're as bright as I've always thought you were!*

An instant before the fusillade of shots would have erupted from the Bekkir ranks, Commander Benjamin Sisko calmly released the Activate button on the phaser grenade in his hand, allowing the button to pop up and close the circuit.

It was a deadman's switch; had the Bekkir shot him earlier, the grenade would have detonated anyway.

The grenade exploded, detonating the bag full of phaser grenades that Sisko had stuffed between his own back and the fusion reactors.

The resulting explosion was so violent, it momentarily disrupted the force shield that surrounded the two reactors.

A moment was all that was necessary. The sudden pulse of electromagnetic radiation, uncontained for the briefest nanosecond, expanded outward from the point source through the entire station and the Bekkir ship.

Every unshielded person on Deep Space 9 died the moment the pulse passed through his or her body, convulsing them like an instantaneous epileptic seizure.

Every momentary survivor whom the Bekkir had missed on their first pass fell dead atop the corpses of the militia who had tried in vain to defend them. An examining physician would have said they all died of massive electrical shock . . . except there were no burn marks.

The nervous system of every unshielded, sentient being on the station was instantly "degaussed," terminating the biological sequence.

The forty-eight Bekkir in the chamber with Sisko received such a concentrated pulse that they died despite their armor.

Some were blown apart a nanosecond later by the explosive force of a dozen phaser grenades, the impact crawling along at only a few thousand feet per second— much slower than the light-speed pulse. But even those remaining did not fuse, for the same pulse that killed the Bekkir also shorted out the incendiaries in their armor.

Eighteen of the twenty shielded Bekkir who were not in the reactor well itself survived the EMP wave. Each was severely injured by the electromagnetic fist, however.

The stunned Bekkir fell heavily to the deck. Injured, near death, they still had just enough presence of mind to press their large "belt buckle" devices to their chests. The remaining two became red oxidation nearly as hot as the reactor itself.

Eighteen had vanished, and the rest were dead.

The Bekkir ship was devastated by the pulse-wave. All electronics were destroyed, as were all crew members who had not donned battle armor . . . including the Bekkir inquisitor-commander. Two of the surviving crew managed to back the ship away from the station and dive, defeated, back into the wormhole, using visual navigation alone.

The device blocking subspace communication was heavily shielded, and the field remained intact. Deep Space 9 was left alone at last, a floating mausoleum, a mocking monument to Sisko's Last Stand.

Jake and Molly huddled up against the door to the weapons-sail control room, waiting, not knowing they were now the only living beings left on board. Jake buried the little girl's face against his chest, wrapped his arms around her ears. He squeezed his own eyes shut, clenched his teeth against the expected shock wave.

They waited, waited. Nothing. After nearly another minute, Jake could not stand the suspense; he opened his eyes.

The short corridor was now absolutely dark. Even the lights on the door's control pad had disappeared. All sound had ceased; Jake stood in profound silence.

Suddenly afraid he had lost his hearing, he smacked the door with a resounding slap, which he clearly heard; then he felt the sting in his hand, and he yelped in pain . . . he heard that, too.

"Can I look now?" asked Molly, already looking.

"Yeah," said Jake. Why not? Apparently nothing had happened except for a power failure. His father had failed.

Wait—did he? How would I know?

Swallowing a lump of fear, Jake realized his only chance was to begin prowling the station, trying to find out whether the invaders were dead or still infesting the station.

Hour after hour he wandered, feeling like Moses in the wilderness. Jake kept a record: his father's deadline had been about 0500 the day after the attack began. After nearly a full day, Molly was crying all the time from hunger. They had slept twice.

In twenty-five hours, Jake had seen not a single living soul—Bajoran, Federation, or invader.

He had tried the replicators; none of them worked anymore. For a while, they still created the bizarre, random "sculptures"; then that, too, ceased, and the replicators were simply dead.

Some of the apartments in the habitat ring had food . . . those of crew members, miners, or other civilians who simply liked to cook. There were a few more than there had been on the *Saratoga;* the replicators on DS9 never worked well, and the civilians tended to hedge their bets.

Somewhere on the station, Jake knew, there must be vast stores of emergency supplies . . . but he had no idea where. He tried all the likely places, striking out.

For the first day after the station died, Jake's heart pounded whenever he turned a corner. Worrying about bumping into invaders was only part of the problem. Each new vision of destruction was more horrific than the last; each tableau of the dead stabbed through Jake's stomach like a knife. What little food he found he gave to Molly; he wanted none.

At last, after they slept again, he was so ravenous he began to eat. The food stayed down.

To keep sane, Jake began to arrange the bodies as he had seen in holos, covering their faces as well as he could. He turned studiously away whenever he saw a body of someone he knew.

It was not long before Jake realized that whatever his father had tried, it had been successful: there were no more invaders left on DS9. Of course, there were no more people, either . . . none except Molly and himself.

Nevertheless, he felt compelled to keep moving, not stay in one place very long. Jake had read somewhere that back in the days when criminals were commonplace on Earth, they often moved constantly from place to place, driven by an animalistic instinct that staying in one spot too long was pushing their luck. They knew they were hunted, even when no predator was in view.

This is exactly how Jake felt: he and Molly would remain in someone's old apartment, in Ops, on the

Promenade for an hour or two; then Jake would hear the heavy tread of the fool-killer coming up behind, and he would take the little girl's hand and roam.

Yet in all his wanderings, he always veered away from the lower core: somehow, he could not bring himself to explore that inferno, lest he find the unspeakable, proving the unimaginable.

The one place he wanted to visit but could *not* get to was the infirmary. Apparently a bomb blast had damaged the doors, and he could not wrench them open. This terrified him, because he had been unable to get himself and Molly into the heavily shielded weapons-sail control room. This meant they might both have received a lethal dose of radiation.

Without a medical examination or treatment, they might *already be dying* one of the most horrible deaths he could imagine: hair falling out, progressive weakness, dizziness. He already fancied he felt the first symptoms . . . but of course, it might be hysteria.

He circled Dr. Bashir's infirmary, coming back every few hours, as if one day he might be able to command "Open, sesame!" and the door would slide open.

What would he do then? *There must be a way to operate the equipment,* he decided; *and if a way exists, I promise you I'll find it, Molly.*

After two days, Jake no longer covered up bodies as he found them; there were too many. His feet began to lead him on *wanderjahrs* that his mind barely noticed. He would wake to find himself standing in his old quarters, talking aloud to a father he would never see again; or sitting in Odo's security office, staring at blank displays and wondering whatever happened to the old constable.

Then, early on the morning of the third day following the attack, Jake returned to the Promenade to discover that a genie had granted his wish, had rolled aside the infirmary doors.

He ran to the door, looked inside: there stood Odo and Quark, Nog's uncle, watching a gruesome log entry showing Dr. Bashir being murdered by the relentless invaders.

Jake stared, desperately wanting to shout out to them —but a sudden dread welled up in his throat, closing off the exuberant shout.

For some unknown reason, he was suddenly terrified that his very existence was about to end.

CHAPTER
19

JAKE FINISHED HIS TALE. Odo made a slow, steady tricorder sweep of the fiery furnace they found themselves in.

"Rest easy, Jake," said the constable; "you are in no danger of radiation poisoning. The radiation released by Commander Sisko's action was electromagnetic, not nuclear; and if it had actually struck you, you would have died instantly."

"But it's so hot!" wailed Molly, squatting on her haunches. She had tried sitting down, but the burning floor hurt her fanny. For some reason, the silly grownups had turned the heat up way too high.

"It's heat-hot," explained Odo, "not radioactive-hot. Whatever the commander did, it must have blown down the force containment shield on the fusion reactors. This would have created a single, electromagnetic pulse wave that would have killed any normal, biological creature within a certain radius not shielded against EMP.

"Then the reactors would have *immediately* shut down."

"Why?" asked Jake.

"Much as Chief O'Brien hates to admit it—sorry,

used to hate to admit it—Cardassian technology is not primitive. They know enough to install failsafes to protect the station in the event of a fusion catastrophe. If the force containment shield disappears, the laser stops. No laser, no laser-induced fusion."

"Then why is it so hot?"

Odo squirmed. This was the tricky part. "Jake, are you sure you want to hear this?"

"No. Tell me anyway."

"For a single moment, there were two exposed, *uncontained* fusion reactions occurring in the chamber directly below us. Each contained a magnetic platform, upon which was a single pellet of carbon that the laser had just flash-heated to several million degrees. There were also beds of superheated silicon and sodium, but my understanding is that they were only a few tens of thousands of degrees, therefore negligible."

Jake stood, backed away. The image began to form in his head even before Odo described it.

The constable continued. "For an instant, Jake, just before they fused, the two carbon pellets were exposed to the air.

"They superheated the air . . . not to the core temperature, or the entire station would have vaporized; but far hotter than humans or Ferengi can tolerate.

"The metal walls reflect and contain the heat, which means the reactor well below us is still radiating heat at eight thousand K, according to my tricorder."

"No!" insisted Jake, putting his hands over his eyes. "Stop it!"

Odo wished he could just stop; but he decided the boy had to face the truth. "If there was anything left of Commander Sisko before the containment shield broke, Jake, there is nothing left now. His body melted into constituent molecules and immediately evaporated into superheated gases—carbon, hydrogen, oxygen—and perhaps some trace amounts of heavy ash."

He paused; the good news seemed limpid indeed compared to the bad. "Fortunately, I think it would take more than eight thousand K to melt the Bekkir armor; so if the EMP knocked out their incendiary devices, we might still recover an intact time key."

For a solid minute, Jake clenched his teeth, balled his fists as if he were about to attack the constable. Odo fretted; in his present condition, he was too weak to fend off the boy.

Then at once, Jake relaxed. His muscles softened, his eyes mellowed; he lost the "haunted, hunted" look he had worn since they first found him nearly two hours ago.

"I still don't understand how *we* survived," he said, putting his arm around Molly.

"I don't know," said Odo.

"I do," interjected Quark, wheezing full-time now. "You—you went up—to the upper weapons sail?"

Jake nodded. "But we couldn't get in."

Quark looked at Jake. "You have the luck—of a Ferengi," he said. "If you had—gone down—instead, you would have died."

"But we weren't shielded! How come the pulse didn't get us, too?"

The Ferengi shook his head. *"Were* shielded."

"By what?"

"By the *lower* weapons sail. It sat—between you and—and the reactor. You were—sitting in its shadow."

For a long moment, Jake stared out the window. Then he smiled. "The luck of the Ferengi," he said, and coughed.

"Why didn't you just go to Ops?" asked Odo, too tired to cause any facial expressions. "Ops is the most heavily shielded point on DS9. Quark, you saw that some of the systems in Ops were still functional."

Jake shrugged. "I—well, *I* didn't know that. Molly said the weapons sail. And how would I have gotten there anyway?"

"Good thing he didn't," added Quark, who had regained some breath by sitting still. "Remember the bullet—holes, Odo? Might have met—Bekkir on the way."

Jake smiled, finally accepting his father's death and finding in it some meaning. The other senior members of the crew had died bravely, but the commanding officer of Deep Space 9 had died the most bravely of all.

Odo pondered Commander Sisko's death. *So at least one triumph came from the tragedy.*

No, that's not fair, he argued with himself. Each *did* triumph in his or her own way:

Lieutenant Dax discovered that the Bekkir were not invulnerable. She proved they could be killed by killing one. And it was her act that allowed Quark and Odo to finally understand what had happened, who had attacked the station, and how the attack might still be averted.

Major Kira performed her duty as a warrior, killing more of the Bekkir than anyone else and leading the rescue mission to the runabout. It was her special tragedy that this triumph was trumped by the inability of the pilot to navigate the ship safely away from the station.

Dr. Julian Bashir kept the Bekkir talking while his medical log recorded the interrogation. From that recording Odo and Quark could reason out the timetable and infer that there still might be a chance to return and stop the attack from ever happening.

Keiko tackled a Bekkir, saving Jake, Nog, and Molly; then her husband, Chief O'Brien, threw the grenades that allowed the children to escape.

Nog sacrificed himself to allow Jake and Molly to live—and it was Jake's special knowledge of what his father did that brought Odo and Quark to the lowest pit of DS9, the inferno where they might still find the tools to set everything aright.

And last, Commander Benjamin Sisko had killed all the remaining Bekkir, who otherwise would have simply killed Odo and Quark as soon as they reappeared—and who might have left behind the keys to returning to their original timeline.

Every single death materially contributed to the one chance they had to prevent all the terror, the anguish, the death and destruction . . . to avert the tragedy.

Each brave death was actually a small triumph; and together, the triumphs added up to a possibility, a fifty-fifty shot.

It was all they could hope for; they had been given a chance to undo what had been done.

Odo stood shakily. He would not allow this magic moment to be lost by his own weakness. Despite the fact that he could barely even hold his shape, he knew what he had to do.

"I'm going down," he announced succinctly.

Quark turned from the window, a curious look on his face—almost like *concern*. "Odo, that's insane. Not even you could walk into an eight-thousand-degree blast furnace and walk out alive!"

"Am I insane? I don't know that I am." Odo smiled. "I don't know what I *am*, remember? Maybe I *can* withstand heat equivalent to the surface temperature of a large star; I don't know.

"But I do know that I'm the only one here who *might* be able to endure. Could you? Could Jake?"

"The keys are probably melted," said Quark, his voice soft and pleading; he desperately wanted to be contradicted. "And if they aren't, then the EMP wave destroyed them!"

"We do not know that. We don't know how tough the Bekkir armor is, or how they shield their emergency beacons." Odo forced himself to stand tall, cross his arms. "Quark, I am resolved. I'm going down: be prepared to help me out, even if it means you burn yourself."

The Ferengi muttered to himself something that sounded suspiciously like "you're *dissolved*, not resolved," but he moved into position near the final ladderway leading down to level thirty-four, where the still-open trapdoor to the reactor well awaited. He turned his face away from the terrific heat.

Odo stepped forward briskly, his indomitable will belying the enervating exhaustion he actually felt. He was scant minutes from collapsing into his liquid state, heat or no heat. He removed everything in his pockets and handed it all to Quark, who tucked the flash and data clip into his boot and dropped the rest on the deck. Then Odo allowed one last shapeshift, eliminating all protruding edges, digits, clothing—anything unnecessary to the final task. He stepped to the ladder, wading through the energy swamp, and descended smartly into Hell.

The normal, "visible light" part of the electromagnetic spectrum was useless. The sodium-silicon bath was so bright that all other reflections in the chamber were off the low end of the scale by comparison. Infrared was obviously useless for the same reason; and Odo had no idea how to change his eyes to observe ultraviolet light, even if it were in any way useful.

Thus, he allowed his eyes to reabsorb back into his head, then let the head join the main mass of body, leaving arms and legs the only protuberances.

Odo reached the bottom of the ladder, stepped off onto the deck. He guessed that he walked on the actual inner side of the hull of DS9, since the normal "deck" would have long ago melted.

He felt a curious sensation with every step; he felt lighter, slightly less massive. With a sick feeling, he understood that some amount of his living substance was frying, sticking to the ultra-hot hull, then pulling loose from his feet as he walked: he was literally leaving "footprints" behind.

Odo visualized the reactor well as it would have appeared before the containment shield disappeared. The working reactors, one and two, would be off to the left, the dead reactors to his right. If Sisko had been standing near reactors one and two, monkeying with the shield, then the Bekkir were probably standing on the opposite side when the shield dropped.

He staggered to the right, lowering his hands to brush along the deck in a sweeping search.

Odo felt his molecules begin to come apart.

It was the same feeling as when he liquefied for the

evening, but a hundred times as strong. The tremendous heat forced a chemical change in his living substance, causing it to lose cohesion. Had he been fresh, he could have withstood the effects for as long as thirty minutes or so; but in his fragile condition, he would liquefy—or possibly *discorporate*—in no more than three minutes.

It would, of course, mean his death, since neither Quark nor Jake Sisko could possibly come down into the chamber to collect the melted shapeshifter.

Quelling his rising feelings of panic and hopelessness, exacerbated by the chemical imbalances induced by superheating, Odo continued his methodical search, sweeping his long, flat flipper-hands left and right, all the while walking a spiraled path like an ancient shaman.

Suddenly, his right flipper brushed a piece of detritus on the deck.

Forcing down his unnaturally intense excitement, Odo crouched, carefully traced the object with his hands. It felt like a Bekkir helmet, melted into a flat disk, as thick as a small stack of pancakes.

Hotcakes, he corrected.

Working like an archaeologist uncovering a newly discovered fossil, Odo moved excruciatingly slowly, feeling the warped and buckled neck gorget, shoulder pauldron, breast- and backplate. He found the two upper-arm articulated plates, felt along them to the elbow couters and forearm vambraces.

Here he finally discovered what he sought: the Bekkir had been lying on its chest, and the left vambrace contained the key.

Shaking and slipping, still losing mass to the greedy deck, Odo extruded a set of three tentacles from his hand, pried the key from the Bekkir's forearm.

Even without sight, he could feel the peculiar warp in the metal: the key was useless; it had melted, and would no longer even fit in the slot.

He tried to stand, instead dropped to a crawl. It was no use; he could not continue.

No! he raged. *Justice demands that I continue. I will not allow my friends to have died in vain!*

He forced himself to shuffle forward, a four-limbed step, then another, then a third. Almost immediately, his hand bumped into another pile of Bekkir armor, scattering it.

Frantically, he felt for the vambraces. The armor lost its original formation when he smacked it; now, the pieces could be anywhere. Odo slapped the ground at several points, feeling the sticky, sucking hull rip off layers of his flesh. At last, by sheer random chance, he happened upon a vambrace.

Sliding his hand down the piece, he discovered it was a leftie: there was a slot, a key.

He tried to slide his nerveless tentacles under it, pry it loose; but they would not obey his command. Incredulous, Odo tried again, with no better luck.

This is insane, he thought. He calmed himself, tried a third time. This time, he almost got them under; then the tentacles became limp, lifeless.

Odo sat, realizing he had lost about ninety percent of all control over his substance. It was no longer *his;* if any mind still controlled his flesh, it was not centered in any one part of his body.

Then his hand moved, seemingly of its own accord. An eyeball formed in his palm, the pupil a vertical slit no bigger than a Ferengi hair.

The rest of his body blocked the metal pool, the source of light; it was enough. The pupillary slit could see the faint outline of the key in the slot.

A simple latch covered the key; that was why he had been unable to lift it. Apparently, the latch had been blown away both on the first body and on the Bekkir Lieutenant Dax had killed. This third body was more intact—a positive sign.

His tentacles again moved on their own, unclasped the latch. Then wriggled under the key, pried it loose.

Gripping it in his self-sentient hand, Odo rose to his

feet, reeling. Disoriented, he careered across the floor in the direction he had come. The eye in his palm, blinded by the sudden light when he turned his body, withered and fell to the deck.

Inferno . . .

Odo's swinging, apelike arms banged against the white-hot ladder, wrapping around it. He could no longer remember who he was, *where* he was, or why it was so hot. He only knew he must get out of Hell *now,* or he would be condemned to spend all eternity there.

The ladder led up to paradise—or at least to a decent halfway house.

The blind, shambling beast that once was Constable Odo lurched up the ladder one faltering rung at a time, deaf and dumb, no more self-aware than a Cardassian *bekkir.* His flesh bubbled, three-quarters liquid already, and that just beginning to boil to a gas.

It reached for a rung, found only empty air. The white-hot *thing* flopped forward, splatting onto the upper deck like so much sewage.

Purgatorio . . .

It humped toward the second ladder like a gastropod. Its sense of time had disappeared: it could have been a day, a year, the lifespan of a universe. The thing flowed like semi-aware molasses up and up, turned a horizontal corner, and found itself in—

Paradiso.

It rolled forward, became a jelly, then finally a thin, bubbling liquid.

At the very edge of the ladderway flowed a puddle; at the rim of the puddle rested a wafer-thin Bekkir key, just the right size to fit the device Quark gripped tightly in his hand.

Quark ran to the key, almost scooped it up into his greedy hands. But he remembered just in time that it was so hot it would probably burn a hole right through them.

He fumbled out his pocket watch; it read 11:30, a scant thirty minutes until they had to jump, until the attack commenced in the "real" timeline . . . or less, if it actually began *before* twelve hundred, station time.

Trembling, Quark said, "Jake—find me something to pick up this key . . . hurry!" He glanced at the puddle of Odo, now spreading thinly across the floor, covering quite a lot of square footage. How wide was the device's field? Would it include all of Odo, or would parts of him be left behind?

The image of a miniature, elfin Odo, pattering around DS9 and squeaking orders, caused the Ferengi to cackle out loud.

I'm getting hysterical, he realized. "Jake!" he shouted, just as the kids reached the ladder. "Bring a mop or something too, to clean up Odo."

At first, Jake tried to let Molly climb by herself. But he saw in an instant that she could never keep up, and if he slowed down to her pace, the window of opportunity would forever close.

"I think I should leave you here," he suggested, but she looked stricken, clutched his leg as if she would hold him back from certain death. He pondered for a moment, thought of a possible solution:

"Molly," he asked, "can you hang on to my back?"

She considered, nodded gravely. "Of course. Daddy always gave me *onmamasan* rides, piggyback rides."

Jake bent, and Molly climbed aboard. They started to climb, and she startled him by shouting "Piggyback! Piggyback!" in his ear.

Up one level was a cargo hold. Jake ran around, trying every storage compartment he could find, but found nothing suitable for either task. He climbed up another level.

Level thirty-one was a crew lounge, with a bank of replicators along one wall, viewports along another.

There were also tables, chairs, and couches. He tried the replicators, thinking he could *make* the necessary tool; they were functionless.

The pair climbed one more level and struck payrock: an equipment storage room. Inside were specialized tools for manipulating the extremely hot by-products of the fusion reactor, including tongs of various sizes. There was even a vacuum, dangling from a hook, labeled for cleaning up sodium spills; it was made of some strange alloy, presumably heat-resistant up to the temperature of the sodium-silicon bath—a few "tens of thousands" of degrees, according to Odo.

Jake grabbed the vacuum and a pair of tongs, dropped them down the ladderway. At the last moment, he remembered that they also needed a bucket; he grabbed one at random, threw it down with the rest of the gear, and climbed down after it. He repeated this sequence twice more, finally dropping the entire kit except for the tongs into Quark's room.

The Ferengi pawed like a goblin at the pile of tools. He picked up the vacuum, stared at it. "I suppose we better clean up Odo first," he said reluctantly.

Quark began to carefully vacuum up the constable, emptying the contents into the bucket as the vacuum filled up.

At last, he carefully sucked up the last drop of Odo, squirted him into the bucket with special care, not to leave mass behind—if he did, would it grow into a tiny, extra Odo? Then he tossed the vacuum aside and held out his hand to Jake. "Tongs," he said.

Jake said nothing, gripped the tongs tightly.

"What are you doing, human? Hurry, hurry!"

"Quark?" asked the boy. "You—you're going to make the last three days never happen?"

"That's the idea," said Quark peevishly. "The station is saved, nobody gets hurt."

"But . . . what about me?"

"What *about* you?"

"Wouldn't that mean I would never exist?"

Quark stared, puzzled. "What are you talking about? Of course you would exist."

Jake shook his head sadly. "No. *Jake Sisko* would exist; *some* Jake Sisko would exist. But *this* Jake Sisko, the one who lived through the attack and took care of Molly . . . he, *I,* would be gone.

"That's worse than dying, Quark. If you go back in time and stop the attack—then he—I—will vanish from the universe and never have been at all."

Quark stared, grinding his sharp teeth. He briefly considered mugging the kid for the tongs, but realized first that Jake was bigger, and second, that the boy might even have a point.

"That's not certain," Quark said quickly. "You may still exist here after I vanish. If so, I would suggest you keep hiding . . . the Federation will show up eventually, one hopes before the Bekkir arrive to find out what happened to their expedition.

"But you're right, human. It's more likely you'll simply never have been. This entire timeline won't exist, because the attack will be averted—I hope."

Jake lowered his eyes. Slowly, he handed the tongs to Quark.

"I hope that's what happens," said the boy softly. "I don't *want* to exist in this branch. I don't want Molly and myself to be orphans. Even if we were somehow rescued, I don't want to live the rest of my life remembering what I saw over the last two days."

Quark accepted the tongs as he would the sword of a defeated general.

He carefully plucked the belt buckle from his pocket and laid it on the deck, as far from the hellish hole as he could get. Then he returned.

Turning his face away and shielding his eyes from the worst of the heat while still allowing them to see, the Ferengi extended the long-handled tongs, picked up the tiny key.

Fearful of accidentally dropping it—perhaps even down the hole itself—Quark moved in slow-motion agony, gently shifting the device away from the ladderway and toward the belt buckle. By the time he got there, his face and arms were burned a bright red.

He laid the pair of tongs on the deck with its precious cargo, laid his pocket watch on the deck beside them, where he could easily see it, and knelt to study the belt buckle intently. But the tongs were built for long-range, gross transport, not fine, delicate work. He could not both manipulate them and be close enough to see *how* to manipulate them.

"Jake, you're going to have to help me." The Ferengi thought for a moment. "You take the tongs; I'll guide you."

The boy dropped his eyes. "All right," he agreed.

Quark said nothing, but he felt a lump in his throat. Jake knew that he was probably helping Quark to erase Jake's entire existence—this Jake, at least. If Quark was successful, this Jake might never even have existed.

The boy could not do less than his father. Benjamin Sisko sacrificed himself to safeguard the Federation; in the end, Jake could do nothing but sacrifice his own existence to save the station . . . and his father.

He took the tongs. Quark gave him quick, terse commands, and Jake rotated or turned the key until it was perfectly lined up with the slot on the belt buckle, then pressed it home.

Quark's shoulders slumped. He felt such sudden fatigue that he almost passed out. The atmosphere was thinner than ever, and Ferengi took a heavier atmospheric pressure than humans.

He breathed as deeply as he could, feeling dizzy and very sick. Then he rose. *I have a duty,* he thought, *and not all the gods of profit or the devil of philanthropy can stop me!*

He walked back to Odo's bucket, feeling the room spin around him. He grabbed the handle, felt pain lance through his palm.

Quark yelped, almost dropped the bucket back on the deck. *It burns!* He realized the mistake: the bucket was ordinary steel, not a special one designed for ultra-hot spills, like the vacuum.

In his haste, Jake had grabbed the wrong one.

Quark ran back to the belt buckle, his hand almost on fire. Gritting his crooked, pointy teeth against the extreme pain, Quark carefully lowered the bucket to the ground, stared at his hand: an ugly, dark band of blackened flesh cut across the palm; his entire arm throbbed in excruciating pain with every pulse-beat.

"Perfect!" he cried. "That's my ear-pricker hand!"

Furious at the universe, at fate, at the Bekkir, Quark plucked the ear-pricker out of his pocket with his good hand. He mastered himself, spoke calmly and quietly to Jake. "Human, you'd better leave; I don't know how far this thing's field extends. Go up a few levels, then shout when you're clear."

Jake did not move. He stood, holding Molly, trying to say something.

"You can be really proud of your nephew," he said at last. It did not seem like what he had intended to say.

"Go ahead," added Jake with resolve; "flip the switch. I hope the next time I see you, it'll be when you're throwing me and Nog out of Quark's Place again."

Quark smiled, looking like a demon from Jake's nightmares. "Goodbye, boy. You remind me a lot of your father."

"Do you really think so?"

Jake had Molly climb aboard for another *onmamasan* ride. Together, they climbed up the ladder. He climbed one more deck, up to the crew lounge, then shouted down to Quark that he was clear.

Jake and Molly stood at the viewports, watching the nearly invisible wormhole slowly slide past their field of view.

CHAPTER
20

QUARK BENT OVER the belt buckle, probing gingerly and clumsily with the ear-pricker. His left hand felt like five thumbs; he had never practiced using the tool wrong-handed.

He cursed himself for a shortsighted idiot, then glanced with concern at the bucket: it was definitely softening, melting. Odo was nowhere near as hot as he had been when he first emerged; the short period stretched thin on the deck had allowed him to cool. But he was still hot enough to melt steel, given a few minutes.

The return combination was much trickier than had been the first; activating the belt buckle had been like throwing a switch—but the Bekkir *key* was fantastically complex.

Even with his good hand, it would have been hard to pick it; with his left, it was virtually impossible, and terribly frustrating.

He kept *almost* picking up a frequency, only to lose it again. He barely managed to hold the combinations as he solved them, twisting the tensor left and right, as if that would make it hold better. Quark worked by feel . . . and it *felt* right to rotate the tensor.

Of course, he thought. *You want to jump away from danger quickly, without a second's thought. The Bekkir can probably activate the signal-jumper with a single motion.*

But they would not want anyone to be able to access the return function but themselves: hence the lengthy combination.

Quark had no idea how long it had been; time had dribbled away with the atmospheric pressure. He forgot about the watch that lay in plain view. The Ferengi could barely concentrate, kept thinking a dozen irrelevant fancies.

Then he felt resistance. One frequency—he did not know how many tumblers in—was stuck, would not budge.

So the question is, he mused giddily, *is it a wrong turn that will destroy the device, or is it intentional, to let me know it's the last tumbler, and one more will activate the key?*

He pondered deeply, then suddenly remembered the pocket watch. He glanced at it: 11:52.

At first, the numbers were meaningless. Then he realized the awful significance. When Quark and Odo jumped back, the Ferengi's watch would again synch up with the station chronometer . . . which meant he had *eight minutes* to get back, get up to Ops, and stop the attack.

"Oh, what the six hells," said Quark; "if I *don't* push it, I'm dead anyway." He twisted the stuck vortex, wrenching it to full field-break.

Deep Space 9 rolled beneath Quark, throwing him to the ground. His stomach felt as if someone had grabbed it and flipped it over for a cruel joke.

He blinked, found himself lying on a cool deck, still on level thirty-three. He crawled to the ladderway, peered down: the trapdoor to the reactor well was firmly shut.

The air was thick and cold, uncomfortable, but the correct temperature for DS9.

Quark stood, sucking in great drafts of air, flooding his brain and body with the needed oxygen. Then he checked the watch: 11:54.

Apparently, the shift forward and backward was not instantaneous, not even subjectively; it had eaten up two more precious minutes.

He jammed the watch in his shirt pocket, then immediately plucked it out and transferred it to a hip pocket. He stripped off his shirt, rolled it up into a tightly coiled rope, and looped it through the bucket handle.

Eventually, the heat from the handle would burn through the shirt; but Quark already had a plan.

He grabbed the ear-pricker and tensor, shoved them out of sight in his boot; no sense borrowing trouble with Sisko. Then he picked up the Bekkir device, carefully avoiding the still glowing-hot key stuck in the slot, picked up his improvised bucket-sling in the same hand, and headed up the ladder.

Climbing was difficult with only one hand, the other dangling a bucket; but the Ferengi managed the task because he *had* to; otherwise, neither he nor anyone else on the station would survive.

When he found the equipment room that Jake had mentioned, he dashed into the closet. There he found the vacuum, and right next to it was a strange-looking bucket, double-walled, like a thermos.

His shirt-sling had already begun to smoke; rather than monkey around trying to pour the bright-orange, still intensely hot Odo from one bucket to another, Quark simply dropped the warping, melted steel bucket into the heat-guarded one.

Just as he dropped it, Odo melted a hole in the first bucket, dribbling through into the new. A few drops hit the rim and splashed out, but Quark managed to save the rest.

He climbed up and up, six levels, finally reaching level twenty-eight, where the turbolift shaft began. He ran to the doors, slapped the control pad, then danced in impotent fury, shaking his fists, while the turbolift delayed . . . undoubtedly carrying drunken miners to illicit trysts (without them even paying Quark for the privilege).

At last, it creaked into view. He jumped aboard, shouted *"Ops!"* The lift began to move.

Quark looked at his watch: 12:06. He prayed he was still in time.

The turbolift ride had never seemed so slow; of course, he had never started from so many levels below, and rarely rode all the way up to level one. He counted the levels as they crawled past.

All of a sudden, the lift stopped, *not* at Ops. The harsh voice of the station computer announced, "Access to Operations is denied."

"No, you stupid machine!" Quark pounded on the turbolift doors. "You don't understand! This is an emergency."

"State nature of emergency," said the voice.

Get ahold of yourself. It's like a deal that's on the verge of going down the volcano—got to keep your ears on tight. "This is Quark . . . I have to speak to Commander Sisko *immediately.* Tell him it means life or death for the station. I have vital information about the Bek—about the ship that just came through the wormhole."

Silence. Quark paced up and down in the turbolift, wringing his hands. Odo still bubbled in his special bucket, his temperature making the entire lift nearly hot enough to be uncomfortable.

All of a sudden, Quark realized he was still shirtless. He gasped—*the entire Ops crew would see him!*

He felt sick again, this time from shame. Ferengi males *never* appeared in public in such a state of undress.

He curled his lip in a Ferengi sneer. "I will bear up under this adversity," he promised; "it's just one more entry in the long list of humiliations one must put up with to deal with the Federation."

"What humiliations?" asked Sisko's voice, right in his

ear. "What are you talking about, Quark? What's this about the Gamma visitors?"

Kira's voice cut into the conversation. "Quark, you worm, we have an emergency situation here! Take your petty problems elsewhere."

"Your emergency situation *is* my petty problem," snapped Quark. "I know who these—these entities are, I know what they want, and I know how to get rid of them."

Silence again; Kira was probably telling Sisko to ignore the Ferengi. *If it's Kira's voice, we're all dead,* Quark thought; *if it's Sisko's, then I'm coming up.*

"All right, you miserable Ferengi," said Major Kira, her voice tense; "come up and spill your guts."

The turbolift resumed, advanced two more levels, and stopped. The doors slid open; Quark had made it to Ops.

Quark strutted into the room, aware what a ridiculous figure he cut: shirtless, dirty, sweaty, and carrying a bucket of boiling constable.

The entire crew stared, and Quark gaped right back. The last time he had seen any of them, they were all dead, shot full of holes or blown into small bits.

"You're alive!" he cried.

Kira's mouth fell open. "No, Quark," she corrected; "we all died some time ago. But I'm sure we'll be resurrected shortly."

"You have to let me speak to the—to the Gamma aliens," demanded Quark.

"Why must I?" asked Sisko.

"Because . . . because I've just come back from the future, and if you don't, they'll attack the station and kill everyone except me and . . . Odo. . . ." Quark suddenly realized that a half-naked Ferengi swinging a boiling pail and babbling about time travel was perhaps not the most credible witness.

Kira turned to Sisko. "He's drunk," she accused. "He mistakenly drank that same Ferengi poison he foisted on me yesterday. Permission to eject the Ferengi?"

"Do you want a lapful of hot Odo?" threatened Quark. Kira stared at Quark in confusion.

Sisko nodded. "Eject the Ferengi," he agreed.

"Wait!" screamed Quark. "They're called Bekkir—ask them! Ask them whether the Cardassians call them Bekkir!"

Quark approached the mind-numbingly lovely Lieutenant Dax. The last time he had seen her, she had a pair of bullet holes in her face and a serene, mysterious smile on her lips. She had killed a Bekkir.

He poked her shoulder.

"Ow," she said, staring at the shirtless apparition with a bucket of boiling glop in its hand.

Iron fingers seized Quark's ear, causing an intense thrill to run through the Ferengi's entire body. Kira dragged him toward the turbolift, unaware of the orgasmic feelings she was unintentionally stimulating.

"Ooooooooh," moaned Quark, almost spilling his Odo right there on the deck of Ops.

Kira suddenly remembered that Ferengi ears were erogenous zones. She let go, gagging as she realized what she had done. "Quark, you miserable little—little—little *altruist*, get off this level!"

The harsh, mechanical, flat-inflected voice from the intercom startled Quark. It was instantly recognizable. "Your minute has expired. You will surrender your prisoner or be destroyed."

"We are still trying to get information on the prisoner," said Sisko, stalling. He signaled the frequency off for a moment. "Quark, I was just about to tell them we had no prisoner from the Gamma quadrant when you interrupted. What do you know about this?"

"Just ask them if they're called Bekkir!" insisted the Ferengi, ignoring Kira's dreadful insult.

Sisko pursed his lips, finally nodded, and Dax restored the line. "Do the Cardassians call you Bekkir?"

"The ones who used to be here call us Bekkir. Prepare to be boarded."

"Please wait a moment," said Sisko smoothly; "I think we may be able to locate your prisoner." He slid a finger across his throat, and Dax cut the frequency.

"Are they doing anything?" asked the commander.

Kira blinked, then hurried back to her console. "No, sir. They seem to be waiting for us to stop stalling."

Sisko advanced menacingly on the shirtless Ferengi. "All right, Quark, you've got three seconds to explain *what* you are doing here, half-naked, and *how* you knew who these Bekkir were."

"I—" Quark began, then suddenly realized how preposterous it all would sound. "I . . ." He stared miserably from Sisko to Kira to Dax, back again. *If only Odo were awake, or I had some shred of evidence, or—*

Suddenly, his face lit up like a Lonat's. "Yes!" he shouted, "I *do* have something!" Carefully placing the constable on the deck, Quark tried to jam both hands at once into his boot. They would not fit, of course.

He sat heavily, began frenzied tugging at the footwear.

"The son of a *sthondat* is stripping!" hollered Kira. She began scrabbling through a pile of clutter at her console. "Phaser, where'd I put that damned phaser?"

Quark hallooed in triumph, held aloft the data clip that held Dr. Bashir's medical log. He hopped one-footed to the nearest console, jammed the clip into the input slot. "Here, I'll show you! Observe!"

Dramatically, he tumbed the control pad. The log began playback.

Sisko, Kira, and Dax watched, mesmerized for a moment. Quark fast-forwarded to the death scene, and all three members of the audience jumped satisfactorily at the gunshots.

Suddenly Kira shook her head angrily. "I can't believe we're watching some tasteless holovision show that Quark cobbled up when we've got a genuine emergency here."

The audio line hummed. "The time allotted for animals is ended," declared the alien voice; "prepare to be boarded."

"Shields up," said Kira instantly.

Quark looked imploringly at Sisko. "Please," he begged; "I know who they are and what they want. Just let me talk to them. The shields won't work."

"They've put a field around the station," exclaimed O'Brien; "it's stopping subspace communications."

"Can you break through it, Chief?" asked Dax.

Sisko took a deep breath. Anger seething just below the surface, he finally agreed. "Let the Ferengi say something to the visitors . . . but if he tries anything, cut him off immediately."

Dax pressed a touchpad, gestured semimockingly at Quark.

"Wait!" he shouted to the Bekkir. "I know why you're here. You received a signal, right? A distress call?"

"We received a signal from a Bekkir captive."

"No," said the Ferengi; "you received a signal *from me.*"

There was a long, pregnant pause. Nobody spoke. Everyone watched Quark in amazement.

The Bekkir inquisitor spoke again. "How did you obtain a Bekkir signaling device."

"I bought it," said Quark. "It was locked in a Cardassian box for at least a hundred years. Check your records . . . can't you tell how old a particular signaling device is? Check them, you'll see I'm telling the truth!"

This time the response was immediate. "The signal uses an obsolete frequency. You say you activated it. How did you activate it."

"I broadcast a signal into the device at—um—oh no, what was that frequency?"

"Boarding will commence in—"

"Nine hundred fourteen cycles per second!" shrieked the Ferengi, frantic. "I have the blasted thing right here . . . do you want to see it?"

"Begin transmission of visual image," said the Bekkir inquisitor. Sisko nodded to Dax, who touched her console.

Immediately, an image of the Bekkir appeared, a

solemn figure wearing a black bubble helmet and black-and-gray armor. It looked exactly like the figure in the chip Quark had played.

Quark raised up the belt buckle, let the Bekkir see it. "I bought it," said Quark. "I activated it, ah . . ." He looked at his pocket watch, made a quick calculation. "Twenty-seven hours and forty-two minutes ago. Does that match your records?"

The Bekkir froze motionless. After a moment, it began moving again. "We are persuaded to investigate. You will hand over the device or be destroyed."

"Gladly," said Quark with a shudder. He scuttled forward, placed it on the transporter pad.

"Chief O'Brien," said Sisko, "will you do the honors?"

The chief shrugged. "I'd like to look at that thing a bit first; but if you insist, sir." He lowered the shields, then tapped a sequence on the engineering console. The Bekkir device faded, discorporated, and presumably reassembled on the Bekkir ship.

Several minutes passed, during which the inquisitor did not move. For a moment, Quark wondered whether the Bekkir had mysteriously died. Then at last, it stirred, reaching out to sever the connection.

"He closed communication," Dax said.

"I can see that, old man."

Without another word, the Bekkir ship rotated its coiled mass 180 degrees, fired its engines, and disappeared back into the wormhole.

Quark collapsed into an empty chair, feeling a terrible pressure explode in his head. All the stress of twenty-eight hours of torment, guilt, and terror released in a single moment. Then it was gone; he felt a delicious lassitude.

Perhaps it was time to . . . visit his own holosuites.

He was summoned back to reality by Sisko's stern voice. "I demand you explain yourself, Quark. What is the meaning of the Bekkir threat? And what did you think you were doing, Quark, sending a signal through the wormhole?"

The Ferengi sighed. There was no way he was going to face prepayment penalties alone. "I refuse to answer," he said, "until I can consult with my counsel."

"And who, precisely, is your counsel?" demanded the commander.

Quark held up the bucket, grinned nastily. "Constable Odo. He's the hottest property around, these days."

He continued to grin, for he had just had his own epiphany: Odo was still so hot that it would take two or three days at least for him to cool down enough to reassemble.

Two or three days with no Odo poking around my affairs! If Quark had not been so exhausted, he would have leaped in the air and tugged on his ears. . . . *In three days, I can* own *this station!*

He blinked, abruptly brought back to his senses. The second-most-beautiful woman on DS9, Major Kira Nerys, gazed down at him speculatively, her arms folded in a very Odo-like fashion.

"Did you ever notice," she asked, "that when you're naked, you look just like a plucked torura bird?"

Quark leaped to his feet, blushing a pale, milky white. Wrapping his arms around his chest, he sprinted for the turbolift. On the way down, he realized to his horror that the only way to get to Quark's Place and his wardrobe was to push half-naked right through the heart of the Promenade.

"You'll pay for this," he muttered darkly; "they'll all pay. *It'll be three days of Ferengi heaven!*"

Odo actually took four days to cool, not three. Major Kira made it her business to ride herd on Quark practically every minute of every one of the four days.

Quark stared at her in horror as she dogged his footsteps, interfered with his business, harassed him, and generally made his life so miserable he longed for the good old days, when all he had to contend with was the supercilious Constable Odo.

"At least Odo let me go about my normal life!" he complained.

"Oh, are you here too, Quark?" she said. "Funny, I didn't notice you. I just happen to be sitting and resting here in Quark's Place. Tum-ta-tum-ta-tee."

"What did you do, take a leave of absence from Ops?"

"Important station business," she said, a faint smile on her lips.

Quark turned back to the Bornic trader who was trying to sell him a cargo hold full of some native Klingon plant, *turach-tai,* used in shamanic rituals—or so the Born said. Ten bars of gold-pressed latinum to buy the lot, and the rest would be pure profit.

Kira leaned in close, and Quark and the trader stared at her. "Oh, don't mind me," she said; "just go on with what you were doing."

"Was not doing no thing," said the Born with a strange look. He slid down off the stool and waddled out of the bar.

Quark let his face fall into his arms. After a long time, he looked up again. Kira was still before him, smiling vapidly.

When Odo suddenly walked into Quark's Place, the Ferengi had to restrain himself from running up and hugging the constable. As soon as she saw him, Kira yodeled some sort of greeting, waved a cheery goodbye to Quark, and motored off back to Ops.

The constable walked straight up to Quark, said, "Your office. Now."

As soon as they arrived, Odo demanded to know every single thing that happened since he decided to climb down the ladder into the reactor-well conflagration. That was the point beyond which his memory ceased.

Quark tried to brush the shapeshifter off, but Odo forced the Ferengi to recount every moment in excruciating detail. When Quark finished, the constable sat on the desk, staring in the general direction of the Klingon clock.

"What an odd ending," said Odo.

"Odd?"

"Decidedly. Quark ends up saving Deep Space Nine . . . in a sense."

"In a sense! Odo, you know very well I *did* save the whole, blasted station . . . every single human, Ferengi, and Bajoran on board owes his life to *me,* to me! And I haven't received the slightest bit of gratitude from anyone!"

"Have you *told* anyone?"

"No, of course not," said Quark. "Not until you and I can talk and get our stories straight. After all, there's money to be made on this—why, the holovision rights alone would pay for—"

"Good," interrupted Odo, "because I've decided we won't tell anyone the details of what happened. It would be too upsetting. I know how fearful you changeless beings are regarding your own mortality, and it might compromise my ability to interact with the senior crew if they knew I had seen them dead."

Quark stared, utterly dumbfounded. "Not . . . not tell *anyone?* But Odo, you don't understand—I *saved the entire station!* I'm a hero! And I'm a Ferengi; you're asking me *not* to make a completely honest killing off of this? You shortsighted altruist," he swore, "it's a latinum mine!"

Odo rose to his full height, or perhaps a little more, and gazed down upon Quark with his huffiest look. "You saved the station from the catastrophe that you yourself brought about. And if you *really* want to get all the gratitude you deserve, I shall be happy to lock you in one of my cells for a few weeks."

"Well, I, for one, do not intend to simply sit around and claim I was wandering lost in a daze for twenty-eight hours. I have a reputation to maintain."

Odo smiled almost Ferengi-like. "Go ahead."

"Eh?"

"Go ahead, tell anyone you want. But when they come

to me to ask for corroboration, I'll tell them I was with you . . . and you were mad with *turach-tai* tea the entire time."

"*Turach-tai* tea . . ." The Ferengi stared, then leaped to his feet. "You did it again! You were doing it again, you unethical spy!" Quark wandered around the room, bent over like an old man, looking for the hidden communicator. "Where is it? What were you disguised as this time, you privacy-invading—police brutality! I'll tell them you broke into my place without a . . . wait!" Quark stood up straight so fast he cracked his back. "Ow! Wait, in the bar! I was down in the bar, and some customer left his purse on the—Odo, this time you've *gone too far!*"

Constable Odo settled back serenely in Quark's own chair, folding his hands across his chest like a self-satisfied Vedek. "Quark, have you not learned yet," he said, "that nothing that you do escapes my attention?"

For the briefest of instants, his features shifted, changed into those of a Bornic captain. Too quickly for Quark to be sure of what he saw, the constable was just Odo again.

He rose, descended the stairs back down to the main floor, and exited Quark's Place.

The Promenade was unusually crowded that day.